BROKEN STEEL

BOOK 3 OF THE JOHN STEEL THRILLER SERIES

STUART FIELD

All characters in this publication are fictitious and any resemblance to real persons, living or dead, is purely coincidental.

Broken Steel © Stuart Field

Layout design and copyright © 2020 by Next Chapter

Published in 2020 by Terminal Velocity – A Next Chapter Imprint

Edited by Tyler Colins

Cover art by Cover Mint

The right of Stuart Field to be identified as the author of this work has been asserted by him in accordance with the Copyright, Designs and Patents Act 1988.

A CIP record of this book is available from the British Library.
All rights reserved. No part of this book may be reproduced, stored in a retrieval system, or transmitted in any form or by any means, electronic, mechanical, photocopying, recording or otherwise, without the prior written permission of the copyright holder.

To the people who have supported and showed me the way throughout my time as a writer.

Thank you.

ACKNOWLEDGMENTS

To Miika from Next Chapter for giving me the chance to get my books out into the world.

To the fantastic people of the New York Police Department, who keep their city safe and inspired these works of fiction. To my fantastic family, who have supported me during me writing career.

ONE

Black threatening clouds loomed over the city. A warning of the incoming storm that was coming over the ocean from the East. The heat of the past months collided with a cold front that had come over from Europe. The air on the east coast of the US was warm and humid. Warnings had been issued days ago of the possible storm. The guy on the weather channel hadn't said hurricane, but people got ready all the same. The year before the Caribbean had been hit hard, leaving millions of dollars' worth of damage, so now people were conscious of anything that could happen.

A strong warm wind hurried down the Manhattan streets, picking up bits of wastepaper, or anything light enough to be swept away in its wake. Steam rose from the vents in the manhole covers, which enveloped the passing cars as they drove over them.

The night was calm with few people risking the weather to hit the streets. This was a quiet part of town, all the tourists and party people were blocks away, or they were tucked up at home avoiding the bad weather.

But the still of the warm New York night air was broken by loud screams of an argument. The heated words between the husband and his wife were muffled by the restaurant's red brick walls and half-frosted windows. The people inside the restaurant got front row seats for their fight. Something none of them would forget for a while. As the restaurant's door swung open, a tall dark-haired woman stepped out onto the empty street. She stopped and bent slightly at the waist as she cradled her head in her hands, letting out a small yell to vent her frustration.

The woman turned around and saw through the restaurant's window, her husband arguing with the manager. The other customers who were watching glanced often at the incensed man. His words were distorted by the building, but it was clear what he wanted. He wanted to leave to check on her, to apologise for being an ass. She could see his face full of regret. But the look changed slowly the more the manager insisted that he had to pay first. A sound argument for rational people, but the man wasn't being rational.

Julie Armstrong had come out for some fresh air and distance; her hope was that he would calm down enough for them to talk. However, the incident with the manager had just made things worse. She didn't want to fight in the street; hell, that was the last thing she needed to hit the press.

High-court Judge Battles with Husband in Street. She wouldn't be able to try any couples' cases any more, that was for sure; the lawyers would have a field day, saying she was "objective in her decision."

She knew she had to put some distance between them for a while. He had been drinking a lot of wine, mostly out of anger. Julie looked over the road and spied the perfect place, an alleyway.

It looked safe enough, but then she wasn't going in that far, just enough so he couldn't find her. Her long hair was carried up by a sudden gust of a chilling breeze as she crossed to the other side of the street towards the mouth of the alley. As she looked back on the fight, she could see his point; he had accused her of cheating. Seeing it now through his eyes, she came to realise how he had arrived at the conclusion he had come to. The long hours at work, the odd phone calls late at night. The odd look here and there from other men in her line of work. Sure, she was a high-court judge who was close to becoming Chief Justice. She had thrown benefits and parties, anything to attract the right people. Julie had worked hard and rubbed shoulders with powerful and influential people. Hell, she was one step away from that presidential seal of approval, but then he had also been working long hours at the school due to cutbacks and the shortage of teachers. He had left the army and a damn good career so he could spend more time with her, but that never worked out the way they had hoped.

Recently, she had become secretive and distant, and for him, that meant only one thing. Julie Armstrong was in her mid-forties and a very attractive woman with a model's figure that many men had stared at with wanton looks. She looked back with hazel-brown eyes that were red with the sting of fresh tears to see if he had followed her, but the dimly lit alley was empty behind her.

Part of her hoped she would hear him call her name, so she knew he still cared, but no sound came. A cold chill bit the air, causing her to pull up the collar on her long coat and arrange the waistband tighter. The temperature was changing; that cold front was near, and the storm with it.

Julie Armstrong started to walk back to the restaurant.

The cool air had calmed her down, and she hoped her husband was still at the table, waiting for her. Julie searched her purse for the car keys just in case he had gone. She had wisely taken the keys off him, just in case he decided to drive back. She had seen him down half the bottle of red wine at dinner, probably for Dutch courage. A sudden noise in front of her made her look up to who was there. Julie had thought she had been alone in the alley, but a shadowed silhouette of a man stood before her.

"I am glad you found me. Look we need to talk ... just please let me explain," Julie began to say. A look of surprise and pain crossed her face as she felt the large blade puncture the flesh of her stomach. Julie stumbled backwards and looked down at her blood-soaked hands, still trying to compute in her brain the shock of the situation. She wanted to scream, but it was as though her vocals had been sliced. Her mouth moved in hope of some sound coming out, but nothing came.

She looked up at the figure with a look of utter confusion and betrayal; why had he done this to her? She stumbled backwards until she fell over a pile of cardboard boxes someone had left there. Julie looked up, and a look of terror crossed her face as her assailant walked calmly forwards with the blood-soaked knife held tightly. The reality of what was about to happen sunk in and she found her voice before the knife quickly silenced her with a slash to the throat.

* * *

AFTER WITNESS STATEMENTS and forensic evidence had been collected, the investigation had taken less than a week. For the detectives in charge of the case, there was only one guilty man, and they were coming for him. The media frenzy was like nothing the small New York community had ever seen. Cameras and news teams who had gathered outside the blue and white family home had turned the residents normal, tranquil lives upside down.

Reporters and camera teams lined the pavement outside Brian Armstrong's house, ready to get what they thought might be that money shot. At first, they stood poised awaiting any action; only the anchor crews stood in front of the cameras, telling of the horrors that had befallen Brian's wife. The press had already cast their dice: to them he was guilty.

A slight easterly breeze cooled the warm midday sun, and birds darted playfully around in the pale blue yonder, breaking up the cloudless sky. Two squad cars and an unmarked black Ford that was sandwiched between them came around the corner and down towards the expectant hordes. Inside the Ford, Detectives Carter and Doyle looked out at the sea of hungry reporters.

"OK, let's do this." He smiled as he spoke. Detective Alan Carter was tall with broad shoulders and face that was chiselled and purposeful looking. He was a career cop, groomed by the powers-that-be; all he had to do was be *that public figure*.

As they got out of the car, the crowds automatically headed for Carter, who nudged his way towards the house. Doyle held back slightly. He was Carter's partner, but that was work, so he had to be. Jack Doyle was a different kind of cop; he was a good man and a damned good cop. Jack was shorter than his partner, but only by a couple of inches. His brown hair was short, and he wore jeans and a black leather three-quarter length jacket over a black T-shirt. He always thought of himself as a cop, not a fashion model.

Moving through the precession of flashes from cameras

and microphones, the two detectives moved towards the driveway, with four uniformed officers following close behind to assist with the crowds.

Doyle looked over at his partner, who swaggered as he went. What an asshole, Doyle thought, shaking his head. The crowd loved Carter, and he knew it and loved it.

Reaching the front porch, Carter stood up tall and waited for a moment. Some would have thought it was because Doyle and the others were getting into position, just in case there was trouble, but Doyle knew otherwise. Carter made a fist and held it poised inches away from the door, ready to slam it against the glossy white door. Carter felt hundreds of eyes on him, and he closed his own eyes to wallow in it. Soon the door would open, and his life would change forever.

In that split second, Carter had recalled the trip over to the house from the precinct how he had rehearsed what he was going to say and how he was going to say it. Everything had led to this moment; hell, Carter had even broken into his savings and gotten a new suit, especially for the occasion. Sucking in a huge breath, Carter slammed his fist against the door.

"Mr Armstrong, this is NYPD, open up and come out with your hands up," Carter yelled, possibly louder than necessary. It had been more show than anything, adding drama for the press.

Doyle just stood at the side of the door. They didn't know what was waiting for them. Part of him hoped Armstrong had a 12-gauge in there and he would shoot through the door and blow this schmuck away. Doyle smiled to himself at the thought. Standing over Carter's bloody corpse and grinning, "Well, you wanted to be on TV, asshole."

Doyle looked back at the crowd to see the press silent

and open-mouthed, like an audience watching a trapeze act; maybe his daydream was too much to ask for, but it would make one hell of a story.

There was no answer and Carter could feel his moment slipping away. Carter looked back slightly, catching his audience in the corner of his eye. He felt he had to do something. He raised his fist once more to hammer on the door. More drama for the press to feed on.

Perhaps this would be better than if Armstrong had opened the door the first time. The more Carter thought about it, the more boring that would have been. Carter made a fist so tight his knuckles turned white. The door slowly opened. Doyle heard a thousand photographs been taken. Carter smiled inside; this was *his* moment. He rested a hand on the door, ready to shove it open and reveal to the world this evil man. The door opened, and a little girl in a pretty pink dress stepped out and stood in the doorway. Carter froze at the sight of the girl who was no more than ten years old.

"My daddy said that he has to go away and that I have got to go and live with my aunty. Why, where is daddy going?" the girl asked, her eyes filled with tears.

Carter said nothing. He couldn't. The man had everything arranged in his head, and this had thrown him; he had lost his moment, and he was angry.

Quickly, Doyle grabbed the little girl and picked her up before Carter trampled her into the hallway carpet. "Hi there, what's your name?" Doyle asked softly as they walked towards a neighbour's house.

"I am Megan Armstrong. Are you a policeman, too?" Megan sniffed and wiped her nose on her sleeve.

Doyle nodded and smiled. From the corner of his eye, he saw a female officer and beckoned her over.

"Yes, I am. My name is Jack Doyle, and I'm very pleased to meet you, Megan."

The little girl smiled, her blue eyes were large and inquisitive.

As the officer approached, Doyle put the brown pony-tailed girl down and knelt in front of her.

"This is Officer Morgan. She is going to take you to the neighbour's house, and you can wait for your aunty there, OK?" Doyle's voice was soft and friendly. He knew this poor kid didn't understand what was going on. What he did know was she didn't deserve to see her dad being paraded away like some freak for this media circus.

Megan looked up at the blonde-haired officer, who was tall and had a nice smile.

"Hi Megan, you can call me Claire."

The child took Officer Morgan's firm hand, and Doyle watched them walk slowly towards the old woman who stood waiting. He smiled at the sight, knowing that she wouldn't understand why these men were taking her daddy away, but Doyle also didn't want her to remember her father being manhandled into a police car.

An explosive sound of voices made Detective Jack Doyle look back at The Armstrong's house. There was the victorious looking Carter and a scared looking Brian Armstrong next to him.

Brian Armstrong was your average looking forty-year-old man next door. He wore a grey cotton sweatsuit and a black T-shirt from when he had been jogging earlier. Armstrong's short brown hair was uncombed and full of sweat. Carter couldn't have hoped for a better picture of the man if he had dressed him himself.

As the cameras flashed, Armstrong paid no notice; all he could think of was his daughter. He didn't care what the world thought. Armstrong searched frantically for her, hoping that she could not see him in the crowds, but never found her. He smiled to himself, happy that she hadn't witnessed his arrest.

Carter held their position long enough for the press to get their money's worth, then dragged Armstrong towards the car. Carter moved him slowly, with a deliberate pace, and as they neared, Doyle opened the back door of the Ford so Armstrong could get in, but Armstrong was still looking around for his little girl.

Doyle stopped him at the car. "Don't worry. I sent her to the neighbours' house. They will look after her until your sister gets here," he explained.

Armstrong smiled and nodded once in appreciation, and ducked down, feeling Carter's hand on the back of his neck, shoving him in.

Carter slid onto the seat with Armstrong next to him, but Armstrong's look had changed now he knew his daughter was safe.

"Wait until the uniforms are back at their vehicles before we take off," Carter said smugly.

Doyle glanced into his rear-view mirror to see Carter adjusting his tie and combing his fingers through his hair. Then his eyes caught the bright taillights of the squad car in front and smiled.

"Sorry, the photoshoot is over asshole," Doyle said to himself as he put the car into drive and made the car speed off.

Armstrong closed his eyes. He knew that this would be the last time he would see his house, the last time he would see his daughter. He closed his eyes tight, as if to burn the images into his mind, something to cling on to … something to hope for.

TWO

Brian Armstrong opened his eyes to the sound of approaching work boots on the steel-grated floor. They sounded like a hammer on an anvil. His cell was dark, less for the light from the small window and the glow from the small television set that sat on a makeshift shelf in the corner.

Armstrong lived alone; all he had for company was his books that he had collected over the fifteen long years, as well as the respect of the other inmates who had named him *Teacher*.

The sound of the night made him think back to that first evening in Rikers. He'd arrived straight from the courthouse; it was late in the day and night shift was just about to start their handover/takeover.

Armstrong had been slapped in a cell with a small cockroach of a man named Gomez – some petty two-time loser who liked to rape old women, which pretty much put him on everyone's shit list from the word go.

Armstrong got up on the top bunk but made sure he was facing the door, and his back was to the wall with the window; he wanted to see if anyone was coming for them during those dark nights.

He had closed his eyes only for a moment before the cell door opened and there stood three large black guys with armless shirts that showed off tattoos and too many hours in the gym. Their shaven heads glinted from the light of the moon that shone through the window. They were not particularly tall men; in fact, Armstrong would dwarf them at six-one, but they had a muscular advantage. The centreman was larger than the others. This was obviously the Alfa of the group. An angry-looking man with a scar that ran down the left side of his face, he wore a red bandana around his neck as though it were some symbol of authority.

"Now then, what have we got here, boys? Fresh ass, I do believe," the man said. his voice gravely but quiet, as though he'd had surgery on his larynx.

The others laughed, but Armstrong didn't. He just stayed on his bunk until he was called. Below him, the rapist scurried across the room to the corner, next to the stainless-steel toilet, and curled up like a frightened kitten.

"Don't worry cockroach, we will get to you, but first we have to introduce ourselves to our new guest," said the other, a bulky man with a goatee and a tattoo of a lion on his thick right shoulder. He was the muscle, the guy they sent in first because his mass could take it.

The insect in the corner giggled with excitement. Armstrong got off his bunk and stood with his back near the wall.

"I don't want any trouble." Armstrong raised his hands with the palms upwards in a stop gesture, but the three men just laughed.

"It's okay, fish. You do what we tell you, and there

won't be any problems. Now get your ass down and get on your fuckin' knees, bitch," laughed the leader.

Brian Armstrong shook his head and moved his right leg backwards slightly. "Sorry, that's not going to happen," he said.

The man to the boss' left sucked his gold teeth and walked forward quickly. He went to grab him, but before he knew it, the goon was thrown to the ground, and Armstrong held the man in an armlock while his foot rested on the back of the man's neck.

"OK, back off, or this guy has to find someone else the cut his food," he growled.

The second goon rushed forwards to try and catch Armstrong off balance and save his friend.

Through the steel, corridors screams of pain echoed along the many floors of the blockhouse, but the guards didn't care if these men took one another apart; they were there to stop riots, and if the inmates wanted to take out each other, that was fine by them. Fewer scumbags to look after in their eyes.

Hell, they were doing society and the taxpayers a favour. The sound of metal springs screeching was the only noise to break the silence as Armstrong got back on to his bunk. The cockroach had left, scurried away to find another hole to hide in.

"You must be the schoolteacher?" came a voice from the cell entrance.

He looked over at the doorway to see a huge form blocking it, but his face was obscured by shadows.

"It seems you are good at teaching, so maybe you could spread some education in here?" asked the shadowy figure.

Armstrong sat up as some other men entered and dragged away the unconscious three. "What did you have in mind?" he asked curiously.

"Maths, English, those sorts of things. This place has lost its purpose. I was hoping you could restore that," said the mysterious man.

He nodded. "Sure, a man's gotta have a purpose, right?" he asked with a shrug.

"Welcome Teacher, and I wouldn't be worried about any more visits; you have definitely demonstrated *that* lesson." The man's booming belly-deep laughter echoed through the block as the doors clanged shut.

* * *

ARMSTRONG OPENED his eyes suddenly and looked over to the small television set that sat in the corner and sighed deeply. The images of the past were now a distant memory, but one he would never forget. The television had a news report on the prison and, at first, his sleepy eyes couldn't make out too much, so he rubbed them a couple of times to let the eyes natural lubrication get to work before opening them again.

The news report was about inmate Brian Armstrong going to the review board at county court along with nine other men, but it was his face that was making the news as it had done all those years ago. The press had labelled him then, and they were doing it now. To them, he would always be guilty; to them, he had stabbed his wife in that alleyway and left her to die slowly.

* * *

THE JOURNEY from the prison to the city would take a good hour. Outside, the rain came down in thick sheets, making driving almost impossible. Bursts of light illuminated the sky as the storm clouds above crackled and flashed with the build-up of electricity. The streets outside the long white armoured prison bus were filled with inch-high water that reflected the lights of the stores and the headlights of the passing vehicles that waded through the ocean on the road, water spewing from the wheel arches as they flew past each other.

Armstrong looked out across the half-empty streets. He guessed that people were smart enough not to leave the comfort and safety of where they were. Closing his eyes, he felt the coldness of the window on his face and the rain as it pounded on the thick grating on the windows as it came down sideways against the bus. He watched the world as it blurred past through water-streaked windows; this was not a world he had known or knew. It was merely one he had passed through several times. He had no idea why, protocol he guessed, the whole human rights crap. Armstrong knew he was going to never get out, not while the press and joe public had a hard-on for him. Who knew, maybe one day when people had forgotten, or the President was making an ass of himself so much that Brian Armstrong didn't matter?

His world had gone, ripped away from him in conspiracy and lies fifteen years before. Now, he had re-invented himself and established himself as a big part of the prison. The large man who had visited him in his cell on his first night had said something to him once.

"You can let this place consume you, or you can become so important that you are hard to be swallowed up by it."

At that moment he didn't understand, but as time went on and he saw the beatings and the stabbings he came to understand. Be someone they respected, not out of fear, no, that was someone else's domain. Become something so different they couldn't do without you; become an influence of a different kind ... a teacher.

Armstrong was suddenly roused from his daydream by an argument between the head guard and the driver. He couldn't make it out as they held their tone down, as if not to alarm the prisoners, but he paid no heed and just went back to listening to the music of the raindrops on the metal.

"OK, ten minutes, people," yelled the guard who stood next to the driver.

Armstrong opened his eyes and smiled. Even if the board never granted him early release, he had still gotten outside for a little while.

He looked casually around the bus, at the other inmates and three guards along for the ride. His gaze evolved into an interesting glare as he took note at the way everyone was settled, almost confused at the seating arrangements. The old soldier in him kicked in. He hadn't noticed it before; he hadn't really had time as they were carted on to the bus like cattle for the slaughterhouse.

He found it curious the way they were settled into two groups and his group was at the back of the bus, seated against the right-hand wall while the others were against the left-hand side near the front. He shook it off as his soldier paranoia kicking in and went back to looking out the window.

The rain had gotten heavier, making it almost impossible to see out of the glass, which was beginning to mist up. The glass, although strengthened, was still breakable; however, the steel caging on the outside of the windows prevented any escape. In addition, all of the men were clamped down by a securing grip that held the leg cuffs in place on the floor.

He stared out of the window as best he could, noting

shapes of buildings blurring past; he realised, in horror, that the bus was moving faster. He turned towards the long gantry to see if there was a problem and everything seemed to slow as the bus skidded out of control when they turned a sharp bend. Those at the rear were thrown to the ground while the men at the front were pinned to the windows with the sudden velocity of the skid.

Armstrong heard screams and then what seemed to be a loud explosion behind them. Glass fragments fell like small diamonds from shattered windows, covering the men as they sought shelter on the floor. Then there was another massive shudder, and their bodies were thrown upwards as the bus was hurled to its side. Prisoners on the left side of the bus screamed in pain and fear as they hung upside down from their leg restraints. He looked up at the men as they struggled to grab hold of something to support themselves. Fountains of water sprayed inside from the broken windows, filling the interior with rainwater as the bus skidded across the deep water-covered road.

The sound of screaming and metal against concrete was deafening. Brian Armstrong covered his ears as best he could and closed his eyes. He knew it would only be a matter of time until it stopped, and the only question was how. He didn't have long to wait for the answer as he felt himself smash against the seats. Another loud explosion burst forth, and the bus came to a halt.

Half dazed, Armstrong sensed himself been carried, then felt the sensation of wet and cold against his skin; he was outside. He looked up through narrowed eyes and saw the two large black men that he had shared the back row with. Suddenly, his body felt heavy, as if he were losing consciousness. Then, he felt himself grow light, as though he was leaving his body. Slowly, he closed his eyes and fell into the darkness.

THREE

It was three in the morning when the storm came. Bright purple forks of lightning lit up the night sky. The thunder sounded more like a massive explosion than the low rumble of the storm the other week. An impressive sight to behold for sure – if you were sitting in the safety of your home or office.

Detective John Steel stood on the roof of his apartment block. There was no rain, to begin with, just the impressive light show that Mother Nature had put on. Steel remembered a lightning storm he had seen in the Gulf conflict of 2003. That had also been an impressive sight. He had to admit there was a lethal fascination with thunderstorms. A beauty that undoubtedly could kill, but you couldn't help but watch, like the Sirens of Greek mythology; their calmness drew you in before they killed you.

Steel's nightmares had kept him up. The recurring memory the night his family had been killed, the day he had died and had been reborn. The wind began to pick up, but he felt little of the bitter wind as his tailored black suit protected his athletic, muscular body. A wool and leather trench coat enclosed the suit, but he preferred to leave it unbuttoned. The tail of the coat flapped in the wind like a mythical beast's wings. There was another burst of lightning, followed by a *bang*; the strike had hit something. Steel looked around at the city. New York at night during a storm. He felt a chill of excitement run down his spine.

The bright flash of the forked lightning reflected in his sunglasses as he watched in awe. The glasses were a necessity due to their special function. More than a glamourous accessory, they were a tactical accessory. Their main function, however, was to cover Steel's eyes. Since the shooting at his family's estate that claimed his entire family, he had been cursed not only with six bullet scars, but soulless emerald-green eyes. A result of his saviour's medication, or something else, nobody could say, but these eyes had come in useful for getting people to talk or get him out of situations. Besides, he liked the glasses; they gave him an even more mysterious look.

John Steel, son of a British Earl, ex-soldier, and now a cop working with the NYPD. Sure, it was more a temporary posting from his usual duties in Britain, but he was having fun. His father's assassination had brought with it several things Steel didn't really want the title of Lord, the CEO of the family's company. He was never any of those things that had been his father, his grandfather, no, not him. He'd been a soldier, and now he was something else.

Steel smiled as he looked out over the view. A buzz from the cell phone in his pocket disturbed his moment. He took out the smartphone and checked the message: *the usual place, half-hour*. Steel replied with a thumbs-up emoji and closed the phone. His smile faded. The message had been from an old friend, someone he'd not heard of for many years. Steel looked back over at the landscape. There was another flash of lightning, and this time it hit something in Central Park that was in front of his building. Steel smiled as he swore; he had felt the electricity from the strike. He thought back to the message, and whatever his old friend wanted, it couldn't be good or end well. He smiled at the challenge.

"I have, indeed, no abhorrence of danger, except in its absolute effect - in terror," Steel said as he headed back inside his building. He had things to do, people to see.

DETECTIVE SAMANTHA MCCALL peered curiously past the shower curtain and listened hard to the faint sound of her cell phone as it rang through the open door of the bathroom. She hadn't gotten much sleep the night before because of a case she had wrapped up. The paperwork had taken her until two in the morning to finish. The case had been a store robbery, where the perp had shot the store owner over two-hundred bucks and a Snickers bar. McCall had always been surprised at people's lack of empathy when it came to human life. Mr Jackson's life was worth more than two-hundred dollars to his family, and the punk who had shot him – some sixteen-year-old teeth-sucking idiot – was about to learn how much the cost was going to be.

The new district attorney was hanging the kid out to dry, an example for the next wannabe gangster. Even though the kid was sixteen, he was going to be tried as an adult and be given an adult's sentence. In the DA's eyes, the kid was old enough to know what he was doing when he went into the store with a gun; he was old enough to know what he was doing when he laughed as he pulled the trigger five times, emptying the revolver's cylinders into Mr Jackson. There was nobody with him, so the defence couldn't argue coercion. The kid even laughed and joked in interrogation, saying how he was a minor so he would be out soon. How wrong could the kid be? The case was due in a week, and there was enough evidence to bury the kid four times over, a slam dunk. The DA was happy he was getting his time with the press at the expense of the kid and the victim's family.

"You have got to be kiddin' me!" She moaned at the inconvenient timing. Getting quickly out of the shower, she rushed naked through the apartment to the sitting room, leaving small puddles on the dull wooden floor as she went. McCall held a towel, which she was quickly attempted to wrap around her athletic form as she rushed for the cell phone.

"What's up Tooms?" McCall asked in an irritated voice after looking at the caller ID. It was Detective Joshua Tooms, who was another detective at the 11th Precinct's Homicide Division.

"Mornin'. Sam, the captain, wants all hands in on this one. There was an accident with a bus from Rikers. I'll fill you in when you get here," said Tooms. His voice was deep and had a natural growl to it. McCall often joked the man had been a brown bear in a previous life; he'd kept the voice but lost the fir.

McCall looked over at the clock that hung over a 32-inch flat-screen television and saw it was almost six in the evening. She grunted as her plans for a quiet evening at home were shattered.

"Okay, where are you?" McCall asked and picked up a pen that sat next to a large jotter pad and got ready to write. He gave the address as being downtown near the courthouse.

"Give me fifteen minutes. I'll meet you there," McCall replied. Placing down the cell, she blew out lungs full of disappointed air.

The address was at the junction of Kenmare Street and Lafayette Street. It was a large built-up area with a bend onto Lafayette. McCall had to park near Petrosino Square – which was a spacious concrete park where people could just relax from their day-to-day. Police tape and barriers closed off the road, meaning traffic had to be diverted to Broadway. The two lanes where full of debris.

"Holy shit," Detective Samantha McCall said to herself as she stopped for a moment, taking in the scene from a distance as she stood at the junction, McCall's head moved slowly, thinking she had walked onto the set of a disaster movie. The rain had stopped, but the lakes on the road and sidewalks remained. Droplets of water fell from overhangs and store-signs, causing ripples in the motionless water.

McCall took out her small digital camera and began to take photographs of the scene, starting at the junction. Satisfied she had enough, McCall moved slowly towards the police tape where a tall uniformed officer stood ready to shun off the press or the over-interested public.

"Hey Tom, how's things?"

The large uniformed officer smiled as he lifted the tape for her to pass under. "Hey, McCall. Things ain't too bad, and at least it's stopped raining," the big cop replied, looking up at the dissipating clouds.

She smiled back at him as she straightened and headed for a group of men who stood around a police vehicle, an unmarked black Dodge Charger.

The three men were Captain Alan Brant, Detective Joshua Tooms and Edgar Marks – who was the CSU tech in charge of this scene. McCall wouldn't move up straight away but would stop and look at the surroundings, taking in notes of what she considered important. The police bus lay on its side, a large slash embedded in the rear of the bus that went from left to right while the back door lay on the ground a couple of feet from the bus. Detective Tooms nodded to the others as McCall walked up towards the men, and Captain Brant and Marks turned to greet her.

"Captain," McCall said, her eyes meeting Brant's to try and find his mood. She could always judge his mood by his eyes; if they were crazy, then she would avoid conversation or seeing him altogether.

"McCall." Brant nodded a greeting as he pulled up the collar on the heavy wool trench coat that covered his blue suit. He was a large built black man in his mid-fifties and had the build of a quarterback and the temperament of a pit bull.

McCall looked around at the carnage that lay before them. "So, apart from the obvious, what happened?" She turned back to face them.

"As far as we can tell, the transport was taking ten prisoners to the Supreme Court for their meeting with the review board, it lost control, and skidded into that delivery truck." Edgar Marks pointed out the route the bus must have taken with an outstretched index finger. Marks was tall, about six feet but with a slim build that made him look taller. The man was in his mid-fifties but didn't look it. He had white hair which complimented his youthful face. Marks adjusted his gold-rimmed glasses.

"After it found itself on its side and heading towards that building, three of them got early release via the door," Detective Joshua Tooms added as he pointed out the damaged backdoor. He pulled his coat tightly around his huge, quarterback build.

McCall looked over towards the bus, and long skid marks torn into the tarmac showed the distance it had travelled before the building stopped it. Pieces of white metal lay strewn across the ground, and the reminisce of the loading ramp lay next to the backdoor of the bus; the large metal ramp looked as though some wild beast had chewed it up and spat it out.

"How many survived?" she asked, shocked that anyone had come out of that mess alive.

"Three got away, and four were injured, five of them didn't make it along with the driver and another guard," Tooms reported, then flicked his notebook closed.

McCall looked back at Tooms with a puzzled look. "I thought they were all locked down by the floor lock?" she asked.

Tooms gave her an awkward look. "Apparently, the device unlocked due to the impact," he replied, shifting his weight as he spoke. The massive detective was feeling the effects of standing outside in the cold and wet for over an hour.

McCall shook her head and laughed at the absurdity of it. "Unbelievable. So, do we know who got away, sir?" she asked.

Tooms flicked open his notebook and read the list of names. "Darius Smith. This guy is a real peach, been in and out of prison most of his life, burglary, attempted murder, murder, carjacking. The list goes on." He looked down at his notepad at the others listed. "Then we have Tyrell Williams. Now, this guy has a good résumé with armed robbery, attempted murder, and murder. He shot a guard, a clerk and two cops," Tooms continued with a frown.

McCall stopped looking at the bus and turned slowly towards the men. "You said there were three. Who's the third guy?" she asked, then saw the look on the Captain's face, and froze. "What ... what's wrong, sir?"

"Armstrong, Brian Armstrong. The schoolteacher sent away for killing his wife," Brant answered.

The men could see the anger in her face.

"McCall, it's our job to take care of the dead; we are investigating the crash, not the breakout," Brant stated.

McCall could feel herself become dizzy with rage. There were two violent men and a killer-schoolteacher on the run. Two of them would be up to their old tricks and probably disappear into the crowd, but McCall knew that it wouldn't be long before they would be making more bodies for homicide to sort out.

Armstrong they would no doubt pick up, wandering the streets, looking lost and scared. She had seen it before: a onetime criminal finds an opening and goes for it, with no plan apart from getting out. Next thing you knew, they were trying to hold up a 7-Eleven or a gas station for quick cash. All they had to do was wait for either their capture or the bodies to start coming in; she didn't want to chase these men. That was for the feds. But she did want to know how the men got free in the first place.

FOUR

Andy Carlson sat alone in his small two-room apartment. He had a can of cheap beer in one hand and a large bowl of chips resting on the armchair armrest. He had lived alone since his old lady kicked him to the curb nine years ago, but he liked the quiet new life. The apartment had a seventies thing going with the outdated wallpaper and imitation furniture. Carlson was once a respected member of the community and a gym teacher at the local school, but now he was nearly two-hundred pounds of disappointment and shame.

An old cop movie with Steve McQueen was showing on a big, ancient television set. Carlson just sat there and watched while he downed half the can of beer robotically. He hadn't chosen the program; it had come on after the last program. He wasn't even watching it. it was noise. He hated quiet because it reminded him he was alone in the world. With a large hand of bloated fingers, he reached into the bowl, pulled out a mass of chips, and shoved them into his large maw just as a news flash came on.

It was about some escaped prisoners and the accident.

Carlson watched with a little interest as it was something different than the normal game shows and old movies. He took another handful of chips, shoved them into his thin-lipped mouth, and began to crush them rather than chew. The screen changed as a reporter named the escaped men and showed recent photographs of them, so the public was aware who to be on the lookout for.

Carlson stopped chewing and sat with his eyes wide in fear. His mouth fell open in a state of shock, and half-eaten chips fell onto his stained grey sweat-suit trousers. As fear set in, he crushed the flimsy beer can, sending the rest of the liquid flowing over his left hand.

The news flash finished, and the movie came back on. Half-dazed by the news, he heaved himself up and looked around for a second, oblivious as to what to do next. His eyes shot towards the front door. As quickly as his large bulk would carry him, he headed for the door to check the locks was on, and the chain was safe across the door.

Andy Carlson breathed a sigh of relief and headed back slowly towards the kitchen, shaking his beer-soaked hand to flick off the traces of spilt liquid. He was still shaking with the shock of the news as he opened the refrigerator door and reached for a fresh beer. He took a knife that sat in a sink full of dirty plates and bowls and used it to pop the ring pull on his cold beer because his fingers were too thick to get under the tab. With a quick sound of escaping gasses and a small spray of foam, he brought the can to his lips and drank half before heading back to the sitting room.

Carlson smiled comfortably; he was safe, and he had everything he needed. As he went to retake his seat, he stopped, and the grin he wore turned sour as he noticed the bowl of chips that lay across the floor. He shrugged and, with a groan of effort, got down on his knees and started to retrieve his snack. There was a noise behind him, a snipping sound as if metal was been cut – and then there was a sudden breeze. Turning, Carlson looked into the dark corner, past the kitchen, to where the front door was. His face became red with panic, his heart beating hard in his chest. Andy started to hyperventilate; his body began to shake. With strained eyes, he waited to see who was coming for him. His blue eyes looked up, full of sorrow, and tears began to form, clouding his view.

"You … I knew you would come." He went to scream, but the bite of a Taser rendered him unconscious. The room fell silent as the dark figure got to work on the victim.

FIVE

McCall stood by the hotdog vendor located just down the street from the precinct. The evening sun was fading, and most of the rainwater had disappeared, leaving dark grey patches on the sidewalks. Some of the streets still had pools of water, but the oceans of rainwater had gone. She'd waited in line for only a few minutes, but it was time enough for her to check on missed text messages. McCall looked up as the woman in front finished drenching onions with ketchup and mustard. The small Indian man behind the stall greeted her with a smile that could cheer a cloudy day.

"Sam, it has been too long. What, you have found another stand?" he joked as she put her cell into her jacket pocket.

"You know I would never do that Sid – you're the closest," McCall laughed.

He gave her a hurt look before handing over her usual order: a loaded hot dog.

"Healthy snack, McCall. Hate to see what you do for dinner."

McCall almost jumped out of her skin as a sudden, soft-spoken voice with a British accent came from behind. She spun to see a tall black-haired man with a pair of face-hugging sunglasses. He was close enough to be her shadow, but not too close to make her notice he was there.

Sid smiled as the man passed him a ten-dollar note and waved off the change.

"Damn it, Steel, you could have given me a heart attack," McCall growled.

Detective John Steel looked at her in amazement while she plastered the hotdog with ketchup.

"Wow, and you're worried about me giving *you* a heart attack!" Steel smiled.

McCall looked at him, scornfully and walked off.

Steel smiled at Sid, and the two men shrugged. He turned up the collar of his long wool-and-leather trench coat as he followed. The leather on the arms and shoulders glistened like the skin of a bat's wing, and the length of the coat flapped behind him like a mythical bird in flight as it caught the wind, revealing his black suit and tall frame.

"Where you been? We missed you at the scene," she lied.

Steel looked down at her and smiled as he saw through the hidden, bitter words. "I had a case a friend asked me to look into; sorry I should have said."

McCall didn't respond and just kept walking towards the precinct building. "So, you done with the case?" Her words bit the air, and he smiled to himself at her question, her voice trying not to sound interested.

"I hit a ... dead end, for now."

She stopped suddenly and turned to him; her mind was conjuring all sorts of images of what he meant. As she faced him, she saw the smirk and slapped him on the shoulder as he carried on past her towards the station house. She finished the hotdog, still wearing an un-amused look on her face and tossed the paper ball into the trash can and followed him in.

They walked through the bustle of the 11th Precinct's lobby and headed for the lifts. McCall pressed the button for the third floor. As the doors closed, McCall gave a quick smile. They got out on the third floor, which was the Homicide Division of the 11th Precinct. She headed for the break room; she needed coffee and lots of it. Inside the room, she brought Steel up to speed on the case as he handed her a cup of coffee he had just poured from the glass jugs from the machine.

Steel had explained how he had heard of the crash from the precinct, but he had been tied up with the other case at the time.

"So, all we have is some dead bodies, three in the hospital and three on the loose," Steel said before blowing on his steaming coffee. He peered through the gaps in the latte-coloured blinds of the room, over at the murder board by McCall's desk. "CSU have any theories about what happened?"

McCall shook her head, making her brown hair flow past her shoulders. They both knew that that report would take time – time they didn't have. "CSU is backed up at the minute, so could take a day, maybe two," she explained as she headed back to her desk.

Steel followed her, then found a perch on the end of her desk.

McCall held the coffee mug with both hands, her long fingers wrapped around the sides as if she thought the precious drink would disappear.

Steel rested his cup on one of the coasters she insisted he used. McCall's desk was immaculately laid out; everything had a place and purpose. He could see something was bothering her; hell, a blind man could see that. There was something that didn't sit right, and he knew enough to know that she would stare at that board until it became clear. McCall wasn't just a detective, and she was a hunter; McCall was tenacious, and that's what Steel liked about her.

"So, how did the three guys getaway? I thought that they were locked down to the floor during transit?" Steel asked.

McCall turned and shot him a look, and then he realized he had asked the very question she was pondering.

"Apparently, the lock disengaged when the bus hit the wall. I don't know, a malfunction or something."

He heard her words, and he could tell she didn't believe it either. "Or something," Steel repeated.

McCall knew what he meant, and although the thought that they had been released on purpose was alarming, she had to keep an open mind. That was until CSU could confirm the facts. Steel's sunglass-clad eyes scanned the photographs of the crash, where everything was, and the conditions of the street. Neither of them spoke; they just stared at the puzzle before them.

"How did the three men survive it anyway? I mean, seven of them were killed instantly, and in a crash like that, I am not surprised," Steel stated.

McCall stared back at him. "What's your point … that the thing is armour-plated?" she asked, not seeing what he was getting at.

Steel looked at the photograph that was taken from one of the building's rooftops and checked every detail on the ten-by-eight.

"Fact is, I'm surprised that more didn't survive," McCall said.

"Do we know where everyone sat on the bus?" Steel asked.

McCall sat back in her chair and took a sip from the coffee. She just stared at him, watching as adrenaline made him as hyper as a kid on a sugar rush. "Not yet, Tony and Tooms are off to the prison in the morning to see if they get any information and, hopefully, they can also explain why the floor lock broke," she explained.

Steel finished his coffee and looked at his watch. It was now seven o'clock, and he had plans.

"Well we can't do anything until tomorrow so I will say good night," Steel said standing up.

McCall eyed him curiously; she could tell something was bothering him and that normally meant trouble. "See you tomorrow then. Oh, Steel stay out of trouble … we have enough bodies." She gave him a warning look.

He smiled and gave a quick salute before turning and heading for the elevator. He had that stone look on his face that held a cold, companionless feel. She pitied the person he was off to see.

SIX

Red wine – and lots of it – chick-flick movies, and Chinese takeout from Mr Lee's was what made up the evening for McCall and her best friend, Medical Examiner Tina Franks. They had both had a hard day – a hard week if truth be told. Now it was girls' night. McCall wasn't on call, so they had the night free – or they hoped. McCall enjoyed these little get-togethers she and Franks did whenever they could. McCall and Franks had been friends for years, ever since McCall had gotten to the 11th in fact. McCall had always been at the 11th. She thought it was because of her dad because he had been a detective at that precinct before he'd been shot during the line of duty. Those were big shoes she had to fill, but McCall thought she hadn't done too bad so far.

"So, who's it gonna be first?" Tina asked, holding up three DVD cases. "Ryan Reynolds, Hugh Jackman, or the Man in Black himself?" she smirked.

McCall raised an eyebrow; she wasn't going to bite. "I hope you are referring to Mr Reeves," she said, pouring full glasses of a lovely Californian red.

"Naturally. Who did you think I meant?" her friend laughed.

"Sam Jackson in that comic-book movie," McCall said sarcastically.

"Girl, when are you gonna get your freak on with Steel; you know that boy ain't gonna be around forever?" Tina asked with a serious tone.

McCall shrugged as if she didn't care. The trouble was, Steel's leaving was always inevitable. She was amazed that he had stuck around this long. He was on loan from Britain, a joint-task force, whatever that meant. No, McCall knew one day he would just be gone, probably as mysteriously as he had arrived. The man was an enigma to be sure. The son of a murdered British earl who had been in the army and now worked for the NYPD. McCall knew if she had that much cash, she wouldn't be a cop; hell, if she were a British Lady, she'd still be in Britain sipping gin and tonics and having champagne with her breakfast in her mansion. Still, that was why Steel was so different – apart from been completely nuts and an action junkie, he didn't reveal much about his past. Which was probably a good thing, because he was scary enough when the shit hit the fan. Fortunately, scary *good*.

"Fuck it, put that hot assassin on," McCall said, getting comfortable on the sofa.

"I wish I could Sammy, but I don't wanna hurt your feelings," Tina Franks laughed.

McCall retaliated with a cushion to the head. They both laughed and settled down to their girls' night.

* * *

THE NEXT MORNING the sun had not quite broken over the horizon as the city began to come alive. A cold blue coloured the buildings and streets, and a crisp wind brought in fresh, unspoiled air through the maze of stone and steel that was Manhattan.

Joggers and dog-walkers set out on their daily routines, and garbage men went about cleaning the streets before the chaos ensued. Samantha McCall lay motionless underneath sky-blue sheets, her athletic body contorted in such a shape, a yoga instructor would have been proud.

Slowly she opened one eye as if the other refused to awaken. McCall turned her head and flattened the pillow beneath her so she could get a better look at the alarm clock; it was four in the morning.

McCall stayed motionless at first, merely lay still hoping that if she didn't move, she would eventually fall back to sleep, but her hopes shattered as she felt her brain click into her morning routine. She groaned disapprovingly as she crawled from beneath the sheets and headed for the bathroom. The wooden floor held a disagreeable chill as she entered the space that was shared by the sitting room, kitchen, and hallway that led to the bathroom.

Quickly, she scuttled inside and shut the door. Seconds later, the door slowly opened, and a very awake McCall looked out towards the kitchen. She felt a cold chill run down her spine as the sound of the coffee machine, and soft music from the radio filled the apartment. At first, the sounds had not been apparent as she was half asleep, but the walk from her room had blown away some of the morning cobwebs. Someone was in her kitchen – her apartment!

She looked over to the large dresser by the front door where she kept her custom Glock 17. It was a good twenty feet from where she was, and she would have to go past the kitchen.

Then her thoughts moved to the backup Smith and

Weston M&P.40 that was in a compartment in her headboard. McCall moved slowly, her gaze fixed on the kitchen door. She could probably take whoever it was, but if they were armed, then they would have the advantage; she was about to change that.

McCall walked back into the dimly lit room. She knew where everything was, how many feet to reach this or that. However, she had backed into something … something that should *not* be there.

She turned quickly; her hands raised ready for combat. She froze as the person in front of her proved to be Steel. The light that crept through the door reflected off his muscular, naked body. She gasped as he pulled her close and looked into her eyes before he pressed his lips against hers. Her body became limp in his muscular arms as he picked her up effortlessly and carried her to the bed. She felt the warmth of his body against hers as he drew closer until they became one.

She threw her head back as passion built, her fingers clawing at his back. She was in ecstasy, and she didn't want it to stop. As she grew near, a faint sound filled her ears, almost like a watch alarm going off: a distant *beep, beep, beep*.

McCall woke suddenly to the harsh sound of her alarm as it grew louder. With an angry swipe, she knocked the digital clock flying across the room. With an animalistic growl, she slammed her head back into her pillow and banged her fists against the mattress.

McCall got out of bed and headed for the bathroom to splash cold water on her face. As she got into the floor space between the kitchen and the bedroom, she stopped and listened, and smiled at the silence before entering the bathroom. The water was cool and refreshing against her sweaty skin. She looked into the mirror and shook her head. "Damn it, not again; this has got to stop."

She cursed her reflection.

McCall showered and changed. The coffee machine had produced its timely pot of coffee.

Tina Franks had stayed over. McCall had left her on the sofa with a blanket and a bottle of water. There was no way she was letting her friend go home so late at night after so much alcohol. Even though they'd both been tipsy, McCall wasn't risking it, cab ride or not. McCall considered herself the big sister of the relationship. Sometimes it was true, but Tina could also prove a cold voice of reason when she needed to be.

Tina Franks, daughter of a black Marine whose family came from Jamaica. He met Tina's Brazilian mother when he was posted in Hawaii. A hell of a combination, but what a package. Sure, she was just under six foot – or rather two inches shorter than McCall – but she wasn't smart and had a hell of a figure, though she had a great sense of humour and a big heart.

McCall woke up Franks with a fresh coffee and a smile – and a bottle of aspirin, just in case.

"Gotta go catch bad guys, so lock up when you're done," McCall said.

She just nodded as she sipped the coffee and rolled her eyes.

McCall smiled and walked up to the dresser near the front door and unlocked the drawer. Took out her Custom Glock 17 and wiped the polished steel top slide with the cloth she kept in the drawer with it. She pressed the button next to the trigger guard and realised the magazine. Pressing her thumb on the top round, McCall checked the tension of the magazine's spring. The hollow-point 9mm bullet moved slightly. She smiled: good tension, full magazine. McCall drew the vented top slide slightly, revealing the glint of brass from the chambered bullet. Fifteen in the mag – one in the pipe, ready to go.

She slid the magazine back inside the magazine housing in the pistol grip and clicked it home. She never slammed it home, too much risk of damaging that first bullet. Besides, it didn't need that extra bit of assistance. This was a lethal work of art with its vent slits at the front, and red and yellow dot rear and front sights. Steel had bought her the pistol, along with a twenty-round magazine, but McCall figured fifteen was enough – not that the twenty wasn't bombed up ready, just in case.

"Catch ya later, Tina," McCall said, turning around, slipping the weapon into the holster at the small of her back. She smiled as she saw her friend shuffling to the bathroom and waving goodbye.

SEVEN

Becky Carlson stood in front of her father's door. Her arms were full; groceries in large brown paper bags were tucked in one arm as she struggled to find her keys with the other. She was a slim, short, young woman with long brown hair, big friendly blue eyes, and a winning smile. Becky would stop by every other day before work to see how her old man was doing. Her mom had thrown him to the curb ten years before, and now he lived here if you could call what he was doing living.

Becky remembered him as a fit man, tall and handsome. In fact, Andy Carlson used to teach gym at the local school, until something happened and then it all changed – *he* had changed. Now he stayed indoors and never came out, never had a visitor. His theory was, "If you don't have a key, you shouldn't be there."

With a sigh of relief, Becky found the large bunch of keys in her bag that hung on her right shoulder. She felt for the special tag that she had put onto the key so it could easily be found using touch, in cases like these. Becky's fingers found the high recesses of the tag and smiled. She lifted the key and scraped it along the door where she thought the lock was until it jammed on something; carefully, she pushed, and it sank home, and the key clicked into place. As she went to turn, a voice from behind her made her jump with fright, and the bags crashed to the floor.

"Morning, Becky."

She slammed her back against the door as she held her chest, trying to calm herself from the shock.

"Mr Edwards, God, you scared the shit out of me!" Becky laughed and shook her head as she bent to pick up the food items she had dropped out of fright.

The ageing black man strained to kneel to assist her with the spilt shopping. "Sorry kid didn't mean to scare you. Hell, I breathe like a locomotive. I would have thought you would have heard that."

They laughed as they started to refill one of the bags.

"Becky, your dad, has had that TV on so loud all night, his hearing has probably gone, but can you have a word?" the old man asked.

Becky nodded with an apologetic smile. "Oh, yeah, sure I'll have a chat with him. Sorry, Mr Edwards." She stood up, slid the key into the lock, and turned it. It had become stiff, which she found odd at first, but still, it opened. As the door swung open, she was greeted by the loud blare from the television set in the sitting room. Becky left the groceries on the floor and rushed in, knowing there was a problem. The apartment was in darkness less for a flickering blue glow that illuminated a path past the kitchen from the television set.

Confused and worried, they ventured past the small corridor and turned past the kitchen with a full view of the sitting room. All appeared normal at first. Becky headed for the heavy armchair to try to find the remote. She stopped, her gaze wandering past the armchair. She noticed the shape of her father on the ground; his body was lit by the glare of the television set. Panicked, they rushed over to him, only to find him motionless on the thin stained carpet. Andy Carlson's cold, lifeless eyes stared up at the stained ceiling with a look of utter horror. Mr Edwards turned and ran out before emptying his stomach. Slowly, Becky moved closer to her father's corpse, the sound of the TV now non-existent to her. The room was spinning as shock took hold of her and tears poured down her face; she felt helpless to do anything. After all these years of caring for him and now – now, she could do nothing except stare. Stare at his cloudy eyes and the bloodied stitching that held his nose and mouth shut.

EIGHT

The morning traffic had built up to its usual madness. People were either rushing to get to work by cab or via their own vehicles. Despite most of the populous using the subway or having the luck of living just blocks away from work, traffic was manic. The sun had risen but had not yet brought its warmth. Commuters huddled in coats that they knew they wouldn't need until later, but they helped with the chill of the morning.

McCall had made a quick stop to drop off dry cleaning; next was the coffee house to pick up a coffee and bear claw before she headed to the station. She was a block away when she got a text from Detective Tony Marinelli, informing her of a fresh body at one of the tower blocks on Water Street. Parking on Water Street was a nightmare; its narrowness enhanced by badly parked vehicles. This meant she had to park down near the bottom, far from the scene.

Despite the distance, she didn't mind, knowing the walk help her think. Finding a spot between an old Golf and a new Ford, she parked her beloved Mustang. McCall sat for a moment, taking in the surrounding view of large brown and red brick buildings, almost as if she were listening to what they had to say. Unfortunately, these were no help, and neither was the tabby cat who was sat in a first-story apartment window.

"Did you see what happened?" McCall yelled up to the cat, who simply shot her a strange look.

"Thanks, big help," she said to the cat jokingly.

The cat meowed a reply and jumped down from its perch. McCall smiled and shook her head.

As she got out of her faded '66 Mustang – which had been her father's, and then McCall's as a graduation present – a fresh morning breeze swept over her face, leaving a tingle on her cheeks. She closed her eyes and breathed in a lung full of the crisp air.

The walk took her around five minutes; she could have done it in two, but she wanted to take in the whole lay of the land. The building itself was large with brown bricks and white window frames. She looked over at the entrance to find Tony waiting for her.

"Hey Tony, so what we got?" she asked.

Detective Tony Marinelli smiled and took out his notebook from the inside pocket of his grey suit and held the door open for her just as she approached.

"Our Vic is a Caucasian male named Andy Carlson; he was in his mid-fifties according to his driver's license. There were signs of forced entry, the front door lock had been picked, and the chain had been cut," Tony continued.

McCall took a mental note of Tony's information as they entered the elevator. He stood next to the control panel and pressed the button for the fifth floor. As the doors closed, Tony flipped his pad closed and placed it in his pocket. "Tooms is in the apartment with CSU," he advised.

Sam McCall nodded as she watched the round buttons on the control pad light up upon arrival on each floor. "Have you been in yet?" she asked, her gaze locked onto the light show the buttons displayed.

Tony nodded as he pulled out a pair of purple surgical gloves and proceeded to stretch them over his hands. "We got the call early this morning. The ME arrived just before you, so she might still be working on him," he said.

McCall nodded silently. She figured Tina had been picked up by the duty ME vehicle after getting a call from the office. She would have driven straight there from McCall's. She just hoped Tina was up to seeing bodies after the state she was in that morning, but McCall knew her friend had a way of looking like shit one minute and a million bucks the next; she hated that about her. McCall knew if she had woken up in that state, it would be late afternoon before she resembled anything human. She sniggered to herself.

The steel box shuddered as it stopped with an unnerving noise from the brakes. The doors slid open to reveal the circus as uniforms made house-to-house calls, trying to build up a picture of the dead guy, or indeed if anyone had seen or heard anything the night before. Down below on the street, passers-by struggled to get glimpses of what was going on as they stood behind yellow police tape.

As McCall and Tooms approached the door to the apartment, a tall black, uniformed officer nodded a greeting to McCall, then passed her the sign-in sheet. She filled in the relevant information: time of entry, name, badge number, etc. She handed it back and shot the officer a quick smile.

"Morning, detective. Not quite the way to start the

morning," the uniformed officer said.

She shot the officer another quick smile. "Never is TJ; it never is," she replied. She stopped just outside the doorway and took in the surroundings. McCall liked to map out things in her mind, get the feel of a place before proceeding.

The doorway led to a small entranceway between two rooms before branching off to the left and right. To the front was what she believed to be the bedroom. Inside, she could see Joshua Tooms' large bulky body kneeling on one knee, talking to a black-haired woman.

"That's the victim's daughter, Becky Carlson, who found him early this morning. Apparently, she visits him every other day before work just to make sure he is OK," Tony explained.

McCall looked over at the girl, and she felt her pain.

"However, today when she arrived, the guy next door was complaining that the TV was blasting all night. After she went in, that's when she found him and called it in," Tony continued.

McCall reached inside her jacket, pulled out a small digital camera and switched it on.

"So, how long had the TV been on?" A sudden voice from behind Tony made him curse loudly. "Jeez … damn it, Steel, where the hell did you come from?" he growled.

Steel smiled childishly.

"The neighbour said all night, why?" Tony answered as he tried to get his heart rate down.

McCall smiled as she took a shot of the hallway. "Because that gives us a timeline; we find out when it got loud and work from there," she answered and her eyes suddenly caught the full view of Tooms talking to Becky Carlson. She stopped. McCall's eyes were transfixed on that moment; memories came flooding back of when she had been told of her father's shooting. She had been no more than eighteen when it happened. He was a homicide detective responding to a shooting in a hotel room. The whole thing had been a set-up to stop his investigation into something he had been working on. A sniper's bullet took him from her and her mom too soon.

"You OK?" Steel asked.

McCall was shaken back to reality at Steel's question. She nodded and smiled at him, then set off towards the corridor. She stopped and looked left, towards what appeared to be the bathroom. She looked right, then smiled at the sight of Tina, and walked past the kitchen, towards the sitting room and the ME crouched over the body.

"Morning Tina ... so what we got?" McCall asked, her tone full of excitement, as though she hadn't seen her friend for a long while.

Tina Franks, ME, didn't turn, merely raised a gloved hand and waved like she did most of the time ... normally every time the girls were not on call the night before.

"Mornin' Sammy. Well, we have a strange one here, that's for sure," Tina said.

McCall looked confused as she neared. The body was not visible at first, not until they had walked past the armchair and the orderlies who were busy taking snapshots of the body.

The detectives' faces contorted with disgust when they got the full view.

"Did someone – *sew* his mouth and nose shut?" asked Tony, struggling not to stare at the dead man's horrified face.

Tina nodded and, using a pen, pointed out the crisscross stitching. "I have no idea what was used to sew him up. What I don't get is why didn't he move or try to rip it out or something. But he just lay here?" she asked, bemused.

McCall took photographs while Steel knelt in front of the man's face, stared, and sniffed. Everyone watched Steel's stone-like reaction, his cold stare as if he were looking into an empty vessel.

"Something you want to share with the class?" McCall asked, her heart skipping a beat, almost in fear of what he was going to come out with.

"Doctor, whatever you do, don't remove the stitching until we get to the morgue if you please," Steel requested.

Tina nodded slowly, terrified at the request.

"Um, why exactly?" McCall asked, confused and little scared.

Steel turned towards McCall and looked up, his eyes hidden behind the dark sunglasses. "Because if I am right, I have seen this before and, believe me, you *don't* want to undo those stitches," Steel explained. His face had that stony expression that they had come to know so well.

Tina stood up, almost shaking at his revelation.

"Is that what killed him do you think that he suffocated?" Tony asked.

Tina shrugged. "I will know more once I get him back, but I am pretty sure it wasn't suffocation because there is no haemorrhaging around the eyes or blueness around the lips. No, our boy was killed by something else," she said, shooting a look towards Steel.

McCall took a closeup photo of the man's face before the orderlies placed the body into the body bag. She turned and scanned the hallway and bedroom, where Becky was talking to Tooms.

"OK. Tony, can you go and see this neighbour and get some details? Steel and I will go and talk to the girl," McCall said.

Tony nodded and headed towards the front door, leaving McCall and Steel, studying the sitting room.

"I don't think this guy has left his apartment in years, if at all. So why would anyone want to kill this guy?" McCall shook her head as she shut down her camera. "Who knows, maybe there is no reason, maybe he just wanted to kill and didn't think Carlson would be found yet. People do strange things…. you should know that Steel," McCall smiled, and looked over at Steel, who shot her a sarcastic smile and watched her walk towards the bedroom and Becky Carlson.

* * *

BECKY CARLSON SAT on her father's bed, which looked as though it had not been slept in for a long time. She looked up as McCall and Steel entered the room and wiped her eyes with her sleeve. Tooms eyed the pair and stood up.

McCall nodded to him, then watched him leave the room. She moved closer and gave Becky a friendly smile. "Hi Becky, I'm Detective Samantha McCall, and this rather intense-looking gentleman is Detective John Steel. We are here to find out what happened to your dad, OK?"

Becky nodded as another cascade of tears flowed. Steel reached into his jacket pocket and handed her a cotton handkerchief. she smiled and took it, her eyes transfixed on his chiselled looks. He didn't look like a cop, more something out of a comic-book or graphic novel.

"OK, Becky, why don't you start us off?" McCall's voice was soft and calming as it carried across the still air.

Becky closed her eyes and inhaled deeply. "Since my mom and dad split up about nine years ago, I have been coming around to make sure he has been looked after." Her gaze switched to the doorway as Tooms returned with a glass of water and handed it to her. She took a sip and smiled at him.

"Every other day, I come in before work." Becky paused as though something had slipped into her thoughts. "I work at the diner just around the corner, so it's on the way."

McCall smiled as though the girl had read her thoughts. "So, this morning Mr Edwards – he's the guy next door – well, he was waiting for me and asked if I could talk to my dad about having the TV on too loud all night," she explained.

McCall could see there was something troubling Becky as she spoke.

"I knew then something was wrong; you see, my dad had problems with his ears. He couldn't stand loud noises. Sometimes if the noise was too loud It would make him blackout," Becky said, her eyes searching, looking to the two cops in front of her, hoping they had answers.

McCall glanced over to Steel, who just nodded as though he had had the same idea. "Didn't he have a job or anything?" she asked, her voice ringing with sympathy.

Becky shook her head and looked into the hallway at the confusion.

"No, he used to be a gym teacher at the local school, but something happened years ago … don't know what … my parents wouldn't talk about it, and after that everything sort of fell apart," she explained, then wiped her tears with Steel's handkerchief.

Steel stared at the girl, his face full of questions. "What happened, do you remember?"

Becky shook her head and wiped another tear travelling down her cheek.

"No, I was only little. I know they used to be happy and then one day – they weren't. They started to argue a lot, he started drinking, stopped going to work and wouldn't leave the house. Then after a couple of months, Mom kicked him out," Becky gazed at the strange detective in his black suit and dark sunglasses, finding something mysterious and dark about him.

"So, if he lived here all by himself, how was he paying for this place?" Steel's voice rang with a soft British accent, which drew her in.

"Dad had come into some cash, he said was for a job he'd done for a friend. We had savings and well, Mom married rich after that, a dentist guy from LA, so she didn't want anything to do with Dad or his money. Benefits helped as well. The doctors reckoned he had bad anxiety about leaving home, so I would pick up his checks and sort out his life, basically." Becky smiled and shook her head.

"So, if your mom moved to LA, how come you didn't go?" McCall asked, having a suspicion about the answer, but she had to ask.

"Didn't really get on with the new guy; he thought money could buy anything. Besides, my dad needed help. I did live there for a while, but after I graduated, I moved back, God I hate LA, too suffocating. I'm a New York girl." Becky smiled and nodded. "It's funny. I remember him when I was a little girl; he was this great powerful man who lived for adventure and the outdoors. He had made plans to go around the world." Shaking her head in disbelief, she looked at the orderlies who were wheeling out her father's body. "What the hell happened, and *why* would anyone want to kill my dad?" Becky's voice trembled.

McCall looked over at the black body bag, her memories flooding back. She had the same questions, but the detective at that time – like McCall now – had no answers.

NINE

Steel hitched a ride with McCall as she headed to the morgue. They were heading there to see Tina before she started to do the autopsy on Andy Carlson. The faded blue '66 Mustang may have been old, but it drove as well as it did when it rolled off the production line. The car had been a present from McCall's dad for her high-school graduation, and after his death, she felt closer to it; this was no longer just a car, it was all she had of him.

An awkward silence hung in the air as they drove down the busy streets. McCall could tell that there was something wrong; there had been for at least a week. Normally, Steel would be his normal charming, annoying self, but he was withdrawn and distant.

"So, what have you been working on? We haven't really seen you for a while," McCall remarked.

Steel said nothing at first, just looked out of the window at the city as it blurred past. Finally, he turned his head slowly towards her and smiled. "Sorry, I picked up a case. I have been busy with that, but it can wait." His voice was deep but soft. His accent rang with a mix of higher education – Oxford or another of those fancy universities and another she could not place. He had spent time in the military, and it was known that they have their own accent. This was a man who had been many places and possibly done many things – a lot of which she knew she didn't want to know about.

McCall shot him a quick, puzzled look before turning her attention back to the road. "I don't remember any cases coming over the desk," she said.

Steel turned back to the window next to him and looked at the world as it whizzed by. The silence was only broken by the sound of the radio, playing a song from the charts.

"It's a favour for a friend; they asked me to look at something," Steel eventually answered.

McCall wanted to dig deeper, but she knew that was all she was going to get for now, but for her, that would not be the end of it. She felt hurt. After everything they had been through, Steel was keeping this one close to his chest, but then that was Steel, as secretive as ever, always with the amour, always in the shadows.

* * *

PATIENTLY, Tina Franks sat on the long stainless-steel counters that McCall liked to perch on. Normally, she would pay no heed to someone's request to put her work on hold, but there was something in Steel's voice that meant it was serious.

Tina stood tall, possessed the figure of a playboy pin-up, but had chosen medicine instead of modelling. Unfortunately, when she was a teenager, her mother had died in front of her after a road accident, and she couldn't do anything about it; this, of course, drove her to become a doctor.

Tina's flawless dark skin stood out in the blue scrubs, which most – including Steel – found very attractive. She looked up at the clock above the door and began to swing her crossed legs back and forth impatiently.

McCall and Steel burst through the double swing doors.

"Nice of you to show up ... thought you weren't coming," Tina sneered playfully.

"Sorry we're late. I had to wait for Mr Happy here," McCall nodded at Steel.

Tina tried to hide her smile by pursing her lips. "So, why is it I couldn't start to cut up our Vic here?" she asked, jumping down from her stoop.

Steel walked around the body, paying special attention to the mouth area.

"In my time I have seen ... questionable things being done to people to either get them to talk, shut them up, or just out of fun," Steel started to explain.

Tina and McCall gazed at each other, fear reflected in both faces.

"Now, one of those things was when someone was a snitch; they would, well," Steel said, pointing to the nose and mouth. He stood up and looked at Tina and smiled. "Could I trouble you for a large container with a lid?" His smile was unsavoury.

Tina smiled and nodded nervously, thinking, "What the hell does he want it for?"

She soon found a container in one of the back stores and rushed back to find Steel with surgical scissors and forceps in his hands. "What do you need those for?" she asked nervously as she approached, her gaze fixed on the forceps.

Steel smiled and got into position at the man's head. Tina stood opposite him with the large glass jar open, ready to receive whatever it was he thought was in the dead guy's mouth. "Are you ready?" he asked with an excited grin.

"Ready for *what?*" Tina yelped, uneasy at the thought of what might be coming out of the deceased's mouth.

"OK, now I have no idea what is in there, I just need you to be ready to put the lid on when the time comes," Steel explained, his expression serious.

Tina glanced at him. Even though his eyes were shrouded with those damned sunglasses, she could feel an air of confidence about him that made her feel less scared. She smiled and nodded. "Let's do this," she said, sucking in an air of assurance.

Steel smiled back and looked down whilst moving the scissors in. One by one, he cut the stitching as close to the lips as possible, so there was plenty for CSU to process. After cutting the last one, Steel slowly forced open Carlson's mouth. He looked into the depths of the mouth until he saw something. Slowly, he slipped the forceps into the orifice and moved around as if searching for something. With a victorious smile, he drew out the forceps.

"OK, not what I was expecting, but nevertheless." Steel shrugged.

Tina moved the jar forwards to receive whatever it was that had been lodged in the man's mouth. As the surgical equipment was slowly pulled out, McCall could see what appeared to be a black tail, then a hard-shiny endoskeleton.

"A scorpion? They put a friggin' scorpion in his mouth, then sewed it shut?" McCall asked softly as if not wanting to alarm the creature.

Steel carefully placed the beast into the jar, then waited until Tina had replaced the lid. They watched as she carefully placed the jar on the counter with over-extended arms.

"Why the hell would they do that?" Tina asked with a high-pitched shriek.

Steel shrugged and moved towards the enclosed evidence.

Tina thought for a moment, then turned to Steel as he patted the jar like it was a good pet and headed for the door.

"What did you mean you didn't expect to find that. What the fuck *did* you expect?" Tina asked, scared.

Steel looked at the jar and then at Tina. "A rat. This guy snitched on someone. In some places, they put a rat in your mouth while you're still alive and let them feed. You can't do anything because –" Steel stopped and thought for a moment before bolting through the door.

"Something I said?" Tina asked, confused by his sudden departure.

Rolling her finger, McCall made a "screwy" gesture beside her head and followed Steel out.

* * *

TONY AND TOOMS had spent hours looking for witnesses and doing the normal door to door, just in case someone did see something. It was almost twelve by the time they had gotten back to the precinct, and Tooms' stomach was feeling the effects, and the loud growls informed everyone else he needed to be fed.

"Man, is it lunchtime yet? I am starved!" Tooms groaned in disapproval.

Tony shook his head in amazement at his large partner

and smiled. "It amazes me how your gut knows what time it is, really," he laughed.

Tooms just smiled as he headed for the vending machine for a chocolate bar or something to tide him over. "We could have stopped at the food stand, you know that, but no, you had to rush up here," he vented, feeling his blood sugar getting low and the unpleasant bubbling from his midsection getting worse.

Tony pressed the call button on the elevator and waited for his partner, who was attacking the machine because it was taking too long. The doors slid open, and Tony blocked the door with his arm. "Hey, you comin' or what?" he smiled as Tooms ran into the steel box while ripping the end of the chocolate bar with his teeth. Tony laughed as the doors closed, and they headed up to their department.

"I'm surprised you didn't just start eatin' with the friggin' wrapper on," Tony laughed.

"Don't go there, baby – you know how I get when I'm hungry," Tooms grumbled.

"Yeah, I know … don't make me hungry, you won't like me when I'm hungry," Tony said, mimicking the Hulk.

Tooms just shot Tony an unimpressed look and flipped him the bird.

THE DOORS of the elevator slid open, revealing the bustle and noise of the Homicide Department. As they stepped out onto the floor, there was a cacophony of ringing desk phones, detectives shouting at criminals, criminals yelling as they got dragged into waiting cells, and lawyers yelling at cops. The only thing that was silent was the large screen TV. Tony nudged Tooms and nodded over to the captain's office where Captain Alan Brant stood with a tall, supermodel woman. She had dark Hispanic looks and long black hair. The two stared in wonderment: just *who* was this woman was with their captain?

Brant looked over to the elevator, saw the two detectives standing there chatting like school kids, and waved them over.

Tony shoved Tooms forward playfully. "Come on, let's see what the captain wants," he said, straightening his tie and combing his hair with his fingers much to Tooms' disgust.

"You did *not* do that; please tell me you did not just do that?" he asked, shaking his head.

Tony turned to his partner after adjusting his jacket. "Do what?" he asked, unaware that he had just groomed himself to get ready for the meeting.

Tooms shook his head and tutted. "Man, I don't believe you. I can't take your ass any place where dere's women." He felt the sugar kick in, and his mood softened. "Don't embarrass me; don't you start with dat shit, not here," he warned, knowing how Tony could get around women he thought he had a shot with.

Tony winked at Tooms as they reached the door and knocked, and the two men entered slowly.

"Captain," the two men greeted Brant before closing the door behind them.

"Agent Cassandra Lloyd, this is Detective Tooms and Detective Tony, and they are working on the bus crash," he explained.

They took turns shaking hands and making pleasantries.

"Agent Lloyd is with the FBI; she is working on the escapees," Brant explained.

Agent Lloyd wore a black suit that screamed government, but her stunning looks said something far different. She had high cheekbones and a full-lipped mouth highlighted with a subtle red-toned lip-gloss.

"We have sent you as much footage of the street as we could, as some of the cameras were either dummies or not working. I hope we can exchange notes and ideas as we progress," Lloyd said, her voice deep and sultry. Her brown large eyes were hypnotic, like dark pools of a forbidden lake.

"Absolutely," Tony blurted like a school kid with a crush.

Tooms looked at his partner in amazement. "If we get somethin', we will let you know, Agent Lloyd. As long as we are share and we ain't doin' all the givin', you know what I'm sayin'?" Tooms' tone sounded distrustful of her promise.

"Absolutely, and please call me Cassandra. After all, we're on the same team, aren't we?" Her gaze fell onto Tony, who just stood there like a rabbit caught in the charms of a viper.

"Sure, no problem," he said with a big silly grin.

Tooms grabbed lovestruck Tony and started to drag him out of the office. "Excuse us, we got … stuff to do, Captain … downtown," he said, shoving his partner through the doorway.

Brant smiled and shook his head, understanding Tooms' meaning.

"So Agent Lloyd, will you be working from here or the Bureau?" he asked, hoping she would say the Bureau.

Lloyd looked around her surroundings and smiled. "Thank you for the kind offer, Captain, but I must be getting back," she replied.

Brant smiled insincerely and shook her limp hand. "Oh, I understand perfectly, Agent Lloyd. Until next time," he said. knowing she didn't want to be around cops, and they most certainly didn't want the Feds around.

She moved quickly across the floor towards the elevator whilst answering a call on the cell phone that had just buzzed in her jacket pocket. Brant watched her press the button several times before disappearing down the stairwell next to the elevator wall.

Brant had the same uncomfortable feeling as Tooms. Was she to be trusted, and how much information would she give up? Was she here to investigate or bury? The elevator doors slid open and McCall stepped off with Steel close behind, their expressions suggesting something was not right.

"What did the doc find on your Vic?" Brant asked, walking halfway out of his office.

Steel offered an easy look and rocked an open palm. "Um, not so much on as *in*, really," he said with a grin that sent a shiver down Brant's spine.

Confused, Brant looked at McCall as she sat down in her chair hard.

"Someone had put a scorpion in his mouth and then sewed it shut," McCall explained.

Brant stood up straight after nearly losing his coffee cup he had brought out with him.

"They did what … why in God's name would they do that?" he asked, horrified at the mere thought. McCall pointed to Steel with her pen as he went to take the seat next to her desk.

"Steel reckons it was some sort of sign, you know … like, 'you're a lousy snitch' type of message," she explained. Steel looked thoughtful for a moment, then shook it off; however, McCall picked up on it.

"What … what you are thinking?" she asked, knowing that look meant *something*.

Steel sat back in the chair and looked at the board. "Why would anyone want him dead? He didn't know anybody. The man lived alone for years, with no contact with anyone for *nine* years," Steel said, rubbing his chiselled jaw.

McCall taped the pen tip on her chin as she tried to come up with something, anything.

Steel felt his pocket vibrate and took out his cell phone, opened the view screen and read the text he had just received. His face grew stony and then a purposeful look came over it. He stood up and headed to a storage room and slammed the door. Brant and McCall looked at each other puzzled.

"What's up with Wonder Boy and why the hell has he gone into the storage room?" Brant's gaze returned to the door that sat between the break room and the corridor to the holding cells.

McCall looked at the captain, just as confused. "Maybe it's this other case he's been working on?" she shrugged. Then she saw Brant's confused look turn to anger.

"What other case? This is the only one you guys have had recently," Brant growled.

McCall realized her mistake and started to head off after Steel.

"Sorry, did I say 'other' case? What I meant was …" she stumbled and offered an apologetic look.

Brant could see she was covering for him and hoped she knew what she was doing.

McCall backed into the old storage room and shut the door slowly, making sure the captain wasn't behind her. She blew out a sigh of relief. "You know the captain's real pissed …"

Her words faded as she gazed around the transformed room. Oak panelling halved the walls and the upper part had burgundy velvet wallpaper. Heavy oak furnishings hid the walls and thick leather chesterfield armchairs sat before a heavy writing desk with green leather topped inlay. Her jaw dropped.

"Oh my God, how did you … when did you?" she asked, stunned, her hands gesturing one side of the room and then the other, her facial expression changing between surprise, confusion and awe.

Steel turned in his red leather vintage cigar office chair and smiled. "I had it done during the holidays when no one was really around, and I picked up the slack while the fitters did their magic," he explained.

She looked around and inhaled the musky scents of oak and leather. She walked up to a sixty-inch smartboard that looked as though it were part of the wall and touched it. The screen immediately came on, a colourful picture view, as though it were a window showing the New York skyline. Along the left-hand side different files sat ready to be opened. Her eyes caught glimpse of one that simply said *missing*.

"So, how many channels do you get on this thing?" McCall asked, impressed by the toy.

"Sorry, I only get porn, not your taste though, I don't think," he joked, causing her to smile.

"Oh, I don't know, you'd be surprised by my taste Mr Steel," she shot back.

Steel raised an eyebrow over the top of his glasses, pleasantly surprised by the friendly flirtation.

"Does the captain know about this?" McCall quickly asked, looking back over her shoulder at the door.

Steel snuck a quick smile and shrugged. "It took a large contribution to the orphans and widowers fund, but it was worth it."

"Yes, but does he *know* you have this?" she asked,

waving her hands as though trying to point out the complete room.

"I asked for a room, and he said I could use the closet, so I did. I think he is under the impression I just sit on a bucket or something, but hey," he smiled and shrugged again.

"Yeah, some friggin' bucket." She looked around before backing onto one of the armchairs and easing into it. The leather creaked with age as she nestled herself into it. "Lucky you got a couple of bucks then." She watched him cross the room to a large wall unit that had several books and other homey pieces on it. He picked up a decanter of pure crystal and poured two glasses of clear liquid into two matching crystal glasses.

"You know we're on duty, right?" She was, shocked he would even consider drinking.

"Don't worry; it's water," he smiled as he handed her the glss. "It's not what's in the crystal glass, it's the fact you're drinking from it that makes the difference," he added with a boyish grin.

McCall took a sip and smiled to herself; she had to agree, but she wasn't going to tell him.

"I take it you told Brant about my little side quest?" Steel asked.

McCall looked at him awkwardly, but he just smiled and sat in the chair next to hers. "Tell him what? I don't even know what you are working on," she complained, holding up the glass and seeing rainbow colours dance in the cut glass. "So, what *is* this case you're on?"

Steel leaned into the chair and enjoyed the feel of the leather against his back. "It is not important; besides, I have hit a … dead end, shall we say?" he responded.

McCall nodded, hoping that didn't mean what she thought it meant.

"So, our Vic, what do we know about him, apart from he hated going outside…ever?" Steel asked, leaning back so the chair tilted.

McCall took out her notebook from her jacket pocket and flicked through the pages. "Well, he was fifty-seven years old, divorced and lived alone. Apart from that, we have nothing until records come back to us. Basically, this guy stopped existing ten years ago as far as the system was concerned," she explained as she put her notebook away and took another sip of water. She watched the rainbow colours collect on her hand as the light from the lamp passed through the glass.

"But he was a gym teacher until ten years ago, so his daughter said, so what happened all those years ago?" he asked.

McCall stood up and placed the glass on the leather part of the desk. "I guess we have to ask the ex-wife."

Steel smiled, having had the same thought,

McCall shook her keys at him as she turned to leave.

"I take it you're driving then?" Steel yelled after her as she opened the door.

"You get a car, and you can drive," she yelled back, causing him to smile wickedly.

"Oh, don't worry, I have a car," he mumbled under his breath.

TEN

It was around half past one in the afternoon by the time McCall had pulled up on the same street as Marie Heller's building. As she got out of her faded blue '66 Mustang, Samantha McCall felt the warmth of the sun on her skin, and a cool breeze flowed down the long street, brushing past her and slightly lifting her shoulder-length brown hair. The whole street had the stench of money, the apartments here were full of lawyers, doctors, and anyone with a large bank account.

"Nice neighbourhood," Steel noted, looking at the ageing architecture as he closed the car door.

"Yeah, even the muggers say please and thank you round here," McCall laughed.

Steel smiled at her quick pun as they headed towards a large building down from where they had parked. Carlson's ex had re-married into money and got as far away from her old life as she possibly could. They stopped and looked up at the towering monument to a greater lifestyle.

"Quite surprised you didn't move here," she quipped.

Steel surveyed the large lobby with its Victorian

furnishings that blended with the modern flooring and long marble-topped front desk.

"Na, too stuffy for me. Besides, it's miles away from the park," he said with a serious tone.

McCall smiled to herself, as she knew these people were either rich through hard work or someone had left it to them. Whereas Steel had to be made rich after his parents' murder, now he was Earl Steel, Lord of the Manor and head of the family business.

They headed toward a tall thin man in his late fifties that McCall figured was either the manager or the floor manager.

The man turned towards them as they approached. "Good afternoon, how may I help you?" he asked in light-toned voice with an accent that rang with excellent schooling. His tall thin frame was draped in a grey pinstriped suit that probably cost more than McCall's car. The man stood up straight as though he had a rod attached to his back. He was prim and proper, everything that money could buy given the correct schooling.

McCall lifted a large A4-sized leather organizer that had her shield pinned to the back. "Detectives McCall and Steel, NYPD. We are here to see Mrs Heller," McCall said, her tone firm, yet friendly. The man smiled and lifted a handset from its cradle, and McCall watched as he pressed a series of numbers and waited. She knew someone had answered. The man desk guy was cradling the handset as he talked, turned to make it look less suspicious.

Steel smiled and shook his head. "Yeah, that wouldn't draw attention would it?" He pretended to look around the lobby.

McCall elbowed him in the ribs and fought the need to smile.

"She will see you now. Take the elevator up to the tenth

floor. She is in room ten-eighteen," The man advised with a nervous smile, and Steel could not help but think he was hiding something – and it had nothing to do with Mrs Heller. He shook it off and followed McCall to the gold elevator doors.

"Did something seem wrong to you?" she asked as they stepped inside the car.

"Yeah, but I think that has nothing to do with what we want. It's either a vice or robbery problem ... ooh, or nark," Steel said louder than normal so everyone could hear.

"You're such an ass," McCall said, offering a stern look.

Steel just shrugged and stood in the corner smirking.

The doors opened after the short journey and McCall stepped off with the smile she had been hiding.

Room ten-eighteen was a short walk from the elevator on the left-hand side of the corridor. McCall used the brass doorbell that set squarely between the doorframe and a watercolour of a waterfall. They didn't have to wait long before a short woman in a black-and-white maid uniform answered the door.

"Hi, I am Detective McCall and this is Detective Steel. We are here to see Mrs Heller," McCall said, flashing her shield.

The maid nodded and opened the door to let them through. "Please, will you follow me?"

Steel could tell by her accent and looks that she was probably from Kosovo or some other Balkan region; he had spent enough time there when he was with the army in the 90s.

"Do *you* have a maid?" McCall asked Steel under her breath.

"No, just a woman who comes in three times a week," he admitted. "Why?"

"Na, nothin', just pictured you as havin' one," she replied, disappointed.

"I do have a butler back at the manor house though, if that helps," Steel said with a grin.

McCall stopped for a moment open-mouthed, then shot him a distrustful look, not knowing if he was telling the truth or yanking her chain. "Butler, manor house, *really?*" she asked flatly.

Steel just shrugged and carried on walking.

"Steel sometimes you're so full of ..." McCall paused, remembering where she was.

The apartment was large and modern with antique pictures and the odd furnishing here and there. The maid led them down a long hallway to the sitting room, where a woman sat on a long white couch.

"Mrs Heller, the detectives are here. Shall I prepare some tea?"

Mrs Heller smiled and nodded.

The maid gave a small curtsy and left the three alone.

McCall and Steel approached the blonde-haired woman who he noticed to be in her late fifties, though cosmetics and good living had been kind to her for she appeared to look in her late forties. The woman rose to greet them. She wore a red dress from Chanel and black-and-orange Louboutin pumps.

"Hello ma'am, I am Detective McCall and this is Detective Steel. We are here because of your ex-husband Andrew Carlson," she advised as she caught tears forming in the corner of her eyes.

Using a handkerchief that she kept in her blouse sleeve, Marie Heller dabbed the tears away before they began to flow down her pale cheeks.

"Please, sit," the woman insisted, pointing to two dark green, brushed leather armchairs that sat on the other side of a glass coffee table. The coffee table was made of bronze, with four sea serpents coming out of an ocean base. She was soft-spoken, with a hint of grace in the tone.

McCall and Steel thanked her and sat. As they settled into their seats, McCall removed her small recorder and placed it on top of a pile of magazines that lay in fanned display. Steel looked at the pile and smiled, knowing that none had ever been read by this family; they were more for decoration. A couple of women's magazines as well as some travel brochures lay amongst several other non-interesting literature, probably something to spark a conversation for when "friends" came around.

The maid walked in carrying a silver tray laden with a large china teapot and several cups and saucers; a silver milk jug and sugar bowl sat neatly on one side. She proceeded to fill all three cups and passed them around, starting with McCall, who thanked the young woman and took out her notebook.

"I presume your daughter has explained a great deal?" she asked and watched as the woman took the cup and saucer.

Marie Heller nodded to confirm McCall's suspicion. "Yes, poor girl. The doctor has bedded her down for a few days due to the shock. Strange," she smiled, making Steel's brow curl with suspicion.

"What's strange?" McCall asked the question for her colleague.

"She wanted to go back to work; she didn't want to let anyone down," Marie Heller said with a vacant look.

McCall could sense an odd tone in her voice even though she tried to hide it. "Can you think of any reason why someone would do this to your ex-husband?"

Mrs Heller stared at the dark liquid that sat inside of her cup. "Detective, my hus … ex-husband never left the house, ever. I don't know of anyone who would want to kill a man who had nothing but a case of cheap beer in the refrigerator to keep him company," she laughed softly.

Steel scanned the brightly lit apartment, various thoughts cascading through his mind. "If he didn't work, where was the money coming from for bills and stuff?"

She took a small sip and placed down the china. "After the divorce, we sold the house and we split it. He got benefits for being medically impaired. He can't go outside, so the state pays him."

McCall looked at Steel, then back at Mrs Heller. She got as far as opening her mouth to ask a question when Steel shot in with a last-minute question. "What happened ten years ago?" he threw out, hoping to get a reaction.

The woman's face dropped, and she stood up; beads of sweat started to collect around her forehead. "Well, detective, I think we are done. Thank you for calling." She made a hand signal to someone beyond the two detectives.

Steel looked around, half expecting to see the tiny maid, but instead, a bulky man with a shaven head and no neck came into view.

"Thank you for your time. I do hope you catch whoever did this. Goodbye," Marie Heller said, her voice trembling with fear.

McCall picked up the recorder and placed it into her jacket pocket and smiled with false gratitude as they turned to leave.

Steel sized up the man as he rose from his chair. Sure, he was large, but he wasn't *too* large. Steel knew he could have the man on the floor and unconscious in a minute, maybe even a couple of seconds.

"If we have any more questions, we will let you know."

McCall turned to face the now shaken woman, who quickly composed herself, straightened, and smiled like a cat.

"If you wish to speak to me again detectives, it will be through my lawyers," Mrs Heller stated firmly.

The large man extended a hand to usher them out. Steel stopped at the sitting room entrance, then turned to face Marie Heller. "Must have shook him up pretty bad when you dumped him for a rich guy."

She scowled, almost baring her teeth. "He left me alone with a child and no support, so I am not going to justify my actions to you, Detective Steel. It was his fault not mine; it was all their—" She stopped suddenly, realising what she had said.

"Their? Who is *their*, Mrs Heller?" Steel asked inquisitively.

"Please leave. If you want to talk to me in future, you can do it through my attorney." She turned and looked out a large, pained window at the stunning Manhattan view before her.

As they entered the hallway, the door slammed behind them as if in some sort of warning.

"Did you get that?" Steel smiled as McCall took out the recorder from her pocket and switched it off.

"How do you know I didn't switch it off before?"

He tilted his head forwards, as if to look down his glasses at her. "Because you knew I wouldn't leave without getting a reaction from her," he replied with a shrug.

McCall grinned as she pressed the elevator call button. "Oh, I think you hit a nerve alright, but the question is, what the hell happened ten years ago?" she asked and a worried look suddenly appeared on her face.

Steel shrugged; he had a head full of theories and none of them made sense.

"OK, so what now?" McCall asked, glancing back at the closed apartment door.

"Can I get a coffee? I never got to even start mine back there," Steel joked.

McCall shook her head in disbelief as the elevator doors slid open. "Unbelievable."

She walked into the mirrored booth and, as the doors started to slide, she thought she saw the face of the maid peer around the doorway with a frightened look on her face. As the doors closed, she knew something was wrong, more than what Mrs Heller was letting on.

ELEVEN

McCall and Steel headed back to the precinct after their little – but somewhat mysterious – chat with Andy Carlson's ex. It was getting up to around four-thirty when McCall's cell phone illuminated in its holder on the dash. She touched the screen and a text from Tina at the ME's office was quite clear: *Get your butts back here.*

The traffic was a mess, with people travelling back from work, the streets an ocean of yellow as taxis travelled with their fares. However, despite the jumble, the journey didn't take as long as McCall had thought.

They found Tina Franks waiting for them on McCall's usual stoop, soft music sounding in the background, and the scent of blood and disinfectant filling the air.

"OK, Tina, what you got?" McCall asked.

Tina jumped down and headed for the body of Andy Carlson. "Once I had removed the stitching from the nose, I found two small tubes in there; someone wanted him to die slowly," she explained, holding up an evidence bag that contained tubes around an inch in length.

"OK, so what now?" McCall asked, glancing back at the closed apartment door.

"Can I get a coffee? I never got to even start mine back there," Steel joked.

McCall shook her head in disbelief as the elevator doors slid open. "Unbelievable."

She walked into the mirrored booth and, as the doors started to slide, she thought she saw the face of the maid peer around the doorway with a frightened look on her face. As the doors closed, she knew something was wrong, more than what Mrs Heller was letting on.

ELEVEN

McCall and Steel headed back to the precinct after their little – but somewhat mysterious – chat with Andy Carlson's ex. It was getting up to around four-thirty when McCall's cell phone illuminated in its holder on the dash. She touched the screen and a text from Tina at the ME's office was quite clear: *Get your butts back here.*

The traffic was a mess, with people travelling back from work, the streets an ocean of yellow as taxis travelled with their fares. However, despite the jumble, the journey didn't take as long as McCall had thought.

They found Tina Franks waiting for them on McCall's usual stoop, soft music sounding in the background, and the scent of blood and disinfectant filling the air.

"OK, Tina, what you got?" McCall asked.

Tina jumped down and headed for the body of Andy Carlson. "Once I had removed the stitching from the nose, I found two small tubes in there; someone wanted him to die slowly," she explained, holding up an evidence bag that contained tubes around an inch in length.

McCall looked puzzled as she gazed at the man's stitch-free mouth. "But the scorpion?"

Tina shook her head. "This one was a Malaysian Forest Scorpion; its sting is about the equivalent to a nasty bee sting," she explained.

McCall looked more confused; in her head it was a done deal: scorpion stings, man dies. "So, the sting *didn't* kill him?" she asked.

Tina rocked a palm from side to side and held an undecided look. "Yes, and no."

Steel noticed a light patch on the man's wrist, where a band or chain had once been. "What if he was allergic to stings; what would happen then?" As Steel asked the question, he noticed tension leave Tina's face, as though someone finally understood.

"He had an allergic reaction to the sting?" McCall felt bad about smiling, but it made sense. "OK, so someone must have known that, maybe someone close to him?" she added as new theories began to build in her head. Steel could see where she might be going with her theory but found it unlikely.

"You're thinking his daughter did it, aren't you?" he asked.

McCall thought for a moment, then bit her bottom lip as if unsure. "She is the only one with a key, and she would know his medical history," she explained as she took out her cell and pressed the autodial for Tooms, then waited. After a couple of seconds, she heard Tooms' heavy voice over the speaker. "Tooms, it's McCall. Get uniforms to pick up Becky Carlson, will you? Don't spook her, just say it's to fill in some blanks; if she calls her mom we won't get anywhere," she said.

Tooms acknowledged her request before she hung up.

Tina waited until she finished, then held up a clear

evidence bag that contained a piece of paper. "Now, for the next surprise. We found this in his stomach. Obviously, someone had made him eat this whole, probably hoping it would be found later," she said, placing it back on the counter.

McCall took it from her friend and held it up. The document was stained, and most of the writing was illegible to the naked eye.

"Something about lies and poison!" was all Steel could make out of the once crumpled piece of paper.

"OK, can you get CSU to get Tech to look at it and try and tidy it up?" McCall asked with a smile and Tina nodded in response.

"Way ahead of yah. It said: *your lies poisoned my life*. Also, CSU found the paper and the pen it was written with." Tina gave an excited smile. "As well as the needle that was used to sew him up. They were all from the victim's house."

Steel looked thoughtful for a second, then looked at the doctor. "So, what was used as thread was too thick to be normal cotton and it was minty... wait! They didn't use what I think they used?" He cringed, feeling the pain.

"If you're thinking dental floss, you'd be right. They also found the empty package in the bathroom. This guy breaks in and uses everything that is available; he doesn't bring the stuff with him." Even though she had explained the obvious, she could feel the next question coming.

"OKk, where the hell did the scorpion come from? Oour guy couldn't look after himself, let alone a pet," McCall declaredasked with a shocked expression.

Tin shrugged and shook her head. "Sorry, that one we don't know," she admitted.

McCall smiled, a little happier there was some sort of progress.

Steel looked at the clock above the entrance; the hands showed it was just after five. "OK, I have things to do and people to see, so until tomorrow, ladies." He gave a short bow and left, leaving the women some quiet time before end of shift.

As McCall watched him leave, she wondered where he was going and was someone ending up in the hospital tonight.

THE REPORTER TOOK the subway to First Avenue because the stop was only a couple of blocks to his apartment on East Seventh Street. The noise of the braking system screamed as the train took bend, but nobody took any notice; everyone was too engrossed in their tablets or smartphones. The odd person would have a book or magazine, but nobody looked up or made eye contact.

Edward Gibbs was busy flicking through his notebook at the story he was about to put together, a story he had been working on for a while, and now he was almost ready to type it up for his editor. He was a reporter for the *New York Herald* and had been for around six years. Gibbs was one of those average guys – average height, average weight and build, average hair colour, brown with hints of grey. An average guy. The perfect look for blending in unnoticed.

Gibbs looked up as a black guy in old army greens got up and started singing. He had to admit the man was good and had no reservations about putting some loose change into an old hat the singer was passing around. The song didn't take long. It had been an old Nat King Cole number, one Gibbs had always liked and was happy the guy hadn't ruined. When the guy was finished, the people applauded and he moved on to the next car. Edward Gibbs smiled as he watched the old veteran start his performance for the audience in the next car.

The train began to screech again and Gibbs looked up, recognising the familiar sight of his station. A warm feeling came over him; he was nearly home.

The night air had a bitter sting to it like small razors hung on every gust of wind. The nights were starting to draw in and everywhere had the feeling that winter would soon arrive. The walk to his apartment block didn't take long as the cold wind hurried him along. His building had black painted fire escapes on the front, almost acting like small balconies for the residence.

Entering the main hallway, the warmth of the building hit him with a pleasant shock, making him shudder slightly; he was home. As Gibbs entered his apartment, he left the door open so the light from the hallway illuminated the room enough for him to find the light switch to the only lights he had to brighten the small apartment. These were a couple of standard lamps, and one sat on a dresser to the rear of the sofa. A faulty wire in the overhead lamp made it impossible to use. The building manager had sent a letter days ago, promising it would soon be fixed. Gibbs wasn't optimistic of it ever been changed.

It was a nice place to live, but the Ritz it was not. Despite the lighting issue, Gibbs was happy. It was cheap and it was clean and didn't need tetanus shots after using the shower. The seating area was shared by a kitchen area, next to which was a long corridor that contained a bathroom and two bedrooms, one of which lay right to the end and was now his office. The walls were painted white, the original wooden floor lay throughout. Gibbs reckoned it was cheaper than carpets, but they looked good and added a little something to the apartment.

He closed the door, then put on the chain and the two

safety bolts before taking off his denim jacket and tossing it onto the back of the brown fabric couch. The room was dimly lit, but he found it to be more homey that way.

The silence was suddenly broken by music; his ring tone blared through his jacket as the loud sound of *Pink* alerted him to his editor's call. Reaching into the front flap pocket, he drew out the phone and pressed the accept button.

"What's up, boss?" Gibbs joked as he listened to his boss' rants about deadlines. "I am nearly there; I just got some more people to speak to and then I should be done. Look, I need to get the facts right here because if I am wrong, he walks and gets away with it; they all do," he explained.

He listened as he headed towards his office down the darkened corridor. Gibbs' hand reached for the handle, but stopped suddenly with something his editor had said.

"What … what do you mean he escaped? No, that can't be. If he got out … look Chief, I have got a lead," Gibbs said, turning and heading back towards the sitting room, the loud rants of his boss booming from the cell's speakers. "Yes, I have proof … what no, it's safe, it's …"

An electric blue flash filled the hallway and Gibbs fell silent. The only noise came from his phone.

"Ed, are you there? Ed, Ed …"

TWELVE

A patrol vehicle pulled up outside Edward Gibbs' building. The officers inside were responding to a 911 call that Dispatch had put through. They didn't have many details, only that someone might be in distress. The sergeant got out and put on his hat, pulling down the peak so is nestled comfortably on his head. The other man came around and stood by him: a training officer and his rookie.

"Come on kid, let's check this out … probably nothin', but just be ready," the veteran cop said.

They entered through the main doors and looked at the row of post boxes on the wall to find the right apartment.

"There it is 4B. OK kid, let's go," the mature cop said gruffly.

They took the stairs to the fourth floor. The building was clean but still needed a little TLC to brighten it up. As they reached the fourth floor, they were greeted by a short dimly lit hallway that twisted round to accommodate the apartments. 4Bwas at the end, on the left-hand side of a long hallway, the walls of which had an off-yellow colour, and the vinyl floor looked worn but clean.

The two stood in front of the door; the sergeant stood with his shoulder to the wall, next to the doorframe. He let the rookie do the knocking. Good practice. The young cop clenched a fist so tightly his knuckles went white and knocked three times to make sure he was heard. The door opened slightly, causing them to move back. Instinct kicked in and they both drew their weapons.

"Police! Is anyone home?" the sergeant yelled loudly through the small gap. He grabbed the radio mic on his shirt and called it in. "Mike four-twenty-one, at site of the disturbance, no response to hails, apartment unsecured and dark, going in for a better look."

The response from Dispatch was a short, "Roger that. Proceed with caution."

They waited for a second before they made their move. The sergeant went in first. Nudging the door with his boot, his weapon was held close to his chest with both hands gripping the weapon. Tactical training had taught them to keep the weapon close to the body, not with outstretched arms; that allowed someone to take the gun away from a person quickly. "Keep it high and tight, and you won't lose it," the instructor had advised.

"Don't shoot me in the ass, kid," the sergeant growled in a low voice.

The rookie nodded as they made their way farther in. The apartment was in darkness, and an eerie silence hung in the air, as though the city had held its breath just for this moment. Using their flashlights, they began to sweep the room. The rookie could feel his heart start to pound as adrenaline started to seep through his veins.

"OK, room clear. We move down and clear the rooms as we go. Make sure your God-damn finger is on the guard and not on the trigger," the sergeant ordered, having had several near misses because of rookies in bad situations, but they never taught you that in the academy.

They had cleared the first bedroom and moved to the bathroom; a subtle *drip, drip, drip* was coming from behind the closed door. The sergeant moved to the left side of the door and signalled the rookie to step to the other. The veteran cop was in his late forties and too much fast food on the job had made him less of a runner. He stopped for a moment and relaxed to get his breathing right as beads of sweat started to collect under his hat. The torches created a halo of dim light around the pair, so hand and head movements could be used with ease.

The rookie could make out the sergeant's lips moving as he counted down from three. As he got to one, the sergeant swung out his arm and forced open the door. A piercing screech filled their ears as a cat came bolting out, past the rookie.

"Jesus," yelled the sergeant, slamming his back against the wall in shock.

The two officers started to laugh at the situation. Then the sergeant's head tilted towards the last room, its door open and inviting. The laughing stopped and their hearts began to race once more.

The rookie watched as the sergeant took point. He could hear every heart thump in his ears and he hung back enough so as not to get in the way – just in case the sergeant had to back off quickly.

The silence was becoming unbearable; he felt like coughing just to shatter the emptiness. The sergeant stopped at the door and backed off slowly, his expression leaning toward sickened. The young cop caught a sight of his boss' contorted face as he turned and moved back to the sitting room.

"Control – this is Mike four-twenty-one," the sergeant said and then paused, catching his breath and trying not to throw up. "Yeah, I need CSU and the ME's office down at that address you sent me to." The Training Officer – or T.O – tried to force out the words.

The young cop watched as the veteran shook his head as if trying to get the image out of his mind. Curiosity begged him to go into the room to find out what was so terrible and he could feel himself leaning towards the door.

"Don't go in there, kid. Just move back to the sitting room and we'll wait for the techs to get here," the sergeant ordered.

The kid, however, couldn't resist. He felt an urge to see what was so bad. Surely it couldn't be *that* bad? Maybe the old guy was overreacting.

At first, the young officer saw nothing. He moved the flashlight around until he found a desk and a chair, and became confused: what had spooked the veteran so much? Then his light hit the large monitor and he saw the reflection and the terrible sight.

The flashlight hit the floor as he ran for the bathroom. The veteran threw his head back and breathed in a lungful of fresh air but dared not close his eyes for fear of re-seeing that image in the monitor that was now burnt into his brain. He heard the kid blowing his dinner into the toilet and shook his head. "Told you not to look, kid."

* * *

IT WAS LATE when McCall got the call on her smartphone. She had kicked off her boots and made popcorn, ready to enjoy a movie marathon. As her cell danced around the table, she simply stared at it at first, not wanting to answer it. Its persistence became unbearable, however, and she broke down.

"McCall." Her eyes fell to the bottle of red she had just uncorked and scowled as she waited for the evitable.

"You need you to come in; we got a fresh one for you," said the nightshift desk sergeant.

"Isn't Tony on call tonight?" she asked, her gaze locked on the popcorn and wine, hoping he had made a mistake and she would be free for the night.

"Sorry McCall, he's there as well. It was the captain who said you should and I quote, get your ass to the address now, unquote" the sergeant explained.

McCall suddenly had a bad feeling. Why so many detectives? Was it that bad? She took down the address, then hung up, and scowled as she recorked the wine. Another movie night ruined.

The streets were quiet, but it was still a pain to try and park near the scene. The street was narrow and made worse by the never-ending line of parked cars.

McCall had to park almost a mile away, or so it felt. The night air was warm with a slight breeze that tickled her cheeks as it brushed past. She had no trouble finding the building as squad cars with their blue-and-red roof lights illuminated the surrounding buildings. Yellow police tape, the ME's van, and the CSU four-by-four confirmed the actual building.

As McCall stopped at the uniform at the main door, she showed her shield. The female officer nodded and gave her the sign-in sheet. As McCall filled out the document, the female uniform went back to watching the street for anyone trying to sneak in for a better look.

Inside the building, McCall followed the precession of uniforms and stopped at the fourth floor upon sighting detectives doing the door-to-door. She headed for what she thought to be the apartment, taking note of the CSU teams getting suited up for the task ahead. As she entered the sitting room, she looked around, taking in the decor of the journalist's apartment and stopped upon sighting a familiar face. She smiled. "Hey, Detective Bennett, you got me out of bed to work your case for you?"

The detective stopped talking to a colleague and turned to her with a large grin.

"Hey, McCall thought you could watch in, see how the real cops do it for a change." The two of them embraced like long-lost buddies.

"Been too long, Sammy. Heard you got a couple of news flashes recently. Very nice." Bennett laughed and McCall slapped him on the shoulder, grinning like a smitten schoolgirl.

"OK, so you didn't bring me down in the middle of the night to reminisce, so what's going on?" she asked, her smile gone and replaced with a serious look.

Bennett's face became grim. "This looks like the work of your killer. Sorry, Sammy. He's struck again," he explained.

McCall finished gloving up and nodded, and then pulled out her small camera and switched it on.

"OK, Carl. Lead on," she said with an open palm gesture.

The tall blonde-haired detective flicked his head in a come-on motion, and she followed him to that long hallway she had seen when she had entered.

Picture frames with news articles littered the walls. She took note and realised it was everything the journalist had done. She nodded in respect of his work, which spanned from Afghanistan to some guy crossing the world on a bike.

Samantha McCall got her camera and nerves ready. For her it was the unknown that was the worst part of this procedure. Not knowing what to expect, sure, she had seen some bad things, especially with the first case she and Steel had worked together, but nothing ever prepared one for that first sight of a body. Inside, she saw the other shift's ME; his name was Fowler, which matched his attitude to anyone with a pulse. He was a heavy man with red hair and round glasses that seemed too small for his large head.

"Hi, Doc Fowler. McCall's here," Bennett said.

The ME looked over and grunted a friendly greeting – or as friendly as he knew how.

"We have an Edward Gibbs, forty-five years old. He was a journalist with the *Herald*," Bennett explained.

McCall walked around the chair to get a better look at the victim. The man sat in the chair with his head back, looking towards the ceiling; cable ties on his wrists and his ankles had fastened him to the chair. His eyes were open wide with a panicked stare and, like the first victim, his nose and mouth sewn shut.

"I take it you're not going to open his mouth here?" McCall smiled.

The doctor looked up and shook his head wildly.

"Unfortunately, because this is your case, it goes to Dr Franks. She can find the special treat if she wants, too," Fowler said with a grin.

Relieved he wasn't opening the corpse, as interesting as it might be, he didn't want to find something worse than a scorpion in there. Fowler waved at the orderlies, who were waiting at the side to bag the body.

McCall quickly took some snaps of the body before they carried him off down to the ME's car that idled patiently. She finished taking pictures of the room and headed out to the sitting room.

"Where you are going?" asked Bennett, following her into the other room.

"I am going to let CSU do their thing, and then I'm going home, I'll be back tomorrow when I have had some sleep," she admitted.

Bennett shook his head in disbelief.

"So, you're leaving the crime scene until tomorrow?" Bennett asked, shocked at her cowboy attitude.

McCall smiled and nodded.

"I don't blame her; she has had a very bad day so far."

McCall and Bennett spun around to find Steel dressed in a black suit and sunglasses; a long black coat was draped over the backrest of the couch. She smiled at Steel's timing.

"Who the hell are you?" yelled Bennett.

McCall raised an introductory hand towards Steel. "Detective Carl Bennett, meet my partner, Detective John Steel."

As the two men shook hands, Bennett's eyes searched Steel's face for any sign of emotion, but the dark glasses hid everything that might give him away.

"Heard a lot about you, man, and I must say your appearance is just what I expected," Bennett laughed.

Steel looked at Bennett in his high-end suit and shiny new shoes, and his frame formed courtesy of good dining and regular workouts. He cracked a smile. "Same here," he said, his face still emotionless.

His words were short but hit a nerve. Bennett released Steel's hand, and he joked, "Only good things I hope?" As he stared into Steel's stony face, the detective broke a smile and shrugged.

"You know some good – some bad." He lost his smile and walked towards the long corridor that led to the bathroom and office. He stood at the mouth of the long stretch and took in everything. A quiet hum from his suit pocket alerted him to an incoming text; drawing it out, he read the message, then slipped it back into his inside breast pocket.

"Well, I would love to stay, but something has come up. McCall, I'll see you tomorrow." Steel turned his head towards Bennett and gave a small bow. "Detective Bennett, a pleasure, and I am sure we will meet again." He turned and hurried out the door and to the street below.

"So, that's the limey everyone is talking about?" Bennett smiled and shook his head.

McCall watched as Steel disappeared to do God knows what. "You mean, is that the right royal pain in my ass, then yes, that's him," she said with a searing look.

Bennett grinned and stuck a matchstick in his mouth. "Huh, he don't look like much to me," he scoffed.

McCall turned, a curious look on her face. "Oh, Carl, you have no idea how looks can be deceiving," she said as she headed for the door, then stopped. "And one thing: don't ever piss him off, because you may not live to regret it." She left Bennett laughing at her statement.

"Yeah, very funny, McCall," Bennett shouted out after her.

DETECTIVE SAMANTHA MCCALL headed back to the car, longing for that glass of wine. A chilling breeze howled down the narrow streets like some demonic hound, carrying with it whatever could be carried and causing loose pieces of paper to dance high in the night air. There wasn't much McCall could do at the moment; she would have to wait until Tina had carried out her examination and, besides, she would just get in the way of CSU. She stopped and looked back at the window. Bennett was looking out across the street below at something, but it wasn't at her.

Steel stopped and put on his full-length wool and leather trench coat. He pulled the high leather collar tight around his neck, so it almost covered his ears. He looked around in time to see McCall speed off in her '66 Mustang, the taillights disappearing into the night. He could feel Bennett's eyes fixed on him in wonderment. The man's question, as if was linked telepathically, would be, "Who the hell *are* you?" Steel didn't look up, just straightened his coat and checked his phone again.

High above, Bennett watched McCall's car leave, but his interest was on this Steel character. He took out his cell phone and pressed the speed dial, then waited.

"Yes, it's me – Bennett. Who the hell did you think it was? Look, she has just gone, but she'll be back on it tomorrow. What … no she's not alone on this; she has a partner. Yes, that's right, a partner. I don't know … some jumped-up British asshole," Bennett explained to the person on the other end, his gaze still fixed on Steel.

There was silence on the other end, a silence that made him nervous.

After a moment, a muffled voice came on, giving him instructions. As he listened, he continued to look down at Steel who had just pulled out a pair of leather gloves from his long coat. A gust of wind carried up the bottom of the coat like a ship's sails on a high sea. Bennett watched as Steel put on his gloves and pulled them tight.

"Yeah, that's the guy. He's got people all worked up, but I reckon he's all show …" Bennett watched as the street lights died for only a second, and when they came back on, Steel was gone, as though he had been swallowed up by the night. He gazed around in fear as a cold shiver raced down his back. Carl Bennett closed off the phone and placed it away, beads of sweat formed on his forehead.

"No way, man, no friggin' way."

Bennett's subconscious told him something was wrong with this man, something very wrong. He quickly stepped back, away from the window, and gazed into the window and the darkened background. This was as good as a mirror. His eyes dropped to the detective shield pinned on his belt strap; he looked hard at its reflection in the window. Suddenly, Bennett felt lost, alone. He gazed away from the reflection, then quickly closed his jacket, as if he didn't wish to be reminded what it stood for.

THIRTEEN

There was an eerie darkness to the night, as though all the stars had gone out. Only the bright lights of the city illuminated the way, stopping the city from being completely immersed in darkness. Steel had walked all the way from the crime scene; he needed time to think about what might come next. The text he had received was an address for some seedy bar on the edge of the bright lights. This was Irish country and he knew he had to watch his back. As he approached, Steel took note of the vehicles out front and in the parking lot next to it. This bar was full of bikers and people who just needed a place not to be found. He had seen a lot of these places in his time and all of them were as dangerous as they came.

Steel flattened his collar and walked in past two heavyset men with biker colours on the backs of their armless jackets. They looked him over for a second before considering him to be not worth the trouble. Steel moved into the bar and looked it over once, making note of exits and other means of getting out quickly, even if that meant the large window with scripted lettering giving the owner's name: Flanagan's.

He took note of a darkened corner with a small table and two chairs opposite a stall that was bathed in darkness and headed over as if he wasn't even there. Even though he had on a full-length trench coat and black suit, he blended into the shadows. He may as well of been invisible to the others. As Steel sat at the booth in the corner, he leaned back so he was immediately engulfed by the shadows.

He took his time looking around, assessing who was most likely to be a threat and, if it came to it, how best to deal with them. The smell of stale beer and cigarettes filled the air, and a thick layer of tobacco smog hung like a morning mist. Loud Irish music blared from the speakers in the corners of the room. Steel's gaze cast to the door as a man in his late fifties walked in and stopped near the bar. He wore jeans and a brown leather jacket, which didn't suit him at all; this was a suit kind of guy, a spook trying to blend in. Steel smiled as the man leaned against the bar and a giant of a man walked over to meet him; the giant had fiery red hair and a long beard to match.

"The owner perhaps?" Steel thought.

The two men spoke before the owner nodded towards the booth where Steel sat. He had to admit he didn't sneak in, but was impressed that the giant had seen him in the chaos of the full bar. The suit walked over carrying two pints of beer; he had a swagger that Steel knew to be "company" walk.

"You Steel?" asked the man.

Steel didn't speak, just pushed out the chair opposite him with his foot so the stranger could sit.

The man placed the drinks on the small table and sat.

The bulge in his jacket told Steel he was packing, probably a Glock or Sig.

"My name is Dalton, a … mutual friend asked me to look you up," the suited man said and waited for a response from Steel, but got nothing, Dalton smiled and sat back on the wooden stool, combing fingers through his short brown hair. "Sorry, you must think me a fool. Echo sent me." All he could see of Steel were his hands, which he pressed together at the fingertips, tapping his two index fingers as if in contemplation.

"Go on!"

Dalton picked up a hint of distrust in Steel's voice. "Echo said from now on I was to be your only contact … it was safer that way," he explained.

Steel said nothing; however, he could feel the man opposite him sizing him up. "The package has gone to ground, but don't worry, I will find it," Steel finally said. "What I don't get is why the company doesn't do it?"

Dalton smiled and took a sip from the condensation-frosted glass. "We just do as we are asked or rather told to do; we never ask why. Sometimes it's just easier that way, don't you think?" he smirked.

Steel sat in silence.

"I will text you later, and that will be the number you will be able to reach me on." Dalton smiled falsely, as though he was enjoying himself.

Spy games, Steel hated them. Too much sneaking around, even for him. "Anything else I should know?" he asked.

Dalton shook his head and took another sip. "No, not at the moment, but keep me in the loop as things progress." He didn't expect Steel to answer and he wasn't disappointed by his silence. A commotion at the bar made Dalton turn around as two men were being escorted out by what could be only described as muscle. "You know, you're somewhat of a legend at the agency. The one that got away, the first." Dalton laughed as he looked back.

He froze as he stared at an empty chair where Steel had once sat. Dalton raised his glass as if to toast Steel. "Good to meet you… Lord Steel."

FOURTEEN

The morning sunrise was a blazing orange that stained the city in deep umber, and a crisp breeze made its way down the maze of quiet streets. McCall had gotten to the morgue early to bring Tina her coffee and they could catch up on girlie chat. The topic was nonspecific, just not work.

"So, I know this really cute guy," Tina started.

Sam McCall rolled her eyes at yet another pitch for a blind date by her friend.

"Hey, look it's been months since Doctor Dave left for DC so who you got to scratch your lonely ass now?"

McCall said nothing; she couldn't.

"What you waitin' on? Prince Charming to wake up and realise you're there?" Tina asked, shooting McCall a questioning look.

McCall scowled at her in disgust. "You're kiddin' me, right? Sorry, but he is the last guy I would be with," she barked.

Tina could see through her lies and just nodded.

"Mmm, you keep tellin' yourself that. My point being: you need a guy," Tina said with a concerned expression.

McCall felt it was time to move on and headed for Edward Gibbs' body. "So, did you find any more friends in our latest Vic?" she asked, looking horrified.

Tina shivered at the thought of a scorpion in someone's mouth. "No, I haven't gotten to him yet, but as soon as I have something, I'll call you," she said, disappointed with the change of conversation.

"You got a time of death?" McCall asked.

Tina flicked through her notes and those of the nightshift ME. "You're looking at a TOD of around eight o'clock last night, give or take," she replied, setting down the file and picking up her coffee mug.

"The guy's editor phoned it in at around ten past, so that fits; anything else?" McCall asked.

Tina shook her head as she pulled on her gloves. "Not yet, but I'll keep you posted," she smiled.

"Thanks, Tina," McCall said just as her cell phone began to ring.

She answered it and walked towards the door. "Steel … yes, morning. Look, meet me at the *Herald* … we're going to see the editor, maybe he can fill in some blanks."

McCall's voice faded as she headed for the elevator at the end of the corridor. Tina watched as the double doors swung back and forth with McCall's dramatic exit and pressed play on the remote, filling the room with dance music.

* * *

McCall pulled up outside the offices of the tower block of the tabloid's main office. The large structure was more glass than concrete. A large LCD display sat where everyone could see. Scenes of current events and adverts flashed on the massive monitor. Steel was leaning against one of the wall pillars, waiting patiently for her to arrive; as she pulled up, he kicked himself off the wall and walked towards her.

"Good morning, detective, how are we today?" he asked in an alarmingly cheerful mood.

Sam McCall looked at him strangely, as he seemed to be in a better mood than the last time they had spoken. "You're in a good mood; who did you beat up last night?" she joked, or at least she hoped she had.

Steel just smiled and headed for the revolving glass doors.

"After you," he said ushering her into the revolving doors.

McCall smiled at him as she walked past and entered the door system. The lobby was a large open floor with a long reception desk to the side and elevators that fitted snugly into the back wall at the far end of the lobby. As Steel and McCall approached the reception, a young woman with long black hair and black-rimmed glasses cut them off.

"Hi there, I am Daphne. You must be the detectives who called?" asked the young woman. She was tall and thin with not many curves but a great behind – or so Steel observed. Daphne's hair was tied neatly and lay over one shoulder. She wore a grey trouser suit with a white blouse. The black-rimmed glasses rested neatly on a cute button nose, their over-sized lenses crowning her attractive look perfectly.

McCall shook the woman's hand first, after showing the shield that sat on her belt. "Yes, I am Detective Sam McCall, and this is Detective John Steel."

The young woman smiled broadly as she shook Steel's

hand, causing McCall to roll her eyes.

"If you would like to follow me please, I will take you to see Mr Cruise."

They headed for the elevators in silence, with only the sound of the woman's high heels tapping the tiled floor. She pressed the call button and turned to face them, her look saddened.

"It is a shame about Edward, he was … a good friend." Daphne's words were soft, with a hint of a Boston accent.

McCall opened her mouth to ask what she meant but was interrupted by the elevator doors sliding open. The smartly dressed woman stepped to one side and ushered them in with an open palm. The ride took but a moment, all of it in silence. McCall wanted to ask her more about Edward Gibbs, especially her relationship with him, but to her disappointment the elevator stopped and the doors opened on to a large room. This was the shop floor – the newsroom. This was where the daily news was written, the predictions from Meg were conjured, and the bleeding hearts of New York asked for help. Inside lay a huge bullpen, full of desks and computers. Telephones ringing and excited shouting reminded the two detectives of their own department at the 11th. Huge side windows allowed plenty of natural light to illuminate the workspace but, despite this, overhead strip lights burned.

Daphne headed to the other side of the newsroom, towards an office right at the end. The two detectives followed her taking in the surrounding bustle of the newsroom. The editor's office was large with glass walls which revealed a large wooden desk and a skyline view.

Daphne stopped outside the wooden door and knocked before entering, Steel and McCall followed her inside and waited for the editor to finish an intense phone call.

Even though he was sitting down, McCall could tell he

was tall; his broad shoulders filled out his white Prada shirt and his brown hair was full and styled. She reckoned he was about fifty but looked amazing for his age. The editor finished the call by slamming the receiver back into its cradle, and then looked up and smiled, and stood up from his leather desk chair.

"Sorry about that, some idiot … never mind, it's not important." He reached forward and shook both detectives' hands.

"Sir, this is Detectives McCall and Steel; they phoned earlier," Daphne explained, introducing the two.

The editor smiled as he took more interest in McCall than Steel. "Thank you, Daphne."

Daphne turned slowly and winked at Steel as she exited, leaving them alone to talk.

"I'm Daniel Cruise, the editor," the man said with a warming smile. "But please, call me Daniel." Cruise's handshake with McCall lingered.

Steel smiled to himself as he felt invisible. He thought about leaving and giving them room, but this was too much fun, waiting for them to realise why the cops were there.

McCall started to say, "McCall. Samantha McCall. We are here …"

"Oh yes, you're here about poor Edward. God, poor bastard," Cruise said, shaking his head. "If I can help in any way." He motioned them to sit as he took to his own chair.

"Mr Cruise, I believe you were on the phone to him when it happened?" McCall asked.

Cruise thought back and nodded, a look of shock at what he might have heard disturbing him. "Yes, he had just gotten home and he called me about a story he was working on. He said he was almost ready to go with it, he just needed one more bit of evidence and he was good to go."

"What was he working on?" Steel asked as McCall set up the mini recorder and placed it on the desk.

"I don't know, something he had been working on for a long time. All he could say for sure was that the proof he had would put someone behind bars forever. Something that happened around ten or twelve years ago," Cruise shrugged and shook his head. "Sorry, that's all I know."

McCall nodded, her eyes locked into his, searching for anything that might indicate otherwise. "How well did you know him?" she asked whilst taking a quick look at the amazing view from the large window behind him.

"Quite well, but then he had been working here for some time; other than that, it was a boss/employee relationship. I mean, we didn't hit the town or play poker on a Friday night sort of thing." Cruise smiled, trying to lighten the conversation, but his thoughts crept back to that call.

"Can you think of any reason anyone would want to hurt him, a story he had done maybe?" McCall asked.

Cruise shook his head as he leant back in his chair and placed his hands together against his lips as if to make a prayer.

"No, there was nothing. Sure, he had done some stories in the past, but that was more Bosnia and Kosovo pieces. Lately it had been cab wars or stories about this and that, but nothing that would get him killed," Cruise explained.

Steel got up and wandered around the office, paying attention to the awards on the walls and photographs of places the editor had been to.

"What about that story he was working on? He must have kept notes or something?" Steel asked as he took interest in a Pulitzer.

Cruise sat up straight and thought for a moment before buzzing his assistant. The door opened, and the woman came back in; her eyes automatically went to Steel who was directly opposite the doorway, and hid a secret smile.

"Daphne, can you take the detectives to Edward's desk, please? They would like to go through his notes."

She had a shocked look on her face. "But the police already have his stuff. Someone came this morning to collect it. They explained someone else would come to do the interview and that they were just sending for his work," the secretary explained.

McCall stared angrily at Daphne, who looked at Steel for support.

"What did they look like, uniform or plain-clothed?" McCall hammered question after question at the startled woman until Steel grabbed the poor woman and pulled her around to face him.

He smiled gently, his words soft and calming to her ears. "OK, Daphne, try and remember what they looked like." Steel's anger at McCall was hidden by a comforting smile.

Daphne looked at her reflection in his sunglasses, wishing it was his eyes she was gazing into. "They were plainclothes like yourselves, and there was two of them. One was a fat guy, kind of short and scruffy looking with black hair that was receding." She thought for a moment. "The other one was kind of tall with blonde hair, and was smartly dressed. He had a moustache."

McCall took note of the men's descriptions as they walked towards the victim's booth.

"I brought them here, they didn't search for anything, just packed what they could into boxes they had brought and just left," Daphne explained.

Steel sat at the desk and went through the drawers only to find the fake cops had taken everything.

"Did they say what they wanted the stuff for or show a warrant?" McCall's voice had softened but still held a touch of a sting.

"I guess I was still in shock when I heard he had been killed. I did try to ask, but they said someone would be back to follow up and answer any questions," Daphne replied, the look of fear still filling her face.

McCall could see that the news of Edward's death was still eating at her and decided not to press her for now. Steel stood up and turned to Cruise, who was rubbing Daphne's shoulders in comfort.

"Do you have surveillance cameras here?" McCall asked.

Cruise smiled and nodded.

"You're hoping they were caught on film?" Steel smiled.

"We can only hope … it may give us a lead on who took his things," she shrugged.

Cruise reached down and picked up the desk phone from the murdered man's booth.

"Brenda, get me security. Tell them I want any footage they got from this morning, thanks." Cruise replaced the receiver and looked to McCall. "I can get it sent to your department if you like?"

McCall smiled and shook her head. "Better if we pick it up, as things seem to go missing," she stated sharply.

Cruise smiled, but it was a different kind of smile; this one was full of admiration. "As you wish, leave me your card and I'll call you when it's ready," he said.

As McCall passed the card, the gesture turned into a long handshake.

"Until next time, Detective," Cruise said smoothly.

FIFTEEN

Detectives Tony Marinelli and Joshua Tooms sat at their desks, waiting for the footage that Traffic was sending over. Tooms shuffled through the files on the three escapes, hoping something might stick out, while Tony was going through the prison phone records to see if any of them had made any unusual calls in the twenty-four hours prior to the escape.

Tooms threw down the file and stretched; he could feel his muscles under his shirt begin to stiffen from all the inactivity and stress from lack of information in the files. "These guys who escaped have nothin' to do with what happened; they have no life, no family who wants to know them, no friends, nothin'. Shit Tony, you could be one of them," Tooms laughed.

Tony replied by giving Tooms the finger. "All these dudes had served at least twelve years, so why break out now, especially when they were coming up for the parole board? Fine, I could understand it happening on the way back if they'd gotten bad news, but on the way there? Na, man, that makes no sense." He tossed down his file and spun round in his chair to face his partner. "I hate to admit it, but you may have a point; these guys had phoned nobody – ever. So if they did bust out, who would they see, and who would help them? They didn't know anyone on the outside as far as I can see," he added.

Tooms picked up his coffee cup and mumbled to himself when he found the thing was empty. "You want a coffee? I need a coffee," he mumbled disappointedly.

Tony picked up his own cup and stood up. "We both could use a break," he said, stretching as he stood.

Tooms nodded but knew that's not what his partner meant. "Any luck on finding the guard who locked them down?" he asked Tony as they entered the break room.

"Not yet. Apparently, he got a call from out of town. His mom had been taken into hospital, so he had to take off for a couple of days," Tony explained.

Tooms shot him a look and replied with a disbelieving tone, "Well that was convenient, don't you think?"

Tony smiled, confirming he had had the same thought. "Yeah, well, I left a message with the Boston Hospital; they will get back to me as soon as they can," he said, filling up both cups and placing the clear half-full jug back into the machine.

"I just don't get any of this. It's too easy man. The bus driver, who takes a different route, a postal truck with no driver, but the tailgate is down, and now a guard whose mother just happened to have an accident the day all this was taking place. Something don't add up, that's for sure,"

Tony and Tooms took sips, their minds adrift in thought.

"I couldn't agree more," said a voice from behind.

The two men almost spilt their coffees in surprise and looked over at the break-room door to see Agent Lloyd standing there. She wore a tight black skirt and white blouse under her black blazer.

"Agent Lloyd, what are you doing back here? Thought you had to go back to your comfortable office," Tooms said snidely as he watched Tony head over to the machine to pour her a coffee.

"Well, I didn't want to miss anything. Plus, your coffee is better," she joked as she took the cup from Tony, her index finger rubbing his upon the exchange.

"Did we hear back from CSU yet referencing the crash?" Lloyd asked.

Tooms could tell she was making small talk; he knew if they wanted, they could tell the ME's office to let them know first, but she was keeping a distance. For some reason, the Feds were not taking charge; if anything, they were hanging back to see how things went.

"No, not yet, they are backed up at the minute; plus, these murders have suddenly taken priority," Tony explained, making his way back to his seat. "However, we have photos out to the media with the escapees' faces, so we are hoping someone will spot them."

Lloyd nodded as she took in the information.

"Any ideas who may have helped them … family, friends?" she asked.

Tooms shook his head. "Na, these guys had no contact with the outside, no phone calls, visitors, nothin'. We checked their personal records, visit logs, even phone records. They'd had no contact with anyone for years. It makes no sense," Tooms explained, before taking a sip from his coffee mug.

Lloyd thought for a moment as she enjoyed the coffee. "Perhaps it was an inside job; they must have paid someone on the inside to arrange it," she suggested.

Tony shrugged.

"It's possible. The guard, who normally locks them down before every trip, had to go out of town quickly," Tooms explained.

They noticed a glimmer in her eye, which could only mean they had something.

"Track him down and bring him in. He might be the key to all of this," Lloyd said excitedly.

The three of them headed for the door. As they walked out of the break room, Agent Lloyd's gaze fell towards McCall's murder board, with its photographs and timelines making a perfect collage.

"Whose desk is that?" she asked, checking out McCall's pristine looking desk.

"That's Detective Sam McCall's, why?" Tony answered.

Lloyd shook her head and paid more attention to the board. "No reason. So what's this detective Sam McCall like?" Her tone had changed; it was almost playful.

"What … um, Sam is, well, not your type really," Tooms smiled.

Lloyd turned around to face Tooms with a confused look on her face just as the elevator doors slid open.

Tooms started the introduction. "Oh, just in time. Agent Lloyd, this is Detective Samantha McCall and …"

Tony and Tooms jumped out of the way as Lloyd's cup slipped from her fingers. Lloyd was frozen in the doorway of the break room, a look of utter shock on her face.

"Oh, my God. It's you, but you're … you're supposed to be dead."

SIXTEEN

Tina Franks, ME, had sent Andy Carlson's and Edward Gibbs' bloodwork to the lab for analysis, and Gibbs' personal effects to CSU so they could get anything off them before they got catalogued. It had been a long day and it was only twelve o'clock. She had finished sewing Edward Gibbs' chest back together before she headed off for lunch.

Music from the stereo in her office played some merry tunes that Tina danced along to as she stitched him back together. She had found nothing unusual about him, just a healthy guy who died from being made to eat a magazine. Tina finished off the stitches and patted him on the head before covering him up.

"OK, you're all done." Tina stopped suddenly when she heard her stomach growl disapprovingly, as if it knew what time it was. Quickly, she tore off the surgical gloves and tossed them into the bio-waste bin next to the office door and began to get ready for lunch. Tina turned at the sound of the double doors being opened, and one of the orderlies stood for a moment, looking around the room for her.

"Yep, what's up?" she yelled, making the young man peer in her direction.

He was holding a blue file and a tense expression. "The results are back from your first victim," he replied hurriedly.

Tina put on her jacket and moved over quickly, taking the file and scanning the results. "Is this right?" she asked, shocked at what was written.

The man nodded nervously. "I ran it three times and it was the same for the second Vic as well," he explained.

Tina gazed at the orderly and smiled. "Thanks Toby, go and get yourself some lunch. You must be starved."

He nodded and made for the door before she changed her mind.

Tina went to study the file more intently when her cell-ring tone sounded in her pocket; it was a message from her lunch date, explaining something had come up. She closed the cell and put it back in her pocket. In a way, she was happy he had cancelled; the results from the lab had made her rethink everything about the murders.

She took out her cell phone again and sent a text to McCall with a simple message: get your ass back over here.

* * *

DC WAS a nightclub owner and a bit of a gangster. Since his older brother had gone and left him, he had to fend for himself and he had done OK. He made his way down the busy streets like it was any other day; he was a man without a care. He was a tall black guy with thousand-dollar sneakers to go with the rest of his overpriced attire. He wore his baseball cap with the peak tilted to one side and a pair of pilot shades to hide his eyes from the masses. He walked with a strut and with purpose, but without haste in his stride. His club wasn't far away from his loft apartment, so a car was unnecessary; besides, he just liked to get out and put on his show.

The sun beat down, and whatever heat it gave off was soon cooled by the westerly breeze, but he didn't care. DC saw his nightclub from across the street and smiled at its large enticing display screen on the outside that would show the public what they were missing. A good marketing strategy if ever there was one. The screen was eight feet by seven feet, with a protective screen in front, just in case someone got angry.

Turning on to the street, DC noticed the black transit van parked down from his club and smiled to himself as he walked across the road.

"Dumb-ass cops might as well have 'we're here' written on the friggin' side," DC laughed as he took out his keys and undid the four locks, then punched in the security code for the door. A green light blinked on and he entered the darkened club. He flicked on the house lights and, as they flashed on, he made his way to the centre of the room and looked around wearing a large grin on his face, proud of his creation.

His grin died as he saw that his office door was partially open and he reached to the small of his back and pulled out the snub-nosed .44 from its holster. True, he wasn't much of a player, but he had still made enemies; this club had also ruffled a couple of feathers since it had opened, so he had to be cautious. As he neared, he heard voices coming from inside, voices he didn't recognise. DC rested his thumb on the hammer of the nickel-plated revolver and prepared to pull it back as he entered. He would have to be quick; hell, he didn't know how many there were or if they were armed. Slowly he opened the door, hoping not to scare or cause the men inside to start shooting out of instinct. When the door opened, he saw two black guys and a white dude.

DC's eyes widened when he saw one of the black guy's sitting on his grey leather couch in the corner of the room, while another man sat in his office chair with his feet up on his wooden desk. DC held the weapon forwards, waving it from side to side, covering the three men. He had seen the men on television, wanted by the cops for breaking out of a prison bus. He recognised one of the black guys as Tyrell Williams. A bad dude that had owned that part of the town back in the day, he was now in DC's club and in his chair. Bad move for an escaped convict. Possibly a large reward for his ass … maybe for all of them. Was today his birthday?

"Hey motha-fucka, you want to tell me what the fuck you doin' with your fat ass in my chair and in my place?" DC growled.

The large man in his chair stood up and walked over to the nightclub owner. "Yo, ugly fucka, y'all got some kinda death wish?"

DC stared at the man who was several feet taller and a hell of a lot wider. "Maybe there's a reward on your asses, maybe I get Five-O down here and bust your behinds, and I get me some green? Hell, get my badass in the papers for takin' you bad mothas down, good for business," DC said, waving the gun around.

The dude started to look nervous. Why had Tyrell brought them there? Was it a setup? Was this revenge? Had this guy sent down Tyrell and he was looking for payback? That was heat he didn't need.

"Yeah, I gotta death wish if I gotta keep listenin' to you yammerin' on all fuckin' day," Tyrell growled in response.

The two men eyed each other, close enough to feel each other's breath on their skin. The air was thick with tension.

Tyrell inched closer and sniffed DC. "You wearin' perfume man?" he scoffed and backed up, laughing, waving his hand before his face as if to waft the stench away.

"It's cologne; the ladies love it. You should have had some inside. You might have made friends then," DC laughed as the two men embraced, leaving the two men on the couch looking confused.

DC and the other man turned to the others, who sat opened-mouthed and confused.

"What you fools starin' at? This is handsome bastard is my brother Adam, but he prefers DC. I guess not many people cower in fear before some guy called Adam," Tyrell Williams laughed.

"DC, this is Darius and Brian," he pointed to the two men on the couch.

The three men shook hands and waited for Tyrell's next cue.

"You should have seen your face, man." Tyrell put on a shocked look to mimic his brother's recent expression and the two brothers laughed, and then headed for the bar.

Brian and Darius just looked at each other, shrugged, and followed the brothers onto the dance floor and into the bar.

"So, I saw your prison break … very nice … but not nice enough. I got the cops watchin' my place; it's bad for business, man." DC shook his head as he poured four glasses of whiskey.

"We didn't do anything but get the hell of that bus, man – fool bus driver was goin' to fast," Tyrell tried to explain.

DC nodded as if he understood the whole karma of

the situation. "So, what you got planned now?" He smiled and turned to his brother.

"Time for some payback, brother, time for some payback," Tyrell said, then turned to the other two and slid the full glasses their way. "Tonight, we rest, tomorrow we hunt," he laughed, then downed the golden liquid in one clear motion.

SEVENTEEN

McCall had sent a text to Tina, telling her she would be there as soon as she could, but for the moment something more interesting was happening. This one reunion she didn't want to miss.

Lloyd stumbled back as if some great weight was attached to her legs. Tony and Tooms quickly sat at the table waiting at ringside, and McCall joined them. Steel made his way to the break room slowly, his gaze fixed on Agent Cassandra Lloyd, a small grin on his face like a cat cornering its prey.

"So, Agent Lloyd, how do you know Detective Steel?"

A strange look came over Lloyd's face as McCall asked more out of amusement than actual inquiry. "Detective John Steel, wow, you went back to your old name," Lloyd said with a curious nod.

The three seated detectives looked at one another, blank expressions painted on their faces.

"Hello, Cassandra, you're looking well and coming up in the world I see," Steel said. His face held its usual stony expression.

She offered him a sarcastic grin. As Steel drew closer, she slapped him hard enough to make the others wince in pain, but Steel just smiled, his cold stare cutting through her; even with the glasses on she could feel emotion burning within him and she didn't need to see his eyes.

"Ouch," Tony let out in sympathy.

"You don't think he felt that do you, not Mr Colder-than-Ice Steel?" Lloyd exclaimed.

McCall could relate to what Lloyd was saying; he had never really shown emotion as such. Almost as if it got in the way.

"You died, I watched you die. You were in that plane when it crashed, so how did you get out Steel?" Lloyd screamed.

Steel just shrugged and smiled as he headed for the coffee machine. The three detectives sat opened-mouthed, wishing they had popcorn.

"There is always a way out, and I have never been a fan of dying, I did it once and didn't like it much." Steel's voice was calm and soft. "It's good to see you again, Cassandra," he said with a warm smile.

Lloyd rushed forwards and kissed him whilst holding him tight.

Steel could feel the whole world staring at them. "Maybe we should discuss this somewhere a bit more ... private." He turned and headed for his office via the far rest-room door of the restroom, with Lloyd following close behind him.

The three detectives waited, poised like alley cats for Steel and Lloyd to leave the room before they bolted after them. Steel opened the door to his office and stood to the side, allowing Cassandra to enter, the smell of her perfume intoxicating as she moved past him slowly, but he never reacted; he just stood firm, then let the door close by itself behind him.

"Drink?" he asked, walking over to the cabinet as she stood in the centre of the room, taking in the decor before moving to the vintage cigar office chair she had spotted behind the desk.

"You know we are working?" Lloyd asked, surprised at his offer.

"Don't worry, it's only $H2O$, not vodka," Steel said, pouring himself a glass.

"In that case, please," she replied, and they both looked over at the door as it burst open, and Tooms and Tony walked in as if by accident.

"Sorry, this isn't the men's roo…" The wit was cut short as they noticed the offices layout.

Tony started with, "Oh my …"

"… God," Tooms finished for him as they looked around the room, mouths open in amazement.

"Please come in, guys; it's only an office, God, you would have thought they have never been here before," McCall joked as if she had been there many times before.

Tooms and Tony shot her and then Steel an evil look of jealousy.

"She's just pullin ya pisser, gents." The two men shot Steel a confused look over the British slang. "She's taking the mickey, having you on…," Tooms and Tooms nodded with an "ooh, right" after explanation became clear. "She saw this place for the first time the other day, and oddly had the same look as you two silly sods are wearing," Steel continued with a smiled.

Tooms made a watching-you gesture with his fingers at McCall who was laughing at their expense. Steel gestured for everyone to sit down and walked to the smartboard on the wall,

"So, what happened. How did you get out?" Lloyd asked as she made herself comfortable in Steel's chair.

He just shook his head and touched the screen, activating the on switch. "That will have to wait I'm afraid. We have bigger problems." Steel said.

The screen showed several icons on the large bright screen, and he touched the one that was entitled "Crash". The file opened to display a series of photographs; moving his hand, he activated one of them, enlarging it so it filled the screen. The photograph was of the scene but from above; the whole area was captured from the corner with the delivery truck to the crash site.

"You have a smartboard. We are using stone-age equipment and you have a smartboard," Tooms yelped with disappointment. McCall slapped Tooms on the back of the head to shut him up as she walked past.

"Focus, will you," she ordered, making Tony smile.

"What channels you got on that – Superbowl for this Sunday?" Tooms interjected.

"Na, but rugby is on, England vs the All Blacks…you in?" Steel joked.

Tooms bottom lip curled up like a disappointed child. "Okay, so we have a bus that somehow crashed, but my question is, *why* did it crash?"

Steel looked around at the thoughtful expressions of his colleagues.

"Bad weather and bad driving?" Tony threw in.

Steel thought for a second then shook his head.

"Just bad luck, wish of the gods … who knows, man. CSU will find that out," Tooms barked, still pissed about the smartboard.

"We find out the why, then we find out the who," McCall nodded in agreement.

"That's great, but we are investigating two murders, not the bus crash, that's someone else's thing," Tooms said.

McCall could see Steel was leading to something; there was always method in his madness. "You think they're related, don't you? You think they may have broken out to kill those people?" she asked with a curious stare. She could see the logic behind his thinking.

Steel didn't say anything, just turned to the others as he stood next to the smartboard. Finally, he spoke. "OK, so I took these photos not long after everyone had left so I could get a clear shot without the masses of cops and CSUs. Question: what do you see?" Steel asked before taking a sip of his drink.

Everyone held a puzzled expression at the question.

"It's the crash site, man; what more do you want?" Tony responded.

Steel shook his head and looked to the heavens for inspiration. "Look closely. What do you see? Look mainly on the road," he urged them.

Everyone got up and moved towards the screen for a closer look, each straining to be the first to find what Steel was talking about.

"Na, you got me, man, ain't nothing there, just the tire tracks and the skid marks," Tooms grunted.

Steel grinned at Tooms as if to tell him something.

"What, the tread marks? You serious?"

Steel nodded and opened up the small bottle of water he had placed on the desk. "The reason the tread marks are still visible is because of a high concentration of oil. Did anyone check what the delivery van was carrying?" he asked.

McCall shook her head. "No, but CSU still have it as part of the investigation," she answered.

Steel pointed towards the board. "This was no

accident, someone planned this. That bus was meant to hit that van so the back door could be damaged. Whoever planned this had it down to a science," he said, his words holding a ring of excitement to them.

Cassandra Lloyd looked closely at the photograph; something she saw troubled her.

"Whoever did this, had massive resources. They would have to get that delivery van, bribe a guard," Lloyd noted.

"Two guards!" Steel corrected her, causing Cassandra Lloyd to glare at him angrily.

"How do you figure *two* guards?" she asked, folding her arms across her chest in a defiant gesture.

"The bus driver changed route when there was no need to. Also, why was he driving so fast? Someone had gotten to him, along with the guard who locked them down," Steel answered with confidence.

Cassandra Lloyd smiled and turned back to the board; she had a sudden feeling like it was the old days. "So, we need to check financials on both the bus driver and the missing guard, see if there is a money trail," Lloyd said, looking at Tony and Tooms.

Tony reached into his pocket and pulled out his cell to read the text he had just received. "CSU want us down there – they say they may have found something." Tony read out the message.

"We'll go," McCall said, remembering the previous text she had gotten from Tina. "I said I was going over there anyway." She showed Steel the message on her cell, which made him cringe.

"We better hurry up then. I have had enough of crazy doctors with sharp objects for a while," Steel declared and shivered jokingly. As he headed out the door, Lloyd cut him off and put her arms around his neck, her look filled with passion.

"You, sir, owe me dinner and an explanation," she said, her voice low and sultry.

Steel smiled and nodded slightly. "Fair enough, when this case is done," he replied.

Lloyd gently pressed her full lips against his, feeling his warmth against her body. "OK, after the case, so no going on any trips," she ordered jokingly.

Steel pulled her off slowly and made for the door, leaving Lloyd with a big smile on her face.

"Hey McCall, make sure he doesn't go on any cruises will you," Lloyd laughed.

Sam McCall turned to Lloyd. "Yeah, well, I don't think ships are his thing at the moment; they doesn't seem to agree with him," she laughed and left the room.

* * *

STEEL AND MCCALL hurried down the white-walled corridors of the morgue towards Tina Franks's office. Tina's message sounded urgent; normally she wouldn't request someone come down unless it was absolutely necessary. Just a couple of lines on a text or a phone call would be enough, but she wanted to tell them personally how this case had gotten weirder. As they neared, Steel stopped McCall by grabbing her arm.

"Hang on a minute before we go in. Did you tell Tina about what just happened?"

McCall's mouth fell open with a look of disgust. "John Steel, I do not believe you would think that I would do anything so …" With that she broke away and slammed through the double doors.

Steel shook his head and readjusted his sunglasses. "Oh great, this will be fun," he groaned. As he pushed his way through the double swing doors, he found ME

Tina Franks with her arms folded and a large grin on her face.

"I heard someone had an interesting day," Tina said with a raised eyebrow.

McCall smiled and stood by Edward Gibbs' head, just out of arm's reach.

"So, you got any more ladies stashed away there?" Tina joked.

Steel looked up as though he was remembering and counted, using his fingers on both hands.

"Yeah, yeah very funny," McCall growled, making Steel crack the side of his mouth with a brief smile.

"We ran some tests and your first Vic and found something unusual – someone had dosed him with scopolamine," Tina explained.

Steel looked confused for a second. "Truth serum! So he was interrogated before he was killed?" his voice rang with surprise. He hadn't seen that coming he had to admit.

Tina tilted her head from side to side as if to say "sort of". "In certain doses, it has different effects; truth serum is one of them. Also, in heavier amounts, it can be used as a good suggestive tonic. It's like a date-rape drug, but the person is awake and has no memory of the event."

McCall looked at Tina with a surprised look. Sure, she had expected something in the system, but not that. "And if the dose is too high?" She had already figured out the answer, but she felt she had to ask anyway.

Tina just gave a look that needed no further explanation.

"Well, that explains why he wasn't restrained; he was knocked out!" McCall looked over to Steel with an excited look. "First piece of the puzzle," she thought.

"It was in your second Vic's system as well," Tina admitted.

Steel had figured as much – these killings were connected somehow and someone wanted them out of the picture, but the question was why?

They stood by the body of Edward Gibbs, who Tina was working on before they came in. "OK, so your boy here was sewn up like the first Vic, and he too had a note shoved into his mouth." She pointed to a clear evidence bag and, once again, inside was a note.

McCall lifted the bag, but the stomach juices had gone to work on it. "How come we can't read this one?" she asked.

"This fine fellow tried to throw up, but the piece of paper stopped the vomit from going anywhere," Tina said, shaking her head.

Steel nodded as he could visualise the effect.

"Don't worry, I am sending it to the lab, see if they can lift anything off of it," Tina said with a less than hopeful tone.

"So, he choked on his own puke, in essence," McCall exclaimed.

Tina nodded as she pulled the sheet back so the detectives could get a better look. Steel saw something on the man's left side near the ribs that made him move closer. "What are these?" he asked, pointing out twelve small round burns.

"I don't know. I took some photographs and sent them to Trace to see if they had any idea," Tina said.

Steel looked at the small marks and tried to work out their pattern. Each was the size of a mark of a ballpoint pen and around an inch apart. He looked up and faced the two women. "I know what this is; he has been tasered," he said.

Tina looked confused for a moment.

"No can't be, it doesn't match any Taser we know of." Her words rang with assurance.

Steel used his thumb and index finger to measure them. "It would fit if he had been zapped several times," he explained, using his two fingers to mimic the action.

McCall's face screwed up at the thought. "Someone really wanted him to suffer!" she said cringing.

Steel nodded in agreement. These were not just killings. These were personal – *very* personal.

"Did you take any pictures of the hallway leading to Edward Gibbs' office?" McCall took out her little camera and flicked through the latest pictures, thinking how lucky it was she had forgotten to upload them on to her computer.

"Um … wait a minute." Steel looked on impatiently as she sifted through her shots from the crime scene. "OK, here they are, why?"

Her question was short-lived as Steel snatched the camera from her and tried to make out details on the inch square monitor at the back of the small device.

"Oh, bugger, You can't see a sodding thing. We'll just have to go there…come on! You're driving," Steel said, rushing out of the double doors. McCall scowled as he left the room, leaving the double doors swinging from his urgency.

"Oh, bye then," Tina shouted after him with a blank expression on her dark-skinned face. As McCall left, she turned to say goodbye to her friend before she went running after Steel.

EIGHTEEN

Agent Lloyd had gone back to the comfort of her office downtown, leaving Tony and Tooms to dig up information on the men on the bus. If Steel had been right, the bus was made to have undergone that crash, and someone on that bus knew about it. Tooms looked around to see where McCall and Steel had stashed themselves.

"Hey man, where's McCall and Steel … thought they would be back from the ME's by now?" He groaned as he looked at the mountain of files on the inmates who had travelled on that bus.

"McCall and Steel are on their way to Edward Gibbs' apartment to work on a hunch; she phoned it through earlier," Tony smiled, feeling his partner's frustration. This case had been more a paperwork exercise than anything: checking phone records and financials once they had gotten through the backlog. Tooms preferred the fieldwork of the job, not riding a desk, and Tony was the same. But this case was all about finding out who these people knew and who had the means to pull off an escape like that.

. . .

When McCall and Steel arrived at Edward Gibbs' apartment, where he had lived and ultimately died, the yellow police tape still covered the door, warning people not to pass. The uniforms that had stood guard at the door had left as soon as CSU was clear from the site and secured it. McCall took out the key she had gotten from the super and unlocked it. There was a gentle click as the bolts disengaged. She took in a deep breath, and with a gentle push, the door swung open freely. The smell of chemicals and dried blood filled their nostrils, making them back off by the suddenness of the stench. They climbed through the tape and Steel immediately headed for the hallway.

"Now, I saw it before but didn't really pay it much notice," Steel explained. He led McCall to a picture that was hanging oddly, one side tilted at though it had been moved.

"You think the killer knocked this in a struggle?" McCall was tired, and she could tell he had a head full of theories.

Steel shook his head and knelt on the ground next to the skirting board. "If you look, you can see scuff marks on the wall, which in itself does not say anything, I will grant you that." He pointed to six marks on the wall that was straight-lined vertical marks.

McCall looked puzzled as she regarded the fresh evidence if indeed that was what it was.

"Oh, come on, how do you know it was made by our Vic? Surely they would be horizontal if he were kicking while he was been attacked?" she asked impatiently.

Steel smiled and lay down on the floor and raised his own boot to the area. "Who said he was standing?" he grinned.

McCall reached down and helped Steel to his feet with a yeah-yeah look on her face.

"The first hit would have put Gibbs down, and the others were – well, to the killer necessary. Look, if you are going to taser someone, you are not going to be holding them." Steel dusted himself off as McCall gazed back at the marks. "not unless you're a complete moron that is."

"But why move him? We found our first Vic had died where we found him." McCall shrugged and eyed him questioningly.

Steel raised a curious eyebrow. "Yes, but that then tells us something about the killer; they have very little in the way of upper-body strength." He thought for a moment, considering the size of Andy Carlson. He was a big man, and it would have taken some strength to move him, but it was possible. "The killer never brings anything that can be traced back. They used dental floss to sew the mouth shut on Andy Carlson."

Steel quickly headed for the bathroom. Moments later, the sounds of things being emptied into the washbasin told McCall he was having one of his moments. She was just about to follow him when he came out holding a case of dental floss, almost frightening her to death.

"He did the same thing here; he used Edward Gibbs' floss to sew him up." Steel placed the container into a baggie that McCall held out for him. He then slowly took in the layout before him, his brain processing everything as he looked around the sitting room.

"What's wrong?" McCall asked, knowing that look all too well. It was one of those that someone had when they were doing a jigsaw puzzle with no diagram to follow.

Steel looked over, and she could see he was working out the series of events in his head as he stood and stared at her.

"We need to know what was on that note," he said with an irritated look.

* * *

The afternoon sun was bright but gave very little warmth to the city below. The air had become still, and the easterly wind had died to nothing stronger than a breath. People went on their merry way, some going to lunch and others wasting the day away. Restaurants and delis lined the street – everything from coffee houses to Chinese food.

A girl dressed in dark clothes with a dark hoodie sat at a window counter with several bar stools; the place was full of people with laptops and coffee mugs containing hour-cold coffee. She sat, pretending to drink, but nobody noticed her; she just blended in. She looked out the window and took note of human traffic as it passed, oblivious to her existence, but she preferred it that way. The dark cowl hid her pretty, young face from the world and the short black hair and pale complexion made her look older than her youthful nineteen years.

She took another pretend to sip from the cardboard cup as she had done for some time; she had to fake it as the cup was empty, a decoy that someone had left for one of the busy staff to clear away. The young woman's gaze suddenly fixed on a black woman in her mid-fifties. The woman wore a black jacket and skirt with a white blouse. The girl's eyes locked on her, daring not to blink just in case she lost her in the sea of people.

Quickly, she got off the chair and made for the door, trying to keep her target insight as she ducked under a man's arm as he opened the door to enter the coffee shop.

The girl looked round in the crowd of pedestrians, frantically searching, and smiled as she caught a glimpse of the woman walking on the other side of the street. She didn't know the woman she was following, but she knew her face from an old photograph.

They walked for what seemed forever, the girl wondering where they were going, then she stopped suddenly as they approached the courthouse, its large majestic form holding a sense of foreboding. The girl shook off the thoughts running through her head and made for the woman, all the while, hoping that her destination was past the large grey-stone building.

The woman walked up the steps, making the girl's heart sag. Maybe she was there on jury duty, she thought along with other hopeful ideas.

"Afternoon Judge Matthews," one of the security guards cried out and gave a friendly wave.

"Afternoon Mr Jeffries, how are the wife and kids?" the judge replied, happy to see a cheerful face.

"Oh, just fine, thanks. You have a good day, Judge Matthews."

The woman waved and disappeared through the large doors at the entranceway.

"Oh shit, she's a judge," the girl thought. She had found her, however, and that was all that mattered for now.

***

THE DAY HAD BEEN a long one for all; much had been discovered but not enough to draw them closer to the killer or find the missing prisoners. McCall peered up from her computer screen and looked out at the dark purple of the sky as the sun began to set. She had not realised just how late it had become, as though the last few hours had been stolen away by sifting through files and records.

She stretched away the pains of deskwork and stood up, hoping to make it home and settle down after a deep bath and a glass of red. She smiled at the thought of a quiet evening, but that soon faded as her desk phone began to ring. McCall stared at it for a moment, daring herself not to pick it up, her hands still on her jacket's collar as she'd pulled it up. She cursed herself as she picked up the receiver and answered the call, hoping it could wait until tomorrow.

"McCall, Homicide." Her inquiring tone was as false as it came, but years of practice pulled off the voice of interest.

"Detective, if you want to know more about the killings, come to this address." The caller gave her the address of a warehouse near some elevated train tracks and, before she could ask anything, the phone went dead. Every instinct in her body told her that there was something so very wrong about the call, but she had to check it out. Steel had left to sort out some "personal" things; however, she sent him a text explaining everything anyway.

* * *

ALL THE WAY to the meeting point, McCall had a bad feeling – the sort of feeling you had when you wished you had a bigger gun. As she turned a corner leading to the street of the meeting, she noticed that the sun had begun to draw down into the distance and was pulling the light of the day with it like a dark blanket. The address was in a large parking lot near the elevated tracks of the subway.

McCall pulled in slowly and then stopped to get a lay of the land. In the distance she saw two large buildings and in the centre sat a red Camaro. The place was bathed in darkness, less for an exterior light from one of the buildings and the odd blast of light from a passing train. She studied the situation and pulled out her Glock 17, pulled back the custom polished steel-top slide, and let it pull forward under its own spring power.

She pulled up slowly towards the other car, taking note of the scattered vehicles in the lot as she made sure they were alone or, more to the point, Steel wasn't hiding somewhere. She stopped and got out of her faded blue Mustang, which she left running just in case she had to get the hell out of there quickly. McCall felt a little better knowing her service pistol, which was back in its holster at the small of her back, was ready to go, as was her .40 Smith and Weston Nano, which was strapped to her right ankle. As she walked cautiously forward. McCall stopped when she heard a car door open, then saw a silhouette of a man – who must have gotten out of the driver's side – come into view as a train rumbled past, the light from the carriages briefly illuminating the lot.

McCall felt a chill run over her as she noticed the car was parked with just the front end visible, making it impossible to see if there was anyone else inside; however, she knew without a doubt there would be. The man began to approach her as a train hurried past, illuminating the area. He was a thin spindly man with a receding hairline and a fashion sense out of the eighties.

He stopped halfway, and McCall halted just short of that, so there were at least four feet between them. She watched the man as he nervously rocked from side to side, his hands firmly imbedded inside his jacket pockets. There was a screech of brakes from the train as it sped by and as the train trundled into the distance, the parking lot was once more cast into near darkness.

"Y-you the c-cop?" The man's voice held a southern accent as he stuttered a few words.

"And what if I wasn't?" McCall replied.

The man looked confused by the question, and she

could see he was no rocket scientist. McCall thought for a moment, then decided playing with him wouldn't really get her very far.

"Yes, I am the one you spoke to, so what you got for me?" Her hand slowly crept to the small of her back, and her fingers tightened around the cold polymer grip. A scream of metal-on-metal filled the air as an outgoing train sped past, the light not as bright, but enough for her to see the man in front of her draw out a snub-nosed nickel-plated .44 revolver and thrust it forwards towards her; she had instinctively done the same.

The two of them held off in a stalemate, each having the other in their sights; however, McCall had the steadier hand and probably more practice.

"OK, so what now?" she shouted at the man, who was now sweating buckets despite the cold night air.

The train disappeared into the distance, taking the light with it.

"What do you think, you dumb bitch? We gonna kill yer cop ass, then collect our money," said the would-be assassin.

McCall knew he would probably fire the next time the train came around, so she had to be either smarter or quicker.

"Well, if I am going to die, can I know why?" She heard a boot scuff the ground, as though he was kicking dirt out of frustration.

"Look, we just paid to kill ya, not chat. Got it?" the man spat.

A shiver ran down McCall's back. "What do you mean … we?" She heard the man yell to the car, then the sound of three car doors opening and closing. The others would be too far away but, hopefully, with the poor light, they would be unable to see anything from their location, even when a train passed by.

McCall could hear the next train coming in the distance; her only hope was to drop to the ground and shoot from there. This would be a one-chance deal. When she heard the clatter of the wheels on the track, she dropped to the ground, ready.

The assassin watched the light sweep the parking lot as if in slow motion, his finger ready on the trigger and a special smile on his face as he could envision her brains leave the back of her head in his mind. He gripped the weapon with both hands, ready to end this cop's existence for good. But his smile faded as the light swept past and illuminated someone else – a large man dressed in black and – sunglasses! The last thought the assassin had: why the hell has he got sunglasses on in the middle of the night? His *very* last thought.

The men by the car heard a woman's loud scream. They laughed, thinking their friend had killed the cop.

A crisp wind blew, and everything went dark as the train trundled off, leaving an echoing melody off the wheels on the track. That's when they realised it was too dark, and they looked to where the building light had given some light off but that, too, was in darkness.

"What the hell's going on, man?" yelled a large, stocky man, who stood near the front passenger door while four men stood by the Camaro, gazing blindly into the darkness.

The sound of the next train approaching gave them a little comfort. As it drew near, a scream from the rear of the vehicle made the others turn, just as the light from the train illuminated the area and the empty space where the man had stood. The men, who were armed with handguns, spun around, hoping to catch a glimpse of anything, but there was nothing … nothing but shadows until the train took its light far off into the distance.

"What's going on, man? This was supposed to be a simple job. Kill the cop and get our money. Didn't say nothing about a fuckin' ghost," yelled the man at the rear of the car nervously.

"Shut your friggin' mouth. There ain't no ghost. Mikey probably went inside to see if he could find a light switch, that's all," shouted the other guy.

A train on the other side of the track flooded the area with an intermittent light, revealing an empty space at the rear of the car where the other man had stood.

"Screw this, I am outta here," the man on the driver's side mumbled as he yanked open the door and slid in. The engine roared to life as his partner got in next to him.

"I'm with you, man, let's get the crap outta here," the man at the passenger side yelled.

The driver nodded and put it into drive. The tires spat gravel as it sped away, swerving past McCall's Mustang and the body of their colleague. The headlights did little to guide the way in the darkened parking lot, and parked cars suddenly appeared as the men hunted for the exit, causing the driver to swerve erratically to miss them.

"I can't see a God-damn thing. Where the hell is the exit?" yelled the driver, full of panic.

As they turned past another set of cars, they saw the lights of the train approaching on their right-hand side.

"Damn it, man, we're going around in friggin' circles." The passenger cursed loudly, slapping the driver on the head.

The driver looked back at him and bared his teeth. "Do *you* want to drive?"

The man was about to answer but screamed out instead, pointing forwards. The driver's gaze shot forwards in time to see a tow truck in front of them with its ramp down. He went to swerve, but it was too late, and the car's left side travelled up and off the back of the truck, flipping the car onto its roof. Bright sparks showed the direction of the car's erratic travel until the building in front stopped it with a loud crescendo of metal and brick.

The night was once more silent, less for the noise of the train fading into the darkness and another sound – the sound of boots walking slowly across the parking lot towards them, scuffing loose gravel and broken glass as they went. The two men sat strapped into their seats, trying to get their breaths back, but anxiety denied them that, and their hearts pounded in their chests. The footsteps stopped; silence filled the air.

"Is someone there, hello?" the driver yelled as he tried to unbuckle the seatbelt, but it was stuck, and so was the one on the passenger side. The silence continued, making the two men even more nervous. What was the cop up to? How had she taken all their men out?

"Hey, is there anyone out there? … Help us, please, damn it." The driver's anger was a mix of fear and annoyance. The footsteps started again, and this time they were much closer. "Hey, you!"

The driver stopped yelling as he heard what sounded like water being emptied from a petrol can. Then, from the dim light of the car's radio, he could see the glint of light reflected in a pool of liquid that had collected on the roof below him. The two men fought with the binding belts, tugging at the material and the locking devices.

"Hi there," came the voice of a man with a friendly British accent.

The two men stopped struggling and breathed sighs of relief.

"Hey, man, we had a bit of an accident; could you get us out?" asked the driver.

There was a pause as if the stranger were thinking. Outside the upturned vehicle, Detective John Steel knelt on one knee, a little to the side of the door so the driver couldn't see him. "Sure, not a problem – oh, wait. Sorry, I can't," said he.

They listened as the stranger began to walk again, then stopped – then the sound of gravel scraping the ground as the stranger turned on his heels.

"Oops, sorry. Nearly forgot. I have a friend who has a couple of questions, which by the way I hope you don't answer because it gives me an excuse to try this experiment I saw on television," Steel said excitedly.

The men suddenly had a bad feeling that things had gotten worse for them.

"Um … try what experiment?" the passenger asked, hoping he was wrong about the answer.

"Well, you see, I have a theory that an emergency flare can light fuel. I have seen it in the movies and always wanted to try it," Steel said with a bounce in his tone.

The men went back to trying to get out of their seats, but they were stuck fast.

"What do you want, man?" cried the passenger to the shadowy figure.

"Answers!" This time it was a woman's voice, and it wasn't as friendly as the British guy's.

The two men froze at the tone.

As McCall walked up to the car, she nodded to Steel appreciatively. He nodded back; no words were needed. "Who sent you?" she asked, her words bitter.

"Oh, shit, you're … you're that bitch cop?" The passenger's words were filled with fear.

"Yeah, and I'm feeling the bitch coming out of me

right about now, so answer the friggin' question. *Who* sent you?" she growled.

Steel could see she was angry but in control. He had to admit her restraint was impressive; if it had been most people, they would have barbequed the two men by now. There was a bright light from a flashlight, which filled the small space of the vehicle, and now everyone could see one another.

"Hey now, you're a cop, and cops don't do that shit. You gotta protect us." The men laughed until Steel came into view, holding the flare pistol. Then they realised their full peril. "You have got to be shittin' me."

Their mouths fell open in fear when they saw Steel's leather-gloved hand holding the emergency flare with a large grin on his chiselled square-jawed face.

"Who sent you?" Steel asked; he hoped the flare in his grasp might encourage them to answer.

"I don't know, I swear. Someone pushed a note under our door at the hotel, and it told us to get rid of some female cop, and we could get 250K. I swear it just gave us directions and a time to here," the driver spluttered.

Steel tapped the top of the flare on the driver's head.

"Where did you get the hardware from?" McCall asked, having trouble believing their story.

"It said everything would be provided at the location … even threw in this car," the driver answered.

Steel looked puzzled for a second before asking. "How big was this bloody note?"

McCall gave Steel a nasty look, then tapped the passenger on the head with the flashlight to regain their attention. "So, you're telling me that someone picked you guys out of a cast of millions to do this?" she laughed.

The two men looked at each other, then back to McCall and nodded.

"Pretty much, that's the truth. Look, we came into the city to have a good time, which didn't work out too well when we got arrested for takin' a leak," the passenger admitted.

McCall looked confused for a moment. "What did you do, pee on a church or something?" she asked.

The two men nodded with an embarrassed look on their faces.

"Did you think you wouldn't get caught? Didn't you think I would come with back-up?" She could see by their expressions that the thought hadn't come into their minds, just the idea of easy cash. McCall stood, shaking her head as she tried to grasp the very idea of it all, turned, and started walking back to her car.

Steel stood and started to follow.

"Hey, what about us?" shouted the two men.

Steel was a good twenty feet from them before he stopped and turned. He aimed the flare and fired it. Everything seemed to slow as the ball of red light propelled towards the screaming men in the car.

McCall stopped and turned, her screams for him to stop mixing with the men's. The bright light illuminated the terrified faces of the men, who struggled to break free of their binds. Everything turned red as the fireball drew close to the car. The men held each other and closed their eyes, as if not seeing it would help.

The screams stopped; silence carried through the air once more. The men in the car opened their eyes to see no flames, no death, just the two cops walking away in the distance.

"You used water, didn't you?"

Steel said nothing, just grinned childishly.

"You're a sick bastard – you know that?" McCall tried

to contain the relief but punched him in the arm anyway as he headed off in the other direction.

"See you tomorrow, McCall," Steel yelled back without turning around.

"See you tomorrow … and stay out of trouble!" She laughed as she pulled out her cell phone to call it in. As she looked back at the upturned car, she couldn't help but wonder who wanted her out of the way and why. Was it because of the case or something else? She got through to Dispatch and ordered an ambulance, a tow truck, and the usual entourage concerning an incident with an officer.

Internal Affairs would send someone to make sure there was nothing untoward. The smile fell from her face when she thought of the men's account of Steel pretending to burn them alive. She shook the thought; somehow, IA was never interested in Steel, almost as if someone were covering his ass from up high. Either way, Captain Brant would have her ass for going alone, but Steel would say he was backing her up. What more back-up could anyone need?

NINETEEN

The darkened streets of Broadway were lit up by store windows and passing traffic. A cold wind hung in the air that nipped the noses or ears of those not prepared for the winter chill. People moved about sluggishly from place to place, some with no purpose other than to get home.

The girl walked steadily, endeavouring to blend in with the crowds of people. The judge had left the courthouse hours ago by taking a cab, so there was no hope of her following her to the next location. No, tomorrow was another day, the girl would get to her then. She pulled down the hood to shield her face as a bitter wind came rushing down the street. She just wanted to go home and sleep so she would be ready for tomorrow.

She stopped at the mouth of an alleyway and looked around before disappearing inside. The alley was dark but free of the biting wind. As she disappeared into the void, a large man who stood casually at the entrance waited for a moment, then headed to a waiting vehicle. He was a large black guy in a black suit with a black polo neck. He got into a dark-coloured Ford, but his gaze never left the alley.

"You know we will have to keep tabs on this place; if she keeps coming back, then we can assume it's home," the driver noted, his Irish accent broad with a deep tone.

The black guy nodded in agreement to his pale, red-haired partner's assessment. "We'll come back tomorrow, then we'll see." He had a feeling she was leading them on, and tomorrow they would find out.

As the car sped away, the girl came from the shadows and stood watching the car disappear, then she cracked a smile. She had made the tail not long after she had left the courthouse. She turned and walked back the way she had come. The place she called home was at least four blocks away, but the long walk back was worth it for the subterfuge. If they thought she lived there, they would be watching there and not her place. From now on, she would come here first, then find a way back. But for now, she would do what she did best and blend into the crowd and disappear.

A silhouetted figure stepped out of the shadows and watched her disappear, but not before taking out a cell phone and taking photos of her. Putting away the phone, the figure started on its way, keeping a distance but never trailing too far behind its target.

* * *

A GOOD NIGHT's sleep had been helped by a large glass of Californian Merlot and a good book McCall had wanted to start for a while. The morning brought questions from the night before – too many for McCall's liking, so she decided to get in early. She wanted a talk with the men who tried to take her out the night before; uniforms had picked them up while she waited at the scene.

McCall had thought it through, and the only thing that

made sense was that they were there because of the recent investigation. Someone had sent them to kill her, probably with a hope to squash the case; however, it was too big and too public now. She stepped off the elevator and headed for the holding cells and her new friends. She made for the back and waited for the guard to open the entrance gate.

"Morning, McCall," greeted the uniformed officer.

"Morning, George, how're my perps doing?" McCall asked.

He looked blankly at her as he turned the key. "What perps? We're empty. Five guys got brought in last night, but some lawyer busted them out not long after."

McCall felt her blood boil. "Who signed them off?"

The guard shook his head. "Couldn't say. I just took over. The guy I replaced told me about the guys. Sorry, McCall," he shrugged closing the half-open door,

McCall looked at the huge guard and smiled. "It's OK, George."

He could tell she was lying but was professional enough not to take it out on him.

McCall headed for her desk, walking as though she had been hit by a truck. Her lead had left the building with a great possibility of never being seen again. She gazed around from her dazed state and found herself in Steel's office. A wicked smile came over her face, and she walked over to the vintage cigar office chair behind the desk.

The leather creaked as she sat on the red leather and a look of a "naughty schoolgirl" crossed her face for those seconds she chose to forget about everything. That was when she realised the power of the room, and she understood why he built it this way. She leant on the green leather-topped desk and tapped the fingers of her left hand on the firm animal skin, and stared at the large monitor on the wall. Picking up the remote, which lay next to his office phone, she turned it on. The screen was filled with icons relevant to different files. Her eyes caught one marked "Escapees". She moved the cursor using the wand remote and clicked onto it, then leant back and put her feet on the desk, using her new position to rock the chair.

"You break it, you buy it," stated a voice from the door.

McCall sat up as if nothing were amiss and found Steel near the doorway, obviously wondering what she was doing. She found the funny side to it and patted the chair as if to check for damage.

"It's fine, really, see," McCall said with a nervous grin, rocking in the cushioned office chair. "So, how much does a knock-off like this cost anyway?"

Steel sat in one of the chesterfields opposite her. "Knock-offs, I couldn't say, but that," he said, nodding towards the chair she was getting comfortable in. "Probably around one, maybe two." He took a sip of the coffee he had brought in with him.

She sat back, refreshed at the news of its cheapness. "Couple of hundred – not bad," she said, patting the leather and making Steel smile.

"Thousand, one to two *thousand*. It's been in my family since the 1800s … the desk also."

McCall lifted her legs off the desk and got up carefully, and walked back around, avoiding everything. "You know I hate you rich guys?" she asked with comical venom.

Steel laughed before he looked up at the board. "I heard your friends made bail. How the hell did that happen, considering they didn't know anyone in the city?" he asked.

McCall shook her head; this whole case was one big run-around. "You know we will never find these guys again – not breathing anyway," she said as she sat on one of the chesterfield's armrests and looked over at her colleague with a lost gaze. She had a tired look on her face, but not the lack of sleep kind of tired. It was the case taking its toll on her.

Steel leant forward and touched her hand, making her shudder as if a pleasant electric shock were going through her system. "Forget about the goons from last night; chances are the people who sent them would have told them as little as possible anyway," he said, his words soft and calming.

McCall's expression returned to her normal stern cop face. "OK, Sherlock, what do you have in mind?" she asked, her eyes holding a fiery excited look.

Steel smiled as if he'd hoped she would ask. "We need to make a connection between the deaths and the escapees. I find it hard to believe that the same day they break out, bodies start dropping."

McCall had the same thought; she found it too much of a coincidence, and she hated coincidences. "You think one of them killed those people?" she asked, hoping for one of his outlandish theories.

Steel shook his head, and McCall looked at him blankly. "So, you don't think one of them did it, but you just said …?" She was confused where this was going.

"I said there was a connection. What if their escaping gave someone an alibi?" Steel put forth.

McCall thought for a moment, then shook her head. She liked her theory best. "We look into the lives of our victims; we are looking for a murderer, not escapees, detective. That is down to Tooms, Tony and Lloyd," she growled and stood up with purpose, and headed for the door, but when her back was turned, she gave a little smile. Thankfully, Steel was there to put her back on track.

* * *

The morning sun shone brightly through the windows of Judge Carmen Matthews' suburban home; sunrays made rainbows on the marble counter of the breakfast bar as they passed through the windows. Matthews walked into the kitchen as she put on her suit jacket over a fresh white blouse, her slender form-fitting nicely into her grey suit. This was a career woman, mother and loving wife. She was on the PTA and a member of a book club that met every Thursday. She smiled as she looked over at her husband, who was busy reading the *Financial Times* and drinking his black coffee. He looked up at her with his eyes and smiled, but his head stayed in position, as if not to lose his place.

"Didn't think you were coming down … thought you might actually take a day off." His sarcasm got a dishcloth thrown at him and a wide smile.

"I know, I know," she said laughing as she moved in behind him, whispering in his ear while she put her arms around his waist. "Tell you what. When this case is done, we send the kids off to your mother's, and we go away somewhere," she suggested.

Alan Matthews turned his head, and they kissed.

"Eww," joked their two teenage daughters, who had just walked in for breakfast.

Carmen Matthews laughed at her daughters' untimely entrance and headed for the coffee machine to fill her Thermos mug. The mood was one of a happy, content family; even the housekeeper was singing happily to herself in Spanish. As she put the lid on her metal mug, something on the small flat television screen caught her eye – a news report of the murder of Edward Gibbs. The report mentioned he had been a reporter for the *Herald* newspaper and that the police were unsure if his murder was linked to the death of ex-gym teacher Andy Carlson. Carmen froze where she was, as though she had seen a ghost. Andy stood up and folded his paper, unaware of his wife's sudden shock until he turned to face her.

"You OK, honey?" he asked, becoming concerned as he noticed her gaze fixed on the television set. "Hey honey, everything alright?" He touched his wife's shoulder, making her jump and scream.

The housekeeper yelped at the sound of Carmen's distress and dropped a glass she was about to put in the dishwasher. The glass shattered and fragments scattered across the tiled floor.

"God, you scared the crap out me!" Carmen held the marble-topped surface for a moment while she got her breath. Alan bent down and helped pick up the broken glass while Carmen found a dustpan. "What's wrong? Is it the murders?" he asked, concerned.

Carmen shook her head and smiled as she kissed him on the forehead. "It's nothing. I was just miles away, that's all." Her gaze darted back to the screen; she could feel her heart sink.

Carmen turned back around with a large, broad smile, but he gave her an anxious look. "No, really, it's nothing. See, I do need a break. I am thinking too much, that's all."

Alan got up from his seat, his smile one of unease. "OK, if you're sure," he said, putting on his suit jacket and grabbing his paper and coffee mug. He walked around to the girls and gave each one a kiss goodbye on the forehead. "Alright, so see you guys tonight," he said before coming back around and kissing Carmen once more. She watched him walk out the door and smiled softly. Looking up at the clock, she saw she also had to go; her Town Car would be there soon, and she had a long week in front of her. After hugging her daughters, she walked to the hallway and got her large leather office bag, and slowly headed for the front door, looking at the family pictures as she went.

As the front door closed, the housekeeper hurried the girls along to get ready for the school bus. As the girls disappeared up the stairs, she took out her cell phone and pressed to call; she stood where she could see the bottom of the stairs from the kitchen and waited for someone to pick up. After several rings, a voice simply asked, "Yes?"

"You wanted to know if Mrs Matthews acted strange, yes?" The woman's voice trembled as she thought about her betrayal. "She saw the news this morning, and she was very upset."

There was a pause.

"Interesting. OK, very good, Marie." The voice at the other end was soft but had a tone that sent a shiver down the woman's spine.

"I told you, so my visa is good, yes?" Marie asked nervously.

Another silent moment made her nervous, and she began to shake, thinking she had been used and her deal with the person on the end of the line had been broken.

"Yes… Marie, I will see to it you spend the rest of your days here."

The phone went dead, and a new fear took over; she repeated his words and trembled.

TWENTY

Steel and McCall sat in one of the conference rooms. The long table was filled with the files they had on the three men who had escaped and the two victims. They hoped that somewhere one of the escapee's history intersected with the two Vic's. McCall was still convinced that it was a revenge killing. The accident could have been just that – an accident. However, it gave one of them a chance to get out and get even.

Steel picked up one file, which was almost two inches thick, and sat down opposite the door. McCall smiled and shook her head.

"What?" he asked with a confused look, wondering what he had done wrong this time.

"Nothing, it's … well, you always sit facing the door," she laughed.

Steel shook his head and opened the massive file. "It's a soldier thing, or squaddie paranoia as my wife used to say." His smile faded as he began to think back at his wife's beautiful smile, her gentle laugh.

McCall could see the pain he was hiding and regretted

bringing it up. "And I thought you were just a nosey bastard," she joked, hoping to lighten the mood.

Steel looked over and smiled. "Possibly a little of that too." He maintained the warm smile that hid his pain. "So we start with the thickest file ... and the lucky winner is ... Tyrell Williams," Steel said, looking at the front cover and typed name.

McCall picked up her coffee mug and took a sip as Steel gave CliffsNotes on their first escapee. "This guy has been in and out of court but was never convicted. Drugs, attempted murder, murder, extortion – basically, if you got a name for it he's tried it, but somehow always got away with it every time," he said.

McCall gave Steel a shocked look.

"Until around eleven years ago, when he was convicted on a murder charge – apparently, he shot an undercover cop in the park," Steel read before looking up from the file and over at McCall, who now had an even bigger puzzled look.

"Hang on, how did they know it was him?" she asked.

Steel smiled like a Cheshire cat. "Get this! They had at least two witnesses, forensics on the body, *and* the murder weapon. You name it, and they had it. The strange thing is he protested that he was set up," Steel said, leaning back in his chair.

McCall leant over and grabbed the file as he passed it over. She flicked through it, shaking her head like it was an impossibility. "So, let's get this straight. A man who *never* gets convicted on anything gets caught. Now, I could understand a little slip-up, but this? No way. This has got to be wrong somewhere. According to this, he did everything wrong. Hell, I am surprised he didn't have it on YouTube for good measure," she said, shaking her head again.

Steel smiled. The same thing had crossed his mind as

well as he had read through the file – something was off and not just slightly.

"OK, so he gets out, and the others just go with him, or they're in it together," McCall continued.

Steel thought for a second, then nodded happily at the theory so far.

"They escape and then what? The first thing they do is kill a guy?" McCall growled with disapproval.

Steel rocked in his chair as he listened. "I know. Personally, I would have bolted to Canada or somewhere but, hey; everyone is different," he said with a shrug.

McCall chewed on her bottom lip with frustration. "What about you – any theories?" she asked, hoping he had one of those crazy ideas that usually made sense.

Steel shook his head. "Not just yet. I think first we should look at the others to see if there are any similarities, then see if they had any connection with our vics. They may be connected, or they may not, either way …"

McCall gave Steel a tired look. "Yeah I know, we have to check," she said with an irritated tone.

Steel laughed as he peered at his watch. "I would say after lunch; I'm bloody starving." He stood up and headed for the elevator, turning halfway and shouting back, "I take it you are staying here?"

McCall didn't turn to face him, but simply raised her hand and waved.

"I'll pick you up something," he said, turning towards the elevator.

* * *

Judge Carmen Matthews had broken for lunch. The case she was working on was a drunk driver hit-and-run with a dispute about who was behind the wheel; unfortunately, one of the two young women had a wealthy father who could afford a top lawyer while the other was in financial trouble.

As she walked out of the courthouse, the impact of the cold breeze made her wince at the initial shock, but she smiled and closed her eyes, letting the crisp air cool her warm skin. The judge made her way down the white stone steps and across the street.

Watching from afar, the girl in the black hoodie sat patiently, her gaze never leaving the judge. She stood and waited for the right moment, then pressed after her. After four blocks, the judge headed inside a large restaurant. It was the sort of place that didn't accept you unless you had a platinum card or were part of the school-tie brigade.

The girl found a perfect spot next to a street vendor and waited; she could see straight into the restaurant without any problems. She watched patiently as the judge was brought to a table by one of the waiters. At the table, Matthews shook someone's hand. The girl could not make the person out as a large supporting pillar obstructed her view; however, she figured it was a man because of the size of his hand compared to the judge's, which was tiny in comparison to his.

Matthews laughed as they talked, then her expression changed to one more serious, scared even. Who was this person who could make a judge nervous? The girl tried to look round the pillar from a different spot, but it was then blocked by the wall, and she growled with displeasure. She would have to wait, but this mystery person interested her. As she watched, the waiter brought the judge's and her companion's meals and placed them down. The girl's stomach let off a jealous rumble. She knew they would be in there for some time, given the way the judge was picking at her salad, so she decided to find a better spot.

Two men came up behind her and grabbed both her arms and lead her towards a black van that had parked not far away.

"Make a sound, and I will stab you in the kidney," said one of them.

The girl was shocked at the sudden abduction. She winced in pain as he gave a quick poke to her side with a knife that was hidden under a jacket he had draped over his right arm. She hoped that someone would notice, desperate that one of the thousands of people would see her dilemma and call the cops. But everyone seemed not to see – or simply chose not to. *Don't want to get involved*, was always the way for some. Not for the fear of paperwork, but they didn't want to be injured or worse. The human condition, fight or flight.

"What do you want? If this is for ransom, oh brother, have you picked the *wrong* kid." She felt another pinch to her side.

"When we get to the van, you get in all normal-like. Mess me around, and I leave you bleedin' here," the man said, his voice rough as if he'd been screaming for hours.

She nodded quickly but with only small movements to prevent another jab from his blade. They walked quickly towards the van in silence, the girl still trying to make eye contact with someone, but everyone seemed to turn to look at the buildings next to them. She felt a tear in the corner of one eye. She had heard about these things: young girls were dragged off the streets to only work them later and, if lucky, it would still be in America.

"I am sorry, but can I trouble one of you gentlemen for directions?"

The girl's heart nearly stopped at the sound of a British tourist. She wanted to turn around and warn the man he was in danger, but she froze. She had second thoughts then; if she turned, they were both dead.

"Get lost," yelled the man to her left.

"Sorry, I am already lost, and that's why I am asking directions." The British voice was firm but had an odd, playful ring to it. Almost as if he were trying to annoy the men.

"I just want to know the way to the Empire State Building," the tourist stated.

She could hear the man to her left start to breathe heavily. He was about to make a move, and the poor tourist would not have a chance.

"Look, you dumb limey bastard, why don't you find a cop or something?" the man to her left growled disapprovingly.

"You know, it is really bad manners to talk to someone and not look them in the eye."

The Brit was getting to the thug on her left, and he turned.

"Look jackass," said the thug as he turned to face the tourist.

There was a sickening crunch, and the man stumbled backwards, blood flowing freely from between the fingers now cradling his broken nose. The knifeman turned quickly, and the girl heard someone being punched hard; the body of the knifeman skidded past her and across the concrete paving. She was frozen in fear, but something – a feeling – made her turn slowly. She was hoping to see the face of the man who had saved her; however, all she found was a crowd of people and no sign of her rescuer.

There was a screech of tyres from the van as it sped off, causing her to turn around just in time to see it disappear down the street before the cops arrived.

"You OK, kid?" asked a friendly voice.

She looked up to see a beat cop standing over her, and she gazed around confused before turning back to the two men bleeding on the sidewalk.

"Yes, I am fine ... these men were ... and someone." Her words were jumbled with confusion. "Who did this, who saved me?" she asked, looking around, hoping her rescuer had found a place to watch from.

"I was hoping you could tell me. I just got called over to a fight. Say, what's your name, kid?" He noticed that the girl seemed miles away, as though she were taking it all in.

"What ... sorry? My name ... I am Megan Armstrong, sir."

TWENTY-ONE

Tooms and Tony stood at the side of the road, looking at the broken safety barrier, beyond the swell of the Hudson River. They had gotten a call from the Coast Guard about reports of a car that had crashed into the river. A witness had seen the car crash occurred after a bout of erratic driving. When the police had taken the witness' statement, she had described the driver. That description sounded like the missing guard. Earlier that day, Tony had put out a "Be on the Lookout" or BOLO alert for the guard, which the Coast Guard and uniforms had reacted to.

As they stood at the roadside embankment, they watched the divers go down into the dank waters of the Hudson. Tooms wasn't sure they would find anything because the river wasn't the cleanest. A good half hour went by before the first diver came up, then moved to a different spot. Then the next one did the same, followed by the other. Tooms nudged Tony and pointed to one diver who raised his arm to signal he had something.

They watched as a large crane manoeuvred over the

spot and lowered its cable and lashing straps into the water while the other divers went to assist. Tony waited for the car to be brought up so they could ID the body. The two detectives stood and watched as the rear end of a car emerged from the deep, and a disappointed look came over their faces as a brand new BMW was placed on the side of the road.

"Thanks, sarge, but we are looking for a blue Ford," Tooms said, kicking rocks into the river out of frustration.

The Coast Guard sergeant leant in to look at the body to confirm whether it was their man. "Well, blue Ford or not, this is your guy." He waved a picture of the missing guard they had sent him earlier.

The two detectives looked at each other, then hurried over. The vehicle held one driver, and that was indeed the missing prison guard. All along Tony had had the feeling the dead mother story was bogus; that was why he had put out an all-points alert.

"I thought this guy would be hundreds of miles away by now," Tooms said angrily.

"Yeah, I wonder why he ain't," Tony replied.

"OK, so he gets himself a brand new Beemer, only to drive it into the Hudson?" Tooms shook his head, confused at the situation.

"Well, if you got to go, you may as well do it style," Tony shrugged and smiled.

Tony and Tooms stood back as the ME – a short man in his late fifties, with white scraggly hair and gold-rimmed spectacles – did his checks.

"Any ID, doc?" asked Tooms, hoping it was someone else who just looked like their missing man.

The ME turned and tossed over a black wallet. Tooms caught it and went through it, and pulled out a driver's licence, then growled. "Yeah, it's our guy. Damn it," he said as he bagged the evidence in a clear evidence bag that Tony held out for him.

"You got a cause of death, doc?" Tony asked as he sealed up the bag.

"Can't be sure. Could be head trauma from the impact, but one thing is sure, he didn't drown," the ME said, taking notes for his files.

The two detectives drew near so they could get a better look.

"How can you be sure?" Tony asked.

The ME pointed to the lips.

"There's no foam around the mouth, which shows the water made it to the lungs, but I will know more once I have cut the poor bastard open," the old ME said, shaking his head at the sight of the trashed German automobile.

The two detectives thanked him and made their way back to their car while CSU folks did their thing with the car. There was nothing they could do there; after leaving their business cards with the ME and CSU, they headed back to the precinct.

"You smell a cover-up partner?" Tony asked as he slid into the driver's seat.

"Actually, I smell hotdogs. I am starved," Tooms said, holding his stomach.

Tony looked at his partner and shook his head as they sped away. "Unbelievable," he grunted. Tooms laughed as Tony took out his cell phone.

"Agent Lloyd? Yeah, it's Tony … Detective Marin … never mind. We have a problem with the guard."

TWENTY-TWO

McCall had gone through Williams' file and still couldn't figure out how a career criminal had become so stupid and gotten caught. What also made no sense was the killing of the undercover cop. This took place in Battery Park, and Williams both lived and worked near Central Park North at the time; so why was he there? The case itself was open and shut, and the prosecution had all the evidence – a couple of witnesses, fibres, ballistics. All roads led to Williams. The case couldn't have been more airtight if they had footage of it; however, something didn't seem right. She had never had a case like that – ever.

Tooms had phoned to tell her about the guard taking a one-way drive, which made his and Tony's life more complicated for sure. But McCall had her own problems. She threw down her pen and stretched just as Steel walked off the elevator, holding a loaded hotdog and a coffee.

"Thought you were eating out?" she asked, disappointed he had not brought her anything,

"Actually, these are for you. I figured you wouldn't have

gone out for anything," Steel replied, handing over the food.

McCall blushed with embarrassment for doubting him. "Thanks," she said, going for the coffee first.

"Any luck?" he asked, hoping she had found something they could elaborate on.

"No, but talking of luck, Tooms and Tony found the guard." McCall bit into the hotdog.

Steel smiled. "Nice, so are they bringing him in?" His smile faded as McCall shook her head.

"No, the coroner's doing that; they found him at the bottom of the Hudson in a brand new Beemer," she replied after swallowing.

Steel grunted disapprovingly as he picked up his empty coffee cup and headed for the break room to fill it.

McCall had finished her meal by the time he returned, but she seemed agitated by her findings.

"So, did you find anything that might shed some light?" he asked.

McCall leant back in her chair and waited for her colleague to sit. "I think our boy here knew it was a set-up and now he's out!" She raised her hands as if she had solved the case.

"Nice. Can we go home now you've solved it?"

McCall scowled, and Steel smiled broadly at his insult. "So, we both agree that his whole case at the time stank of a set-up," he said, looking puzzled. This whole case made no sense whatsoever. "What I don't get is why didn't anyone else pick it up? I mean, for any judge or prosecutor this must have stuck out like a spare prick at a wedding."

McCall had to agree that it was odd, but sometimes as a cop, you welcomed gift-wrapped cases, but never this good.

"We need to look at the others, see if anything pops there. What if someone is setting up killers and drug dealers? But is it such a bad thing if it gets them off the streets?" Steel added.

McCall could see his reasoning; however, one thing made it wrong, not just morally, or even by the fact it made a joke out of the justice system. "It is if innocent people have to die," she answered.

Steel smiled, and she knew he was baiting her. he reached over and picked up the file on Darius Smith. The file was just as thick as Tyrell's and with just as many "no convictions". He looked it overusing his finger as a marker, not relying on his eyes to do the checking alone.

"Well, our boy here, Darius Smith, was no saint either – the usual shopping list for a career criminal, but again never convicted. Well, not until eleven years ago when he got busted for killing some kid in a hit-and-run."

McCall stared at Steel as if he had told a bad joke. "Really, a hit-and-run!" She almost fell off her chair at how absurd it sounded – that he should be taken down by such a charge, considering his criminal career.

"Yes, eyewitness, forensics … the lot."

McCall picked up her coffee and drank some to get rid of the bad taste in her mouth as Steel went through the rap sheet. "OK, I can see the frustration re a case when it falls through because of some stupid little trick the defence had up its sleeve but planting evidence, or actually killing someone to do it, naw. You've lost me on that one," she growled as she started to get the feeling that file number three was also set-up.

She picked up the file that lay next to the others. "This one's different: schoolteacher kills his wife in an alley after a heated argument in a restaurant. Again, they found enough evidence to convict. It reads the same, but this was a normal guy, not some scumbag from the streets. This doesn't fit at all," she said, shaking her head in confusion.

Steel put down Darius' file and leant forward with interest. "OK, so one set-up, nice – but wrong. Two set-ups are a bit adventurous – but three? No, something is going on. We just have to find what ties these three men together and which one is the killer before he strikes again," Steel said.

McCall nodded in agreement, and they both took a sip from their coffees.

Brian Armstrong sat in an armchair, staring at a photograph he had of his family; it was old and had white creases where it had been folded and unfolded many times. It looked timeworn, but he didn't mind as long as he could still make out the faces.

He had changed out of his orange jumpsuit and now sported a black sweat-suit with a hooded top. They had all been moved to an old abandoned tower block that Tyrell used to hide out in if things got a little hot on the street. The rooms were powered by generators, and the windows were blacked out so no light could escape.

Armstrong looked at the door as Tyrell walked into the room, wearing a grey pinstripe suit with a sky-blue shirt.

"Very nice, who's your date?" he joked as Tyrell swaggered like he was on the red carpet.

"Hey, man, *you* had a chance for some nice threads, but you picked that shit. God knows why," Tyrell said, smiling as he eyed himself in a mirror.

Armstrong stood and followed Tyrell into the other room where Darius was watching the news.

"Well, looks like we made front-page news. You know it will be a while before we can make it outta here?" Darius asked, pointing the remote at the television.

Tyrell nodded and patted his colleague on the shoulder. "Patience, man – everything is gonna be fine, just real fine," he said as he walked over to a couch lined along the sidewall and sat heavily.

"Might as well relax, Teacher; my brother will bring some food later. In the meantime, there are plenty of books in that room you were in," Tyrell said, looking over.

Brian Armstrong spun and walked back into the room to search for the so-called books. He had a feeling they were all going to be mystery novels or romance novels. He smiled as he found something of interest and sat after picking it out of the pile. In the other room, Darius leant over to Tyrell and beckoned him forwards.

"Where did the teacher get to after the crash? I mean, sure, we all split, but I followed you?" Darius asked.

Tyrell shrugged and looked at the doorway that led to the next room. "Maybe the brother had business. Maybe he went to get a fuckin' hotdog. Point is we are all safe now and hopefully out of the country soon." He smiled happily at the thought of spending his days on a beach somewhere.

"So, the police are trying to say them killings were done by us. What's with that, man?" Darius asked as he leant forward, took a glass, and poured himself a large glass of the Bacardi Rum that sat in the centre of the table.

"Who can say, man – you know the cops. They'll try and pin anything on us now, but we must be smart and keep low," Tyrell said thoughtfully.

The two men knocked glasses and downed the contents in one swift motion.

"Oh, man, I missed that shit." Darius laughed and winced as the alcohol hit home.

"Don't worry, man, no one is looking for us here," Tyrell's words sounded confident, and Darius was hoping he was right.

TWENTY-THREE

Several hours had flown past since Tooms and Tony had returned from the accident site at the Hudson embankment. They had joined Steel and McCall, who sat at the conference table comparing notes on the off chance that something slotted into place. They knew, even though it was two different cases, that they must be related somehow.

McCall stood up to get another coffee and, after peering into the empty vessel, stopped and took the cell phone from her pocket when it buzzed violently, alerting her of a new text message. She smiled and ran her fingers through her hair as she read it.

"Message from your boyfriend?" Steel asked with a large grin.

"She doesn't have a boyfriend ... do you?" Tooms turned to McCall, hoping for new information.

McCall ignored the school kids at the table and sent a reply. "If you must know, that was the editor of the *Herald*. He said that the disc was ready and I – we – can pick it up," McCall said, feeling herself blush. Steel raised an eyebrow and cracked a smile.

"Okay then, so we'll see you when you get back," he replied, giving her a sideways salute and grin. McCall looked puzzled.

"You're not coming?" Her voice held back relief that Steel was not tagging along.

"No, sorry too much paperwork, plus have you seen the time? Hey, look, you go and have – you know what I mean." Steel tried to seem serious as he picked up a file and held it up to hide his face.

"OK, jackass. So *I* will get the files and be *I* will be right back," McCall turned and skipped to the elevator as someone was getting out.

"Hey bro, how come you didn't go?" Tooms shouted across the table.

Steel put down the file and turned. "Because it's probably a long walk from his house from his," he replied, giving him a stony look.

"I thought …" Tooms started to reply. A puzzled expression crossed his face.

John Steel shook his head as if he knew what Tooms was about to say. "If you had seen the two of them together you would understand; she will be going to his house, I'd put money on it." And, with that, Steel slapped a twenty-dollar note onto the table.

"I'll take that bet," Tooms grinned, tossing a twenty-dollar bill onto Steel's cash on the table.

* * *

McCall arrived at the house of Daniel Cruise, the *Herald*'s editor. She had phoned his office first, but they had told her that he was at home and insisted that she meet him there. McCall had found it strange but, then again, she was curious how a man like that lived.

It was a large house with a Tudor feel. A large front-drive began with electronic gates that had camera feed so he could see who was at the door. She drove slowly up the driveway, taking in the view as she went, and smiled to herself as she'd always imagined Steel having a place like this and not a park-view penthouse – that she still had not seen.

She parked and got out, her gaze not leaving the awe-inspiring house. Of course, the bright full moon in the cloudless sky helped add a little something to its ambience.

"Glad you could make it," Cruise said.

McCall stood there with a half-shocked, half-daydreamy look on her face while he stood at the open front door. "Your house is ... well ... wow." She felt angry with herself for her unprofessional behaviour as she entered the hallway until she saw the interior and her jaw dropped even further.

"Can I get you something to drink, Samantha – sorry, Detective McCall?" Cruise asked.

She gave him a quick, embarrassed smile as she followed him into the sitting room. "No, thanks. I am only here for the disc you promised me." She tried to sound in control, authoritative, as they walked down the long hallway into the sitting room.

The lounge area was huge, with antiques in glass Elizabethan cabinets, paintings that almost filled the entire walls, silver ornaments, and vases from some dynasty long forgotten. Despite all the luxurious antiques, her eyes fell upon the small dining table between the veranda doors and a huge stone fireplace – a table that was made up for two.

"I'm sorry, I didn't realise you're expecting someone.

I'll just take the disc and get going." Her voice held a hint of disappointment. Why had he brought her here if he was expecting someone else? What a cruel bastard, she thought. Cruise smiled and poured a glass of champagne, then passed it to her. "Yes, I was, and now you are here," he said with a childish grin. McCall smiled and took the glass, her eyes sparkling with the light from the candles that were positioned around the room and broke up the darkness.

"You're very sure of yourself, Daniel … sorry, I thought we were on first-name terms now." She tried to give the impression he was overstepping boundaries, but her eyes gave her away.

He stared into her deep blue eyes, filled with emotion. She blinked and looked towards the fireplace, hoping the break in visual contact would change the mood and make him rethink his strategy.

"So, no butler?" she asked casually, adding to the wall she hoped she had put up.

Cruise smiled and shook his head at her stubbornness. "No, it's Simon's night off," he stated.

She gave him a strange look. "Your butler is called Simon? I thought he might be called Albert or Alfred," she joked, taking a small sip of champagne and walking around, looking at photographs of past and present relatives. "So, Daniel, you're getting me here, the champagne, the alone time. This wasn't a date, was it?" she asked as she held a picture of what could have been him and his parents when he was around ten years old. She put down the picture and closed her eyes as she felt him draw closer.

"That depends on you, Samantha; do you *want* it to be a date?" he asked, his voice deep and sultry. She turned and kissed him hard on the mouth, all her passion and longing vented in that brief moment. Suddenly, she pulled away, realising what she had done.

"Sorry, that was …" McCall went to turn, embarrassed at her display. Daniel took her into his powerful arms and held her tight. They moved onto the large plush couch and fell upon it, their bodies hungry for each other. McCall gasped as he started to unbutton her top and kiss the bare flesh as it was revealed. Her fingers grasped his hair as he moved down, undressing her as he went. Her body shuddered as he tasted her, his lips exploring her body as well as his hands. Slowly he moved up, and she wrapped herself around him as they became one. Their hot, sweaty, lusting bodies writhed and enjoyed each other – until finally, with groans of utter bliss, they collapsed holding each other. Their bodies glistened in the glow of the fireplace.

"Where did that come from, detective? I thought you only wanted the disc?" he joked.

McCall slapped him playfully before climbing on top of him. "I just had a thought: won't dinner be spoilt?" She motioned the table setting.

Cruise shook his head and grinned. "No, I didn't order it yet." McCall looked confused, and then a playful smile came over her face as she felt him stir once more. "Good, we can order breakfast instead." She leant forward and kissed him as she moved down, feeling him once more.

Hours faded with animal passion. They lay on the floor, on top of a large snuggly blanket Cruise normally used wintery nights. McCall looked at the mantel clock; it was a quarter to three in the morning.

"Damn it, I have to go," she yelped.

He gazed at her as he pulled the blanket over himself.

"Was that it—"

"I have to be at work in three hours," she shot him a

scowl. "You know, catch your man's killer!" She grabbed a pillow that had fallen to the floor and tossed it at his head.

He caught it and placed it behind his head as he leant back with his arms crossed behind his head.

McCall finished dressing and blew him a kiss, and headed quickly for the door, stopping halfway and rushing back. "You don't have that disc, do you?" she asked with an awkward smile, almost forgetting why she had come there in the first place.

TWENTY-FOUR

Steel closed his eyes and fell into a deep, unsettling sleep. He could almost hear the screams and the gunfire that haunted his memories. Men had come to his home – the reason why he still didn't know, even after all these years. They had come and killed as many as they could at the garden party. That warm summer day, his homecoming. So many family and friends went in a blink of an eye. Until he came and hunted them down on the grounds and in the house – until he reached the attic. There, he thought he might find his beloved wife hiding. Her cold limp body rested in his arms, her eyes closed as though asleep. Steel's body tensed as the next memory bit hard. As he stroked her hair, her eyes opened; she was alive! The sounds of the hand cannon rang through the attic. At first, the pain didn't reach him, only the sight of the bullet passing through her head. Bullets passed through them both. Six shots echoed in his ears, but he felt only the pain of losing his wife. The darkness passed over his eyes and those voices – voices of the men who had done this.

Steel sat up with a start. The plastic glass bounced gently on the floor, and he got up from the window-side chair that he so often fell asleep on – or what little sleep he could get. He smiled ruefully as he picked up the plastic glass; breaking crystal had become expensive, so he'd come up with the idea of plastic a while back. He peered out the large panoramic window of his penthouse suite and took in the splendour of New York City at night. He headed for the door, taking a quarter-length leather jacket with him. He needed air and something to take his mind off the dreams.

Steel had just left the lobby of his home when the cell phone rang; it was one of the many eyes and ears he had in the city, people he used as connections, mostly the homeless. They were a good source of information; they could go anywhere unnoticed, hear things, see things. He paid well and looked after the group of people. One person – known simply as Mouse, had a tip that a snitch was held up in an old building in the Bronx. This snitch apparently had information on his private case. He put the phone away and hailed a cab.

The night sky was dark and almost starless in the clear heavens above, and even the wind had died down, but still, a chill remained. A yellow cab pulled up, and he got into the back and told the driver the address. Every nerve in his body told him that this was a trap, but he had to make sure. Besides, he needed the exercise.

The driver parked a block short of the destination at Steel's request. If it was a trap, he wanted to know the lay of the land. Taking out his cell phone, he checked the internet for a satellite view of the area. He studied the feed and the surrounding streets, then smiled as a plan came into play.

The building Steel was looking for was on the next street, behind the one he was on. To get there, he would either have to go through the alley a few feet away or go back several buildings to the junction. He checked the layout of the numerous structures. There were two rows of buildings to the east and west, and both covered the exits and entrances. The buildings that had once stood at the side were gone and now had rows of bins on one side and rubble on the next. There were only two ways in and out.

The buildings to the east and west of the one he was interested in were tall residentials with flat roofs, not good. Perfect for him, and also perfect for anyone wanting to get eyes on someone entering or leaving. Steel had to admit that whoever planned this planned it well; it was a perfect killing ground.

He picked one of the structures that faced the buildings and tried the front door: locked. Steel looked up and down the street and then picked the lock. He thought about climbing up the side, but why waste the effort? Besides, the last thing he needed was the cops being alerted. He went all the way up to the top floor, to the door that led to the roof. Unsurprisingly, the door was unlocked. Why anyone would want to lock it he had no idea; either way, he was now on the roof.

He needed a rooftop view, and this would be perfect. Steel knew he would have to stick to the shadows; if someone were watching, he didn't want to spoil the party. He moved quickly and quietly towards the edge of the building to check the coverage of view and stopped. At the edge of the wall was a stack of military green sandbags and equipment bags. Next to those was a sniper's shooting mat. This was a long thin, padded mat which looked more like something used for camping. This had been laid out behind the sandbags, and a spotter's scope next to that. Steel recognised this as a sniper's nest. He had set many up himself when he was in the service, and plenty more afterwards. Whoever had planned this wasn't simply observing, they were meant to take out whoever was going to the meeting.

Taking out a small monocular from his pocket, Steel surveyed the land. Was he early? The other rooftops were clean; however, Steel figured they had not yet arrived. Slowly, he gazed over at the building in which the meeting was meant to take place. It was six stories high, a disused tenement building with lots of windows and little cover from one sniper, let alone two or more. From what he could make out, given the amount of foliage growing around it, it had been abandoned for years.

He couldn't see any signs of life as he scanned the building and the surrounding ones for other possible shooting locations. The building he was on and the one next to it were perfect for coverage. The other buildings next to his were too tall and had the wrong angles, no clear line of sight without hanging over the edge. No good for a sniper, possibly good for a light machine gun or assault rifle, but not for a static gunman who was laid down. The structures opposite had the same set-up. If he were planning it, there would be four snipers, two on each side. And if that were the case, he would have only one chance to clear one side and hope that the alarm wasn't sent before he got inside. This was going to be a get-in and get-out operation. Besides, by the look of things, they were expecting resistance and an agent or cop – but not Steel.

"Mmm, nobody home," he thought, disappointed his contact had been wrong about the location. Then he heard the voices. He looked down and saw three men in black running in different directions: one went to the next building, the second to the alleyway between the building where Steel stood, and the third was on his way up to the nest where Steel was.

The roof door opened and the man dressed in black tactical gear walked quickly forwards, ensuring he was low and did not create a silhouette against the night sky. Once at his position, he swung the long bag off his back and took out the silenced sniper rifle.

The sniper unfolded the front bi-pod and laid down the weapon; adjusting his position, he got ready for the job. Steel appeared from behind a ventilation stack and headed towards his target, all the while keeping silent and to the shadows. He was fast but quiet as he moved like the shadows of the night.

The sniper didn't hear anything, only felt the hands on his head before it was twisted, making a loud crunch as his neck was broken. Steel gazed over at the second man on the other rooftop, keeping the man in his gaze as he grabbed the communications set from the dead sniper. Steel disappeared back to the shadows and put in the earpiece so he could hear every move and every order made by the section commander.

Steel needed to take out that other sniper and then the guy in the alley before even thinking of going inside the old building. He made his way to the back of the building where there would be less noise. The jump was at least seven feet, and there were loose chippings on the ground. He knew he had only one shot at this, so he had to make it count. There was a quick succession of white-noise blasts as if someone were pressing Send but not talking. He nearly ripped out the earpiece; it was annoying and bloody loud.

Steel smiled when the burst over the headset gave him

an idea. He walked back to give himself a good run-up. After a few exhalations through his mouth to boost confidence, he started to run. As he neared the edge, he pressed the Send button until he landed on the other building, rolled, and slipped into the shadows.

"Whoever is doing that, make sure you're not sitting on the damn thing, OK," growled an angry voice into his earpiece.

Steel smiled as he headed for the next gunman and whispered, "Don't worry, that's the least of your worries."

After taking care of the second gunman, he made his way down the stairs. He knew going down the old drainpipe was too risky, and it was too high to jump from the roof. The night air felt somewhat warmer down on street level, and there was definitely less of a breeze. As Steel approached the alley, he could see the third man watching the target building and the surrounding structures through binoculars. He moved up slowly behind him at first, waiting to see if the man felt his presence. Seeing his chance, Steel moved forwards towards his next target.

"We are all clear in the alley. I'll let you know if the target arrives. Out." Those were the man's last words as Steel grabbed him and held him in a neck lock, stopping the blood flow and knocking the man out cold. Picking up the body, Steel moved him to a darkened spot and, using the man's own PlastiCuffs, bound him and then checked for useful items.

He walked over to the spotter's position and picked up what at first appeared to be regular binoculars. "Oh hello … beautiful," he said softly, admiring the military-grade thermal-imaging binoculars.

He took off his sunglasses and held one of the arms in his mouth. Pressing the binoculars to his eyes, he checked the windows and saw heat signatures of more than a dozen people in the building, the guards and the snitch. This was no longer a meeting; this was a rescue operation.

Sticking to the shadows, Steel made his way to the building after he had checked the other rooftops for more uninvited guests. The bulk of personnel was on the third and fourth floors. Unfortunately, he could only speculate where the informant was, but he figured he was on the fourth floor. Steel had made out at least seven men on that floor and another seven on the floor below. Even though he had seen the thermal glow from their body heat, he knew that they would be heavily armed. He would have to get in unseen and take out as many as possible before getting the informant out.

Most of the windows of the tenement building were boarded up, apart from three; two were small bathroom windows that only a cat could get through, and the other was a bedroom window. That one held a piece of chipboard large enough to fit the window; however, squatters or tramps had worked it free, so it was suspended by one bolt and swung to the side with ease.

Inside reeked of a stale building that had been left to decay and urine. Each room was bathed in darkness, less for the odd shard of light that broke through gaps in the boarding; this gave enough light to make out items in the rooms. Steel moved slowly so as not to create any noise as he headed for the staircase. He saw the elevator had power, but that was far too obvious and climbing it was out of the question. He'd seen enough films to realise the close calls you could have with a moving elevator.

He walked through the apartment and stopped outside the bathroom, and saw one of the guards heading in to do a room check. The man was alone and armed with only a small machine pistol, but still, he was armed.

As the man moved in, Steel pounced and grabbed him by the scruff of the neck. He dragged him forwards, thrusting the man's head towards the back wall, hoping to knock the man unconscious. There were a crash and a cloud of dust. He looked puzzled, instead of the usual crunch of bone against the tiled wall, the man's head broke through the rotted plasterboard wall.

The man stumbled backwards, dazed by the impact, but Steel finished him quickly with a straight leg kick, which sent the man crashing back through the wall. He pulled the unconscious man from the rubble of plasterboard and noticed that the gap between the outside wall and the bathroom wall was large enough to fit a person. He hoped that he would fit.

Carefully, he tore at some layers of the wall until the hole was big enough, then climbed inside. This was his way up, unnoticed. On the fourth floor, men stood ready with the butts of their automatic rifles tucked into their shoulders – ready for whatever, whoever might come up the staircase.

Each floor had a large landing and a stairwell that ran up the back wall, and a long corridor branched off the floor space with two apartments in each corridor. Decay had made some of the walls crumble, and they lay as rubble on the floor, opening up the apartments, so they were one big space. The flooring had hidden holes in them, ready for unexpected guests to tread. The whole building itself was a massive trap, courtesy of natural decay rather than the mercenaries inside.

Steel made his way up to the fifth floor using the wooden beams as a climbing frame; dust and cobwebs clung to his black outfit, turning him a sandy colour. He stopped and looked through a hole in the wall next to the washbasin. There stood one of the mercenaries, taking a leak. He was whistling a merry tune as he pissed merrily into the toilet, shook it, and buttoned up. Steel shook his head in disgust as the man walked out without flushing or washing his hands.

He had to get out of the wall without making noise and drawing attention to himself. He thought for a moment, then made his way over to see what was in the next room – hopefully, another peephole with which to observe the next room. He noticed that most of the walls had either fallen or been pushed down the drywall dividers by someone, which meant there was no chance of cover for him to hide behind. Despite this, he could see everything they were doing and where everyone was.

Steel needed a distraction to cover the noise and pull the men away from the hostage, who sat near a large window, tied to a rickety wooden stool far from the staircase. He remembered the cell phone he had taken off the spotter and moved slowly back to the bathroom. He tapped McCall's number into the phone, then crammed it between the boards and the bathroom wall, and smiled wickedly as he slid back to the hallway wall and waited.

If this didn't work, he would have to think of something else, and that was time the snitch didn't have. He found the peephole once again and waited for the phone to ring.

Steel smiled as one of the guards went to the bathroom; it was exactly what he needed. The man walked in and yelled back abusively at the last one who had used it as he unzipped and rested one hand on the wall as if to balance himself. He looked up and closed his eyes, relief on his face.

As the man pissed, he heard a faint noise, like distant music tickling his ears. He stopped and stepped back, grabbed his UMP machine pistol and held it ready to fire, a red dot from its laser sight trailing on to the wall.

"Boss, get over here!" yelled the guard, prompting a larger man with cut-off sleeves to walk over to the mercenary in the bathroom doorway.

"What's the matter. Can't you find it?" yelled the boss.

The others laughed as the boss approached the bathroom.

"No – sir! Get in here quick," yelled the guard again, this time a little more softly.

"OK, dipshit, what is it?" The boss stood inside the doorway next to the alerted guard.

"Listen!" The guard held his hand up as if to shut everyone up.

The boss was just about to shout at the man for wasting his time when the music began again. The two men looked at each other, then stepped back, weapons held ready.

"Fuck me, there's someone in the wall – the cop is in the friggin' walls," yelled the boss.

They opened fire and walked in, flashes from the weapon barrels blinding in such proximity. Others joined in, hungry for blood. As the walls exploded with rapid-fire, the men were oblivious to the fact that behind them, in the hallway, a wall had been broken through and a man dressed in black was closing in.

One mercenary who stood in the doorway but was unable to fire, watched excitedly. Steel grabbed the man from behind and held him close as he grabbed the weapon slung from the man's shoulder, and opened fire on the others. The men screamed in agony as their kneecaps ruptured from .45 calibre bullets from the UMP machine pistol. Steel slammed the man's head against the doorframe several times, knocking him out cold. He knew he would not have much time before the others came rushing up the stairs. He checked the men's vests for ammunition and ran into the hallway just as the next couple of men reached the top of the stairs.

Steel jumped and opened fire on the men – two of which were hit full in the chest and legs – and the other two who had been behind the injured men dove for cover by rolling down the stairs. Blind gunfire from the stairwell cut up walls and doorways of the floor where Steel was, and flash-bang grenades were tossed equally blindly in hopes of catching the intruder. There were loud explosions followed by blinding flashes as stun grenades detonated, but Steel wasn't there; he had made it to the hostage, who sat tightly tied to a chair with a bag over his head.

Steel approached cautiously and took the bag off, and the man looked at him, confused at what was going on. "Are you part of the rescue team?" The man's face displayed hope, his brown eyes reflecting the flashes of light from the flash-bangs.

"I am a police officer, and I am here to get you out," Steel said reassuringly.

The man's face fell as though he knew something. "They said you would come. Please, I have a family," he said, his face full of regret and fear.

Steel walked backwards, towards the staircase, and opened up on the four men who had reached the top of the stairs. The lack of return fire had led them to believe they had gotten the perpetrator, and now they paid for it with their knees.

Steel went behind the man, ready to untie him, and froze as he saw the reflection on the floor: a red, flashing LED light. He knelt and saw the detonator strapped to the bottom of the wicker padding of the chair. He stood just as two men rushed to the top of the stairs and spotted the bodies in the bathroom. Steel called over to the men, making them look around before they too lost their knees.

The prisoner in the chair ducked his head from the harsh noise and falling red-hot brass casings. "Hey, man, can you shoot that somewhere else?" he complained.

Steel smiled and changed the magazine. "I can let them shoot you if you like?" he joked.

The man thought for a moment, then shook his head as though it didn't really matter. "No, no, I am good," the prisoner replied.

Steel rushed over and unburdened the men of their ammunition as more bullets from the floor below cut the walls.

"So, what's your name?" Steel asked, tucking away the full magazines he had repatriated and picked up a flash-bang from one of the men. He smiled as he flicked out the pin and casually tossed it over the balcony to the floor below. Screams of pain and shouts of "my eyes" followed.

"Garry Sanchez, sir," replied the man.

Steel noted he was in his mid-fifties and that his black hair and beard hid most of his Hispanic facial features.

"So, Garry Sanchez, tell me, why are you in an abandoned building with a bomb strapped to your arse?" he asked as he walked over to the man.

Sanchez shrugged and held a puzzled look. "You know, I have been asking myself the same question. I was meant to meet a cop here who had information on my missing daughter," he explained.

Steel checked outside the windows to see what was below on the street, hoping for something to land on, less for the concrete floor. They were too high up to try for a pavement landing and too far away to attempt to jump to the next building. He smiled as he saw the half-full dumpster below them; it was a chance, a slim one, but a chance. More than staying and waiting for the bullets to runout or someone to set off the bomb remotely.

"I take it she went missing? Or did she run off?" Steel asked, walking over to the wall near the staircase.

Sanchez nodded. "We had a fight a couple of days ago about her no-good boyfriend. Anyway, we both said stuff, and she took off, and I have been looking for her since, but no luck. That's why I went to the cops and filed a report," he explained, his voice full of regret. "But you know all this because you're … ?" He paused as he scanned the strange cop. "You're not the cop I was waiting for, are you?" he asked, finally filling in the blanks.

Steel shook his head.

"So, if you're not the cop I'm expecting, what are you doing here?" he asked, confused.

Steel raced over to a flash bang that had just landed and kicked it back down the stairs before it exploded. He smiled wickedly as he heard the screams from below.

"Oh, you know, nothing on television … so I thought I would rescue some guy with a bomb strapped to his arse. A usual boring night really," he joked, hoping to calm the man down. "I was actually meant to meet an informant here. I don't suppose you have seen one?" he asked, watching the staircase. The man shook his head, and Steel shrugged. "Oh well, worth a try, I suppose."

A perplexed look crossed Steel's face as more gunfire and explosions rocked the floor the two men were on. He suddenly looked angry, as he knew he had been played.

"Funny, they got it wrong!" laughed Sanchez.

Steel looked over at the man, and a sickening feeling came to his stomach. "What did they get wrong?" he demanded.

The man nodded at Steel as he stood there changing

the magazine after emptying a clip into the next set of men who had dared to come up the stairs.

"They were expecting a female cop," Sanchez said with a strange chuckle.

Steel turned and cut down two more men when they risked rushing up; they fell to the ground, grasping their shattered knees. He heard the screech of tyres and knew more were on the way, and they were nearly out of time and ammo. There was no option: they would have to use the dumpster.

"Okay, Garry Sanchez, here is the plan. We are going to jump out of the window," he said slowly, as though he if he were explaining something to a five-year-old.

Sanchez stared at the strange cop dressed in black and saw his own terrified look in the cop's sunglasses. "Are you friggin' nuts? That's at least a fifteen-feet drop," he yelled in panic.

Steel grabbed the back of the chair and pulled him towards the large window that stretched from ceiling to floor. Sanchez began to wriggle frantically as he was dragged to the edge.

"Now, Garry, stop squirming. That's only a detonator, not the explosive, so if you keep still, it won't go off …in theory," Steel mumbled.

He froze in the chair. He didn't know which was worse: being held by armed men and strapped to a bomb or being rescued by a lunatic.

Steel felt his cell vibrate in his pocket and he took it out, and looked at the caller ID; it was McCall.

"Steel, where are you? I just got a tip from an informant. He's waiting at an abandoned building. I'll send you the address!"

Steel's face stiffened as he realised it was a set-up for both of them. "McCall, how far out are you?" he asked, drawing out the words as though hoping for a good answer. McCall looked at her phone, confused at the question before she started having that unsettling feeling she had when she knew something was wrong.

"You're there, aren't you?" McCall said with a panicked and angry tone. There was a brief silence before he answered.

"Yes, you need to stay away. Don't come for us," Steel yelled over the noise. McCall heard the line close, then as she looked down the street, there was a blinding flash, and a fireball engulfed a building twenty feet away. The Mustang skidded to a halt, and she looked at the inferno, her jaw-dropping. "Oh my God … *Steel*!"

STEEL CLOSED the cell phone and stood in front of Garry Sanchez, who was shaking with fear. "Now Garry, I am going to count to three, then we are going out the window, but first I got to check to see …"

Steel looked at the staircase, and Garry's eyes followed. A huge man appeared, he was very tall and very wide – like a sumo wrestler. But the man's size didn't interest Steel, it was the massive machine gun he had brought to the party. The brutal-looking weapon was a light assault machine gun called a chainSAW due to the front-grip handle, which was just like a chainsaws safety grip. A long flat belt connected from the weapon to a backpack, the pack was the magazine, a big magazine of nearly a thousand rounds of 5.56 mm. This meant continuous fire without changing ammo belts or boxes – this also meant that they had to leave – and now!

Steel turned swiftly as the man released the first un-aimed volley of bullets and ran full pelt at Sanchez and tackled him in the chair, sending them both hurtling out the window and towards the dumpster. The windows shattered with automatic gunfire and pieces of brick and more rained down as the gunner fired after them as he walked slowly forward. Above them there was a series of deafening explosions, then came the fireball. As they hit the huge dumpster the heavy, metal lid came crashing down on top, closing them inside. They felt the heat as the flames engulfed the dumpster. Sanchez cried out in panic, thinking they would perish in there. Loud hammering filled the dumpster as masonry fell upon the lid, covering the exit.

McCall looked at the building; the flames rose high, painting the surrounding streets with an orange glow. As she stood there feeling hopeless, she felt the cell vibrate in her jacket pocket. A smile of joy came over her face, and a tear trickled down her cheek as she saw the call was from Steel.

"Steel, I am not going to ask how the hell you got out of there, but I am glad you did." She eyed her phone; she could hear an argument with what appeared to be a Hispanic man, as he was swearing at Steel in Spanish.

"Oh, will you shut the fuck up for a second. God, some people! You throw them out of a building, and they are so ungrateful." Steel words sounded as if they were meant for himself more than anyone else. "Ah yes, Sam... uhm, my new friend and I seem to be in a bit of a pickle. You couldn't drive around and get us out of a bit of a jam, could you? We are slightly buried under something ... uhm, possibly half the building," Steel said with a strange tone of amusement at the situation.

Puzzled, McCall and got back in her car and restarted the engine. As she drove up to the building, she got back on the phone to Steel. "Where are you? I can't see you anywhere ... all I can see is a... you're in the friggin dumpster, aren't you?" McCall said, her tone was full of anger.

His awkward silence confirmed that, making her even more pissed.

"Steel, that thing is covered in half the building, and it's on fire," she yelled as she pulled up at a safe distance.

"Really? I hadn't noticed. Is there anything there you can use to get the building off the top of this thing?" Steel asked, trying to convey urgency.

McCall looked around and just saw empty streets. Her fingers tightened around the steering wheel, and she put her foot on to the accelerator. The wheels spun until they were smoking, then she slammed the changer into drive, forcing the Mustang to launched forwards, and towards the dumpster. At the last minute, she rolled out of the car – in time to see her beloved car smash into the heavy dumpster and propel it out of the way. The brickwork fell and buried her car.

There was the sound of metal being thrust aside and loud scraping as the lid of the dumpster was thrown backwards. She saw two figures appear from the flames: Steel and another man who appeared to be tied to a broken chair.

"McCall, are you okay?" Steel asked as she looked at him from her position on the ground, a small line of blood trickling from her forehead.

She eyed him with a mix of anger and confusion. "Am I *okay*? You just got blown out of a building, and you're asking if *I* am okay?" McCall laughed, unsurprised at her partner's way of prioritising a situation.

Steel reached out and helped McCall to her feet, and looked around, wondering why she had been on the ground in the first place. Then he saw the rear end of her

Mustang just before flames took it in a massive fireball. "Oh, shit, Sam, your car … you used your car!"

They stood for a while, all three of them, as they watched the burning hell. In the distance, fire-engine sirens filled the empty street. They stood there silent as if to mourn the loss of an old friend.

TWENTY-FIVE

It didn't take long before the fire department, and the police had blocked off the area. Bright orange flames licked at the blackened sky, and thick black smoke billowed upwards, filling the air.

The heat from the inferno could be felt nearly a hundred feet away, and firefighters surrounded the building and launched a torrent of spray, hoping to control the blaze while others sprayed the closet buildings in hopes of preventing the spread of the white-hot flames. Steel stood at the ambulance where Garry Sanchez was being checked after his ordeal.

"Oh, thank you, officer ... uh, detective." Sanchez realised he had no idea who his saviour was. Steel smiled and took a long sip of bottled water.

"You're not going to tell me, are you?" he asked. Steel looked over and let the heat of the inferno warm his skin; he smiled again and turned to Sanchez.

"Nope." Steel said with a quick grin and patted the man on the shoulder. "I'll tell you when I find your little girl." A flood of tears ran down Sanchez' face – he finally had hope and knew this angel in black would find her. Steel saw McCall talking to Tooms and Tony, who had just arrived on scene and headed over to them.

"So, what the fuck happened here? Steel, is this *your* fault?" boomed Captain Brant as he walked up behind the group.

"I had a tip there was an informant waiting in the building, but instead I found a shitload of mercenaries and some poor bastard with a detonator strapped to his arse."

McCall looked at Steel, horrified with a sudden realization. "I got the same tip. I should have been in there as well!"

Steel nodded to confirm her fears. "We were both meant to be in there. Anyway, what kept you?"

His tone was serious, but she knew he was yanking her chain. McCall blushed and said nothing in reply.

"So, medics are nearly done. We will take Mr Sanchez back to the precinct until it's safe," Tooms interjected, and Brant nodded.

"Oh, and I will need a car. Can't really catch bad guys without one, sir," McCall said, bouncing on her heels.

Brant looked puzzled and gazed around for her Mustang. "McCall, you know that they ain't giving you any more cars, not for a while yet anyway. Besides, where's your car?"

McCall and Steel used their thumbs to point behind them at the burning building and the debris covering the dumpster.

"She used it to … um, get me out," Steel admitted through gritted teeth.

Brant raised his eyebrows in surprise, not much wanting to ask where Steel had been to warrant rescuing. "Where the hell was – never mind. I don't think I want to know. McCall, I'll put in the paperwork, but I can't promise anything; besides, *he* trashed your car, get *him* to buy you a new one," Brant joked wryly while McCall stared at Steel with folded arms and a look that could kill.

"Thank you," Steel said. McCall didn't need to ask why; however, she wanted to hear him say it. "What for?" McCall smirked. He could see her trying to hide a smug grin, and he smiled at her childishness.

"For saving my arse." His words rang with sincerity.

She shrugged as if to say, "It was nothing." She laughed. "Oh, it's fine. In fact, I am getting used to it by now."

As they headed for the subway station, the sound of a friendly argument about who had saved who the most times disappeared with the noise of traffic. Steel returned to his apartment to shower and change, as the mix of garbage and smoke was beginning to make him nauseous.

The apartment was a loft with a balcony and a view that came at a high cost – but was worth every penny. Inside was a mix of old and new; most of the furniture was antique, sideboards and cabinets from the 1800s, and pictures that should be in a stately home rather than a New York apartment. However, these were a few items he had brought from his family's estate in Britain to remind him of home.

He opened the front door and stepped directly into the sitting room, which was large with dark oak flooring and a large Persian rug. There was no long hallway, just a huge open space that served as the sitting area. In the centre of the floor was a large, brown, comfortable-looking couch which sat opposite a large fireplace; above it was a wall-mounted sixty-five-inch flat-screen television on which he mostly watched the British sports channels for soccer, rugby and occasional MMA matches.

Next to the kitchenette ran a long corridor, which

contained three bedrooms and two bathrooms. A large panoramic window gave a breath-taking view of the city and park below. Since his parents' murder some eleven years ago, he was now Lord of the Manor – the Earl and executor of the family businesses. He did not need to be a cop or work for the agency.

Steel could have stayed in Britain and taken over things there, but that was not who he was. Steel had served with the British Special Forces, but after the shooting, he knew he had to disappear for a while – until he was ready to hunt the people responsible. His wife had been the daughter of an American senator who had a lot of clout in the Pentagon, so he helped Steel join the U.S. SEALs.

Steel had been a soldier, and now he was a cop but, in the end, he was merely a man who wanted justice for his family and for all those that the organisation known as SANTINI had killed that day – the organisation that had hunted him for so long. But now he was the hunter, and they were the prey.

* * *

STEEL SLOWLY STRIPPED the tattered clothing from his muscular body and threw them to the side instead of the hamper; they were as good as rags now, tatty and torn from the night before. Using the touchscreen controls on the outside of the walk-in shower, he adjusted the water temperature. A large two-way display screen built into a long-tailed dividing wall also doubled as a television so he could watch the news or sports while he showered.

Steel stepped under the warm water and let the water flow over his tight body, his muscles tensing and then relaxing as the soothing water flowed over him. His body was more like an athlete's, with every strand of muscle like steel cabling under tight, tanned flesh. He stood for a moment with his arms against the wall and let the water pass over; it felt refreshing, but Steel knew he could not stay in there forever – he had work to do.

He towelled off and then wrapped it around his middle before wiping steam from a large mirror that hung above the sink. He stared at his reflection with sadness, and his fingers trailed the round scars on his body. Six exit wounds, one in each shoulder and one in his stomach. These ran down in a V shape. Three in the centre near his sternum were shaped like a number 1.

The mark of the Phoenix his Japanese gardener and saviour had called it – not that Steel could ever see that, but then he was never good at seeing the star configurations either, no matter how many times his father had shown him pictures of Taurus, Pisces, and the others while explaining how the brightest stars joined to make an image. Personally, he couldn't see how a couple of bright stars created an image of a bull.

He smiled as he thought back to his dad's frustration every time little John Steel shrugged and told him "I don't get it" – to which he had to admit that most of the time it was simply to annoy his father.

Steel had always felt that he had died that day along with his family, but something dragged him back to the land of the living, and so began the rebirth. Others said he was too stubborn to die. As he stared at himself with dead, soulless emerald eyes, his vision began to blur, and he slipped into another place: a memory.

He saw darkness at first and then a bright light as if a torch were shining directly at him. Then he felt the warmth from that summer day as if he were there, the day of his return from the tour. Steel knew about the surprise party, even though he wasn't meant to; his mother had let it slip to ensure he would be there.

The driver of the black cab was chatting away about something, but his mind was elsewhere as they navigated down the long drive to the family home. *Home.* He often smiled at the thought of the word; everyone else had a home, but he grew up in something people visited on the weekend.

The massive estate had been in the family since the time of Charles I and so had the lordship. He stared out the cab window as he rested his head against the cool glass, taking in a surreal view of trees and greenery, things he had taken for granted until he had spent time in the desert.

Steel's hands gripped the sides of the washbasin as his memory took him through gunfire and death. So many lay dead on the back lawn of his home as the masked gunmen went through, killing all they could.

He had taken out many of the mercenaries in the garden, enabling several to escape the horror, but many he'd been too late to safe – including his beloved father, who lay dead on the patio. His memory took him to a dark place: the attic. The darkness of the room was broken by streams of light that beamed through small skylight windows.

He stopped and before him lay a woman with her back to him, but he knew who it was: his beloved wife. Steel's knees buckled under the strain of the sight. Slowly, he made his way to her as if some great force was pulling him and he fell to his knees before her, then picked her up and stared into her pale, beautiful face. His cries of anger and emotional pain rang through the attic like the cry of a wounded beast. His heart stilled as she opened her eyes – and her pale blue eyes stared at him with a look of fear and joy.

A loud explosion filled the air, and six shots rang out from a hand cannon. Laughter, pain, darkness – then a voice which kept repeating one name. *Santini*.

Steel cried out and stepped back from the washbasin, but no tears came; he had lost those as well. He was a shell of a man. Torn by revenge or punishment? It was something he hadn't yet decided. His gaze caught the reflection in the mirror of the monitor that was in television mode; it was the news. The report was on the three escapees, but they hadn't linked it with the deaths of the schoolteacher or the guards. The report ended, and Steel moved to the bedroom, which was above the kitchen area. He needed fresh clothes, and he also needed to get back to work, but most importantly, he needed to complete the case his friend had asked him to solve. *Find the package.*

TWENTY-SIX

The figure of Megan Armstrong was bathed in shadows as she stood next to a group of street vendors and blended in as though she wasn't there. She had followed Judge Matthews for most of the morning, and now she sat in the same restaurant as before, having a coffee with her mystery man. Megan knew it wasn't an affair; to her, it looked more like a business talk.

She watched for a while, still hoping to catch a glimpse of the man's face or anything to identify him, but he was hidden by a giant support pillar. Her gaze shifted to the street now and again, just in case the goons from the other day came back. She was still puzzled as to who they were and what they wanted. At first, she had thought it was some detail that the judge had put on herself just in case, but that would mean the judge knew about her and, given Matthews's activities, that didn't seem to be the case.

Megan's gaze fell back on the judge who had a look of sheer terror on her face as she stood, then the terror turned to anger as she stormed from the dining room. She smiled at the judge's misfortune and got ready to continue the pursuit. A black Town Car pulled up, and she watched with disappointment as Matthews got in. She bit her bottom lip out of frustration and decided to call it a day; it was past lunchtime, and she was beginning to feel hungry.

Megan got her bearings and smiled fondly as she knew a block away from her uncle – no relation, just a hotdog salesman who'd taken her in and looked after her – had his stand.

She started to walk, keeping to the crowds of people. The walk would take her a good ten minutes if she was lucky. She approached the main street and turned the corner, and stopped halfway to watch as a man in a black suit talked to Uncle Vince. She waited, observing from afar as the man gave her uncle a roll of cash before disappearing into a black sedan, which then sped into the daytime traffic.

Megan slipped back around the corner, her back against the hard stone of the building for support. Had she been given up by the very man she trusted so dearly? Maybe it was nothing. She knew that Vince was more than a hotdog salesman. A *lot* more. The man was connected and did favours for people. To say mob was a little strong, but possibly not that far from the truth. That was probably why she felt so safe around him.

Megan exhaled a large lung full of air as if blowing out the bad thoughts. If she was going to know what the exchange was about, there would be only one way, and that was to simply ask him. Megan walked around the corner and headed towards the vendor with a smile; as she approached, she could see Vince mixing the onions that were keeping warm in a small metal insert.

"Hey, Uncle Vince! What's on special today?"

He looked over and saw the girl walking towards him. "Megan, where the hell have you been? You found another hotdog stand?" he asked, putting on a fake wounded look. The two of them embraced, and Uncle Vince stepped back to his stand where he put together a chilidog for her. "So, what you been up to? Not seen you in a while."

Megan nodded and took the fully loaded hotdog from him. "I got a job. It's only night work, but still, it's a job," she replied before taking a bite.

Vince looked at her with a proud smile on his face. "Good for you, kid. So what is this job that keeps you away?"

She finished a mouthful of chilidog. "It's a cleaning job at a school. The pay isn't much and the hours suck, but it's a start," she explained with a shrug.

He nodded the proud look still on his face. "You know, if you need anything, you just have to ask, OK?"

The look in her eyes was a mix of happiness and relief – relief that he was not who she suspected him to be. The cash was probably for something else and not her. Megan gave him a hug and a small peck on the cheek. "I have to go, but I'll come back tomorrow, OK?" Megan shouted, moving on.

The big man laughed and waved goodbye as she ran off, back the way she'd come with the half-eaten chilidog clutched in her slim hand.

His face became serious as he took out his cell and pressed the icon for the person he needed to speak with. He only had to wait a few seconds before some picked up. Uncle Vince said, "It's me ... she was just here, and she said she'll be back tomorrow."

* * *

DETECTIVE JOHN STEEL arrived back at the precinct around eight o'clock after he had showered and changed.

His stop at the coffee house had taken longer than expected.

McCall turned as she heard the ding from the elevator and saw Steel holding two coffees in takeout cups as he stepped out. She raised her watch arm jokingly. He just gave her a smile and shrugged as though he didn't care.

"So, did our guy say anything?" he asked as he passed her one of the cups before sitting in the chair next to her desk.

McCall smiled as he made himself comfortable –it was a warming smile, as though things were back to how they used to be.

"What?" Steel asked with a grin, trying to imagine what she was thinking, but only rude thoughts came to mind.

She shook her head quickly as the daydream was shattered, realising he had said something. "Oh, nothing really, just what he had explained to you. It seems to be some poor bastard they had set up," McCall explained with a serious expression.

Steel looked over as a still shaking Garry Sanchez was led to a waiting room and handed a coffee by a large black-uniformed officer. He nodded as if to thank the giant of a cop before being left alone to gather his thoughts.

"What are you thinking?" she asked as she could sense Steel thinking hard about something.

"He said that he was contacted by a cop to meet him there, that they had information about his daughter," Steel said as he sat back in the chair, his black leather quarter-length jacket creaking as it pressed against it.

"Yeah, so, someone lied to get him there, using a cop to lure him there." McCall was tired; it had been a long day, and she wanted to go home and relax in a deep bath.

"Yes, I get that, but how did they know he was looking for his daughter?" he asked.

McCall slumped back in her chair and shook her head, her brown hair gleaming as it caught the light from the ceiling lamps. "I don't know … maybe they followed him – maybe they have his kid, and that's how they knew to set him up!" She took a sip of coffee. As she looked at him, she saw a grin appear on Steel's face, as if he had had the same thought all along.

In a way, she was relieved that he wasn't going the dirty cop route, plus the proposed scenario made more sense; however, that led to the question of how did they know to take that particular kid? There was nothing special about her or her father.

Steel drank as he eyed the whiteboard. "There is something wrong here, and we are *not* seeing it." His words rang with concern and McCall gave him a puzzled look as he studied the board. "Someone is going to a lot of trouble to stop us from looking into these cases, don't you think?"

She had to admit things had been a little close as of late; like the meeting in the parking lot, then last night. "I know one thing: the new chief of detectives wants constant updates on this." She nodded towards Captain Brant's office.

At that moment, they noticed Brant waving his hands in anger as he spoke on the phone; the two detectives could only imagine it was the chief on the other end.

"Are the other two at the morgue?" Steel asked, looking over at Tooms' empty desk.

McCall spun to look in the same direction. "No, they have gone to the security guard's apartment, hoping to find something. Think your girlfriend went as well," she said as she smiled wickedly.

Steel scowled at her. "Trust me, she is not my girlfriend," he said with a bitter tone.

McCall could feel his anger.

"Yeah, well, whatever. So, they are looking a lot closer at him. If he did have anything to do with it, there might be a trail they can follow." Steel stood up and studied the pictures of the victims once again, this time more closely.

"Why were they injected with truth serum? It doesn't make sense. They didn't know each other by all accounts, so why do it?" McCall asked as she studied the board.

Steel shook his head; he had a million theories, but that's all they were. The killer could have been smart and done it just to add a false clue, but Steel felt that unlikely – they knew something.

"Yeah, very cold war stuff, you know KGB, CIA … hey, why don't we ask your …" McCall stopped. She could see that the joke had run its course and he had real anger in his face. This led to another question: what the hell had she done to him all those years ago?

McCall quickly apologised, planning to change the subject. Hell, the last thing she needed was an angry John Steel. She had seen a glimpse of it, and she didn't like what she'd seen – the sort of rage you would see from a rabid T-Rex at that time of the month. "Anyway, they stopped doing that years ago … right?" She chuckled, and Steel leant over and grabbed the files on the victims.

"Ten years ago … something happened to these men ten years ago. Look, our schoolteacher leaves his job and turns into a hermit, and our reporter starts doing a story from something that happened – *ten years ago*."

McCall sat still, her cup half tilted towards her mouth as she listened to his idea, a theory that made a lot of sense. "What if *nothing* happened ten years ago?" she asked thoughtfully.

"Believe me, McCall, *something* happened, and I bet you dinner – or a hotdog – that at least one of the escapees had something to do with the schoolteacher," Steel said, tapping the board.

"You mean his murder?" she asked, finally taking a sip of coffee.

Steel shook his head. "No, what I mean is … possibly they were friends, one bought drugs from another – I don't know. But they knew each other," he affirmed. He looked at the stack of files in the briefing room, most of which they had managed to get through.

McCall stood up and headed for the room to start wading through the piles of files. Steel watched her sit at the table and start reading, then picked up the phone on her desk and pressed an extension number.

The phone rang on the other end for a couple of minutes before being answered by a high-pitched female voice.

"Hi, Detective John Steel here … oh, hi Betty, yes, can I ask a favour? Can you get me the financial and telephone records of the following person …" His gaze fell on McCall. He felt bad about what he was doing, but he had a gut feeling. He waited for the clerk to get back to her desk and get a pen. "Hi, Betty, yes I'm still here. Yeah, the name is Daniel Cruise, the editor of the local tabloid."

The hours ticked by, and much coffee and street food had been consumed during them. Tooms and Tony were still out, pursuing inquiries, but McCall knew that meant they were keeping their heads down while she and Steel waded through the paperwork. Unfortunately, new files arrived from downstairs – financials, prison visitor records, anything and everything to get a pattern on these men's lives. It was getting late. The hours passed quicker once the new information had come in. If anything, the new files produced more questions.

Armstrong had nobody in his life except his daughter, and she had disappeared off the planet. The others had no contact with the outside world whatsoever, so if one of them had planned it, how? Armstrong didn't have the finances to set up a lemonade stand, let alone something like a major escape. The others, maybe, but escape to what? They had no life outside; other gangs and handlers had taken over since then.

Steel brought over two more coffees and placed them on the table. McCall shot him a smile. "Anything?" he asked, hoping in the ten minutes he had been away she had cracked the case, or at least found a breadcrumb.

"Nope, just the same-old-same-old," she said, stretching her upper body.

As Steel sat, a petite woman with dark curly hair walked in with another set of files and slapped them on the desk, and one of them she placed in front of Steel. They smiled at each other before she winked and left. McCall rolled her eyes and took a sip of the freshly brewed coffee.

"I can't believe how much crap happened ten years ago, and most of it involved these guys," Steel growled with frustration. "But only the other two … Armstrong only gets flagged at the killing of his wife," he added as he picked up the file the woman had given to him. "Hopefully, the new files will add some new light."

McCall shot him an evil look. She had plans – more specifically, she had plans with Daniel Cruise. "Look, Steel, I have plans. We can worry about all this tomorrow," McCall said with a disappointed look.

Steel looked at the time; it was getting on, and it had been a hell of a day. He nodded and shot her a smile. "Go home. I'll take care of this." He grinned, and she blew him a kiss to thank him. "So, who is the lucky man?"

When she didn't reply, he considered it. Then his jaw dropped. He shot to his feet and grabbed McCall. "It's that editor bloke, isn't it? You can't go out with him! He's a suspect," he barked.

McCall appeared bemused. "Since when?" she asked suspiciously, the whole thing sounding like a sordid plan of Steel's to ruin her evening.

"Since phone records showed that Edward Gibbs called his office, but he never picked up; however, he tried your boyfriend's cell phone and Cruise answered the call."

McCall grabbed the piece of paper with the information on it and read the damning facts. Her face went pale as she read.

"It says here it pinged off a tower near the victim's location. In fact, he was close to both victims' locations the night they died." Steel felt bad about telling her, but she would find out sooner or later.

McCall sat hard in her chair, making it slide back, her eyes staring into nothing as her brain tried to sort out a simple explanation but came up short.

"Look, I am sure there is a simple explanation for this, and he is innocent; however, for now, we have to treat him as a suspect," Steel said calmly.

McCall nodded and shot a broken smile. She knew he was right, and he was only trying to save her from a massive mistake. She glanced at the Edward Gibbs' file, which lay on top of the stack. "What the hell happened ten years ago that started all this?"

Steel went to answer just as Captain Brant came out of his office, looking as unfriendly as usual after a conversation with the chief. "The boss man wants updates, so what we got?" Brant asked, hope on his face.

McCall sat back; her hard composure had returned.

"We think something happened ten years ago and these men are paying for it. P, probably someone is shutting them up," Steel answered. He had no proof, just a theory, but the chief didn't need to know that. He needed an update, so Steel gave him onehe got one.

Brant nodded. It was a sound theory, and he had something to feed to the nchief to shut him the hell up. "Where's Tooms and Tony?" He nodded towards the pair of empty desks.

"They are checking out that security guard's place to see if something comes up."

Brant nodded and looked across the sea of half-empty desks. "OK, detectives, keep me apprised of any further developments," he said as he headed back in his office.

McCall and Steel could see the look of apprehension on his face – the man was under serious pressure. The chief was obviously squeezing this one, probably for his own professional gain.

"We need to find out what happened ten years ago." McCall's voice sounded as tired as she looked.

"No – I need to find it, and you need to go home and relax. You can catch up tomorrow," Steel said with a serious expression.

McCall smiled and stood; she gave no argument, as there wasn't any. She was beat, and an early night would be good.

Steel looked over to Garry Sanchez, who sat alone, nursing a cup of coffee.

"What happens to him tonight?" McCall watched as two patrolmen walked over to him.

"He's going home, but with a protective detail."

Sanchez waved at him and McCall with a broad smile

and mouthed "thank you" at them. Steel and McCall waved back and watched him disappear into the elevator.

"How are you getting home?" Steel asked, also getting ready to head out.

"Subway I guess, unless you want to take me car-shopping?" McCall asked jokingly.

Steel laughed as she logged off on her computer. "See you tomorrow, Detective McCall." Steel bowed regally and walked towards the stairs.

She shook her head with a large grin and made for the elevator.

* * *

SAMANTHA MCCALL STEPPED out of the station house into the unwelcoming cold wind that held a nasty bite. The sun was almost gone; however, the dull light would remain for another hour or so. She looked around to see if there was a cab approaching, but the drivers were either blind or occupied. She stood next to a black Town Car that was parked with a Hispanic man in a driver's uniform waiting patiently by the back door.

"Hey, buddy, you know you can't park there, right?" she asked politely.

The man smiled and shrugged. "Sorry, but I was told to wait here and pick up a detective. My boss said that the guy who paid would take the slack." Again, the man shrugged and smiled.

McCall shook her head. She had a feeling about who this cop was; hell, it had Steel's arrogance written all over it. He was being picked up by a driver while she had no ride because of him.

"So tell me, who are you picking up? Some arrogant

British jerk named Steel?" she asked, waiting for Steel to come around the corner and climb in.

The small driver shook his head and shrugged. Suddenly, he smiled awkwardly as he remembered he had forgotten the calling sign and turned towards the front passenger side. "Oops, sorry." He laughed as he pulled out the sign and held it proudly as if nothing were amiss. "Thanks for reminding me, ma'am. That could have been embarrassing." He chuckled.

McCall looked at the sign, and her jaw dropped as the small board clearly read *Samantha McCall.*

"You're picking *me* up?" she asked, shocked.

He looked at the sign, then back at her, and shrugged with a broad smile. "Now, *I* am embarrassed. My name is Felipe, and I will be your driver," the man announced proudly.

McCall shook her head and laughed at her harsh thoughts as the chauffeur opened the back door. He was shocked when she got into the front. "OK, Felipe, I am Samantha. So whose dime is this on?"

His smile remained as he shook his head.

"Never mind, I can guess. So, you ever been to Canada, Felipe?" Her joke confused the poor man as he got into the car.

TWENTY-SEVEN

Brian Armstrong sat in an old but comfortable armchair in one of the rooms that the disused apartment had to offer. The stiff maroon coloured cloth had a stitched pattern, possibly very old, but probably art deco. He didn't care; the straight back gave him lumbar support and the cushion was soft enough, giving a pleasant contrast. He sat alone, reading a book he had found amongst the many that lined a bookshelf to his right.

The room was small – it had probably been a child's bedroom or a study before the gangs had taken it over as a safe house. The whole apartment was sparsely furnished with a couple of beds and sofa beds in the rooms, trying to create sleeping quarters the best they could. One of the rooms had been made out into a sort of sitting room – or lounge – in which sat a couple of sofas and a big old television. It had the comforts of a shithole and more, but it was safe and secure. This was, after all, a safe house and not the Ritz.

Armstrong had left the door open, not so much as he needed company – he didn't – but more a case of keeping an eye on the others. He looked up from the pages to see Darius walk in with a plate of hot food – nothing fancy, just franks and beans, but it was food.

Darius looked at the book cover as he entered and raised an eyebrow when he saw it was a book on poisonous insects.

"Readin' up on nasties, Teacher?" Darius laughed.

Armstrong smiled as he took the plate and the fork.

"Got to keep the mind active. Who knows when it will become useful? Besides, out of the many books there, this was the most decent," Armstrong shrugged.

Darius nodded and shot a quick, nervous smile. Something had changed in the teacher; he was focused on something, and Darius knew that could be dangerous.

"So, where'd you get to after we all took different directions to throw off the cops? I know Tyrell went lookin' for his brother, but you were gone for some time, man – damn, we thought the cops had got ya ass," Darius said, aiming for friendly conversation, but his facial expression let him down.

Armstrong stared at his food and stirred it for a while to cool it, but he never looked up again, even as he spoke. "Everyone has secrets Darius, even you. Where did you go and why the interest? Afraid I may have done something – rash?"

Darius felt a shiver run down his spine as the teacher's cold eyes met his. He backed off and shot him a quick smile.

"Hey man, ain't no thang really, we just chattin'. That's all. Teacher. Just chattin'." Darius left Armstrong to his food and book. Even though Darius was taller and bigger than him, he still knew not to mess with him. He went back to the kitchen where the others were playing cards.

Tyrell looked up and saw the concern on Darius' face.

"You OK, man – what he didn't like your cooking?" he laughed.

Darius gazed over in the direction of Armstrong and then to the others, his smile false and nervous. "No, no it's cool, his … everything is cool," he blurted.

Tyrell watched Darius head into the room with the television and closed the door, then his gaze fell on Armstrong's door, and he wondered what the hell he had said to spook Darius.

* * *

DANIEL CRUISE HAD SAT in the interrogation room one for over an hour. Steel hadn't rushed the uniforms picking him up; in fact, he had waited an hour before calling it in. It was a usual tactic to let the suspect stew, overthink things; however, this time, Steel had done it more out of spite than anything. He had noticed people did things while they thought they were not being observed – things they wouldn't do in the actual interrogation. Some would be calm, some nervous. One guy actually got on the table and fell asleep a while back. However, what Steel was interested in was the change in body language: would they stay calm or become defensive before knowing what they were there for?

Cruise looked good in his blue pinstriped Burberry London suit, and he knew it. He sat there with his left leg resting comfortably on his right knee, and every so often he would calmly brush invisible dust from his knee, but the one thing he did more than anything was he would check his Rolex as if he were late for something.

Steel sat and watched; his gaze did not wane even as McCall came in to watch the show. "I thought you had gone home hours ago?" he asked, his eyes still on his prey, waiting for a sign of weakness.

"I did, but I remembered you have my date for tonight."

Steel smiled at her sarcasm.

"So, what do your instincts tell you, Steel – is he a bad guy or a good guy?"

He could smell fresh perfume, and her heels had sounded different, more high heels than high boots. He was tempted to look around, but the image he had in his head was enough for now. "My instincts say he is a lying bastard, but he's not a killer. He is an editor of a major paper, so he has it all, even if it came crashing down, and he would still come out with a bank account full of cash. No, he is not a killer. He would lose everything, and this guy needs everything he has."

He leant forward and stared harder into the room. Again Cruise checked his watch and Steel smiled to himself. "So what time were you two planning on going out, just so I can get him out in time?" he asked inquisitively.

McCall looked at her watch. "Around nine-thirty, my idea. We didn't know when we would be done for the day," she answered with a sigh.

Steel nodded in a show of understanding. It was nearly seven, and he had a bad feeling about his instincts. He stood and saw McCall for the first time in her going-out outfit: a tight black sleeveless dress with a collar to support the top half. Her figure looked amazing; *she* looked amazing, but he dared not tell her.

"Why, detective, you scrub up nicely." He smiled amiably and gave a courteous bow.

McCall smiled at the compliment and wished she was wearing it for him.

"McCall … Sam, do me a favour, will you? Go out, but take Tina with you, have a good time. My treat."

She was unnerved by his request. "Why? Do you want to get rid of me, Steel? Afraid I will watch you shoot him or something?"

Steel shook his head, a saddened look on his face. "No, I'm afraid that *you* will shoot him." His voice rang with concern.

She eyed him, puzzled, and crossed her arms in defiance. "Do what you got to do, *Detective* Steel, but I can guarantee you that he didn't kill anyone," she growled defiantly.

Steel nodded. "It's OK, McCall. I believe he has an alibi; in fact, I would be shocked if he didn't." He walked from the small viewing room and headed for the interrogation room but, before he reached for the handle, he looked back at McCall, now sitting on the table, ready for the show.

* * *

JOHN STEEL FINISHED SENDING a text as he entered the interrogation room.

"I have been waiting here for over an hour. I don't know what game you are playing, detective, but by the time I am finished with you, you'll be …" Cruise started to say, his voice holding the tone of a man who thought he held all the power in the world.

Steel remained silent and didn't look at Cruise at first; he put away his cell phone and slammed a large file onto the desk, creating a loud metallic thud. "Sit tight, Mr Cruise," he yelled.

Cruise looked at him, shocked that he had yelled with such venom, and sat like a frightened child.

"So, Mr Cruise, on the night in question you said that you spoke to Edward Gibbs on your office phone; is this correct?" Steel's voice was calm and soft, as though he were making general enquires.

Cruise looked puzzled at the question and scoffed. "You brought *me* down here to ask me that? Are you serious?" He laughed as though he had been too important to be brought to a police station like a common criminal.

Steel sat opposite the smug Daniel Cruise, imagining how many bones he could break in the man before someone came to stop him. "Sir, are you saying these facts are correct?" he asked calmly, his expression was like stone.

Cruise looked at his watch again. "I want a lawyer. I am not answering any of your ridicules questions," he said with arrogance.

Steel sat back in his chair and rasped his fingernails on the hard table surface between them. "You have that right of course, but that will take time, and as you are only here to help us with our inquiries, I am sure it will be a waste of your time and money."

Cruise looked perplexed for a moment. "Wait … so you're *not* charging me with anything, and I can go?" He seemed shocked.

Steel shook his head and offered a smile that widened as he spoke. "Sir, you just requested a lawyer, so that means before we do anything, you have got to wait for counsel."

Cruise's face dropped. "OK – OK. I don't want a God-damn lawyer, so can I go now?" he asked, throwing up his arms.

Steel rocked on the back legs of his chair for a few seconds. "If that is your wish, I cannot keep you," he admitted.

Cruise stood, wearing a smug grin once more, as though Steel were beneath him.

"However," Steel started, his tone self-assured. "I will say that we asked you to come down to clear up a matter in a civilised and less public way. If we find that you have lied to us, we will be forced to do it publicly, by arresting your smug little arse. So if you walk out of that door now, I will make it my mission to find every little secret you have, every dodgy deal you ever made, and I will bury you. So please leave." His tone was venomous.

Cruise was halfway standing when a lightning bolt of reality hit him, and he sat down hard on the chair, his face full of panic.

"You see, your phone records do *not* show you talking to Edward on your office phone, but your cell phone records do … and you weren't at the office."

Cruise smiled as if there was a simple explanation; Steel could see the lie was about to leave his mouth but didn't have time to humour him.

"Mr Cruise, if you tell me you were in the building when the call came in, I will charge you with obstruction and put you in a cell with Brandy, who is a seven-foot, three-hundred-pound bloke who leans towards boys more than girls, and who is also coming down from a bad trip. You should see the bloody size of the man's feet – and you know what they say about big feet. So, the truth please."

Cruise closed his mouth and embarrassment crossed his face. "Look, I went out that night, and this girl came on to me … and, well, one thing led to another, and we went up to her room."

Steel got ready with a pen. "Where was this?"

Cruise froze; his face turned pale as he realised something. "My phone, you traced it to his apartment area?"

Steel nodded slowly, and Cruise gazed into space, as something came back to him.

"It was an apartment building down from some church. I went up to the room to have a good time, and the bitch had roofied me. At first, I thought it was just a wallet snatch, but now …"

Steel put down his pen and watched Cruise's face for signs of lying. "So why didn't you say anything before, report it to the police?"

Cruise eyed Steel with a shocked look on his face. "And what would your partner have thought, that I just go with anything with a pulse?" he snapped.

Steel watched him check his watch again. "Well, Mr Cruise, I am glad we could clear that up. I don't want to keep you from your date with Samantha," he said with a calculated grin.

Cruise looked lost at the statement. "I am not seeing her until later. I have a … well, another appointment shall we say?" he winked.

It took all the strength in Steel's body to stop him from throwing a punch that would probably rip the jaw off the man. "Well, we wouldn't want Sam to think you were a two-timing piece of shit now, would we? But hey, it doesn't matter, because you just told her." Steel sat back in his chair and nodded towards the two-way mirror.

Cruise gazed over, and his jaw dropped as he heard a tap on the two-way glass. The colour drained from his face as he realised he had blown it.

Steel got up and put the paperwork on the desk together. "Mr Cruise, I am afraid you are going to have to stay here until we have had time to check out your story. In the meantime, I suggest you call one of those expensive lawyers you probably have on a leash." He picked up the file.

Cruise took out his cell phone from a pocket, his hands shaking from the ordeal.

Steel walked out of the room with a straight face until he had closed the door behind him, then an evil grin crept over his face as he passed the small viewing room and saw the young black janitor mopping the floor whilst listening to music on his phone, the end of the mop carelessly knocking things as he went along.

"Couldn't have timed it better if I had set it up myself," Steel said happily to himself as he headed back to McCall's desk, where he found a Post-It note stuck to her computer's monitor with a message: *Gone out with Tina. See you in the morning. Sam.*

It was still early in the evening, so Steel decided to check out Cruise's story himself. He thought there was no reason to disturb McCall; she had been on the case since it had started and she hadn't really had a break, so a girls' night out was what she needed to help her unwind.

He had spoken to Tina earlier and asked if she could help get McCall out for the night, and the selling point was a limo to taxi them around as well as a table at a hot new restaurant in town called *The Blue Bottle*. Steel had to hold back the smile when Tina had agreed, as if under some form of duress, but he had seen her do an air punch as he left the morgue. He had wondered how long she would have waited until she had called McCall with the news, but he had asked Tina to make the call after she had received a text from him. For the time being, she was having a good time with a friend and that self-righteous asshole was in lock-up so, in his view, everything was right with the world.

Steel had gotten the address from Cruise, as well as a description and name: Kirsty Tennant. He had painted a picture of a tall, beautiful redhead with a figure to die for and sexy pouting lips.

Cruise had said that he had met the woman at a bar that was at the end of the street, but he couldn't remember the name of the place, only that it was near an old church. Steel had come to the street from Second Avenue, and the church stood proud with sandstone walls stretching up the towering bell tower.

The bar was on the other side of Seventh and not easily missed as it was right on the crossroad. Steel had turned on to East Seventh and followed it until he'd reached the building. The streets were narrow with a mix of red and grey brick buildings with fire escapes clinging to their sides, and tall thin trees lined the sidewalks. Edward Gibbs' apartment was at the end of the street, and this mysterious woman was in the middle – probably why GPS had picked him up near the crime scene.

Steel stood in front of a red brick building and checked the address on the piece of paper Cruise had written the details on. Yes, this was the right address. He walked up to check the names on the call buttons and there, near the bottom, was Kirsty Tennant. He reached down with a gloved hand and pressed the buzzer, but nothing came over the intercom, so he tried again; still nothing.

Steel looked around and put his finger at the top of the row of buttons and ran it quickly down to buzz everyone in the building. A click sounded, and the door was released, and he shot inside as yelling from the intercom started with people was asking who it was.

Steel made his way to the fourth floor and the apartment of Cruise's alibi. The man couldn't remember the apartment number, only that it was the last one on the left. Cautiously, Steel made his way down the hallway, following the directions. He stopped in front of the door and knocked. Nothing. He tried again, and this time he could hear faint sounds of movement emanating from within. He put his ear against the wooden door to hear better. Sounds of something been dragged slowly across a floor came through the wood. He reached under his quarter-length jacket to the small of his back and the Glock 33 holstered there.

"Hello ma'am, it's the police – are you okay in there?" Steel yelled through the door.

The sounds became louder as they drew nearer. He moved close to the wall so he could move quickly to cover if something happened. The metallic sound of door locks being unlocked echoed through the hallway, then slowly the door opened to reveal a small lady in her late seventies. He blew out a quiet sigh of relief and laughed at the situation.

"Good evening ma'am, I am with the NYPD. Do you know a Kirsty Tennant?" he asked with a friendly smile while showing his shield.

The woman grabbed the ID badge that Steel was holding and drew it close so she could see it better. "NYPD? But you're British?" She seemed confused.

Steel didn't have time to explain, not that he was in a rush to release Cruise either. "Yes ma'am, it's a long story, but going back, do you know Kirsty Tennant?"

The woman eyed Steel from top to bottom and smiled. "Yes, I do. Would you like to come in and discuss it?"

Steel could see the wicked smile and stepped back nervously. "No, I am good right here, thanks."

Her face crumpled with disappointment. "*I* am Kirsty Tennant – why, what's wrong?"

Steel glanced into the apartment to see if anyone else was there. "Do you live alone, ma'am?" he asked, and the grin came back to the woman's face.

"Why yes, I do, detective. Why do you ask?"

Steel took another step back, almost in fear of this over-lonely woman. "Someone said they were here last

Thursday night; do you have a niece or a neighbour that is also a redhead?" He had a sudden horrible feeling.

The woman shook her head with a confused look on her face.

"Last Thursday you said? I was in Boston visiting my son." The woman looked around the apartment from where she stood. "Well, nothing has been moved or taken. Why? Was someone here, in my home?"

Steel didn't want to tell her that some scumbag of an editor was lured here and drugged. He smiled and shook his head. "Sorry to waste your time, it was obviously a mistake in the information I was given. Have a good evening,"

He quickly headed for the stairs. The apartment was a bust; whoever the woman was, she had done a good job framing Cruise. She didn't need to blame him completely. She just had to make the police waste their time.

Steel walked out into the street and gazed around to see if there were any cameras anywhere close so he could get some footage, but the street was empty of watching eyes. Then he looked back at the way he had come in at the crossroads of Seventh and Second and smiled. This was a major junction and was bound to have footage, but then another question came to mind as he made his way to the junction to see if he was right. Someone must have known the old lady and, if not, had they picked her specifically or chosen her random? Yet … *somebody* knew she was going to be out of town.

Steel had found enough to release Cruise. Someone had framed him, but why him? He stopped at the junction and looked at the cameras as he pulled out his cell phone to call Traffic Division. Whoever had planned this had done it to the last detail, the same sort of planning as the bus escape. It was too much of a coincidence that all this was happening: the bus crash, the murders, and now the framing of Cruise. It was obvious to Steel they were linked, and all he had to do was find out how and why.

Suddenly, he received a text from a source: *Found her for you, she is in a disused tenement in Hell's Kitchen.* He nodded as he read it, then dialled Traffic Division to request the footage. He had found her again but now had a bad feeling. If he could, so could they – whoever *THEY* were.

TWENTY-EIGHT

Megan Armstrong had followed the judge for most of the day, but now she was hungry and tired. By blending in with the crowds and ducking into alleyways, she had made sure that she had not been followed by the two goons that had tried to take her the other day. The men had tried to take her for a reason, and she wondered who had sent them. Not the judge; she was oblivious to the fact she was being followed. So it meant someone else was after her, but for what purpose?

Megan quickly turned into a quiet alley that ran between two abandoned tenant buildings. She stopped and looked around before shimmying up a drainpipe that ran next to a rusty fire escape with a broken ladder. She stopped part of the way up before leaping for the first balcony of the metal construction.

The loud thud of flesh hitting metal could not be helped, but she hoped nobody had noticed. Megan made her way to the top of the building, then opened a bedroom window before quickly disappearing inside, closing the window behind her and locking it.

The whole place had been abandoned five years ago after a project manager bought the building and paid off the tenants to move. Unfortunately, his permission to tear down the building failed, and so it remained empty with the furnishings the old occupants had left behind.

Inside, the building was dimly lit by the streaks of light that had filtered through the dirt-covered windows. Speckles of dust hung in the air, which was illuminated as they floated through sun streaks, making them stand out like plankton in the ocean.

Megan moved from the apartment and headed down the corridor to another room, one she had a key for. She slipped the key into the lock and turned it until she heard a familiar click. She had gotten the apartment a while back; it was safe, clean and fully furnished. The windows had been blacked out so no light could be seen from the outside, and electricity was run from a streetlamp near the building. The only other person who knew about this place was her uncle – after all, he was the one who had found it for her and had the power re-routed.

Megan had figured it had once been a safe house for associates of her uncle, but she'd never asked. For now, it was her home. She took off her backpack and removed the small number of groceries she had gotten on the way: milk, cereal, bread and eggs.

She glanced at her watch; she would have a couple of hours before she had to be at work, so she made herself a bowl of cereal and settled down on the old couch after lighting a couple of candles for light.

MEGAN HAD FALLEN into a deep but troubled sleep. Suddenly, she was awakened by the sounds of someone creeping along the hallway. She opened one eye and listened – the sound of someone moving slowly as if to minimise the noise. It could have been another squatter looking for a place to crash, but the footsteps told her otherwise; if it was a squatter, why move so stealthily?

She looked at the front door to make sure the dining chair was firmly pressed against it and still rammed into place under the door handle. The sound of crunching – like someone walking on eggshells – echoed through the building. This sound filled her with fear; she had sprinkled broken Christmas ornaments onto the floor, the perfect warning system to tell her how close an intruder was. The sound she heard now meant they were close – too close.

Megan shot up from her position on the couch, grabbed her jacket and the small backpack as she headed to a back bedroom. She quickly shut the door and placed a dining chair under the door handle, so it acted as a wedge before moving to a window. A knotted rope, which had been secured to the radiator, lay neatly on the floor. She opened the window and tossed out the escape rope.

She turned as she heard voices yelling, followed by the sound of running. She had no intention of finding out who it was or what they wanted. Hastily, Megan climbed out of the window and grasped the rope; she looked down at the drop, which probably looked further than it was, but she knew it was a good thirty feet to the bottom of the alleyway. As quickly as she could, Megan made her way down. She peered through one hallway window as she passed it to make sure nobody had seen her climbing down. Fortunately, the only thing the hallway was filled with was badly wallpapered walls and cardboard boxes filled with junk.

A loud crash above made Megan stop and lookup. An expression of fear came over her face as she realized that they were in the apartment. She began to move quicker, in the hope that she would reach the bottom before they found her escape route.

The cold of the evening began to bite at her fingers, making her grip that more difficult, but she had to ignore the sensation in her hands. Another crash emanated from above, and she understood, in horror, they were in the bedroom.

"She's here," a loud voice shouted as she felt the tug of the rope from above.

She looked up to see the grimacing smile of one of the knifemen who had tried to kidnap her. He leant out the window, the rope firmly clasped in his hands as he began to pull her up. His movement was slow and deliberate, almost as if he were enjoying watching her fear. She looked down at the grey concrete below and weighed her options: drop and probably die, or be dragged up to God, knows what fate?

Megan closed her eyes and prepared to let go; she breathed slowly, taking in the sounds of the world, which seemed to be clearer but somehow sounded slower.

There was a loud sound of breaking glass and a scream. She opened her eyes in time to see a man fall past her and land awkwardly on the dirty concrete below. Puzzled, she gazed up to see the face of the man in sunglasses.

"If you drop, he should break your fall," John Steel yelled down to her. Above him, she heard the knifeman yell commands to the others in her apartment.

"There's some hero below us. Get him before he gets the girl," a man shouted.

Steel didn't move. He just looked down at the scared girl on the rope and smiled as if everything would be alright.

Megan looked down; the drop looked further than

before. She began to climb down, but the knifeman was now in a hurry and pulling her up faster than before. She stopped climbing and gazed to the window where Steel had stood, but he was gone.

Her gaze fell upon the knifeman as he pulled the rope, his body halfway out of the window to get more leverage. As she came into line with the broken window, she looked in, and her eyes grew saucer-wide as she saw a man dressed in black running at full pace towards her. Her mouth fell open in shock as he dove out of the window, straight at her.

Steel grabbed her and turned, so his back was to the glass of the window of the building opposite. With both girl and rope firmly in his grasp, they hurtled through the adjacent apartment window.

The sound of her screams was dulled by the noise of shattering glass. The knifeman watched as they disappeared safely through the window of the opposite building and his teeth bared in anger but, suddenly, his look changed to one of horror as he realised the rope had tightened in his grasp and he was pulled out of the window.

The knifeman smacked the brown brick wall headfirst as he was wrenched out of the building. Skull met brick, and it cracked like an egg, leaving a deep red splotch over the weathered wall.

As he fell towards the alleyway, his body ricocheted off both buildings like a pinball; upon each impact, he left a little something of himself before joining his colleague on the ground in a bloody mess. Slowly, Megan eyed the body of the man in black. He grabbed her and spun so he would take the impact of the glass and fall.

Quickly, she stood and backed away from him. Had he given his life for her? If so, why? She didn't know him. She leant down to poke Steel's motionless body to see if he was dead. "Are … are you dead?" She repeated the question to herself, and then chided herself for asking a dumb-ass question.

"Well, if I am, you'd probably be shitting yourself about now," Steel said, sitting up carefully as glass shards fell off his leather jacket. He groaned as he moved, every muscle in his body ached from the impact. He was scratched but not badly, his reinforced clothing took most of the wear of hitting the window, but he still felt it. She slapped him playfully for scaring her.

"Who *are* you?" Megan asked, knowing he wasn't one of the men out to get her.

Steel said nothing at first, just smiled before turning his attention to the loud cries from the other building.

"You're the one who saved me from the men the other day, aren't you?" she asked, her eyes squinting as if to discern a reaction.

"I suggest we leave this party before they find us," Steel said.

Megan nodded and helped him to his feet.

Steel knew they didn't have much time; all he had to do was get her downstairs, or as close to it as possible so she could get out. As they headed down, they began to hear voices from below; they were here. Steel put a finger to his lips to motion for silence, and Megan nodded. They moved down the stairwell, sticking to the wall as they went. At the second floor, the voices became louder, followed by the heavy stomping of boots as the men began to move more quickly. Steel opened the door to an apartment and pushed her in.

"Lock the door, and if you can get out, do so. Go to this address; you will be safe there. Just show this card." He shoved his business card into her hand. She turned it over to see a handwritten address and then peered into the face of the man who had saved her so many times. She saw a cold, stony face – someone focused, exuding raw power.

"Will I see you again?" she asked, almost terrified at the thought of losing her angel. She went to speak again, but a bullet hitting a lamp on the wall signalled trouble. They had found them.

Steel extended his right arm, and his Barretta Storm Bulldog firmly gripped in his hand. There were a roar and a spit of flame from the weapon as he put two rounds into the gunman before pushing the girl into the room and slamming the door. He stood back and kicked off the door handle; now, there was no way in for them.

Megan grabbed what she could to barricade the door. Gunfire rang out, making her flinch with every explosion. She stopped suddenly as she heard screams of pain followed by more gunfire. She looked at the door, and a lonely tear ran down her cheek as she wondered what would become of her angel in black.

She glanced at the card and looked at the address and smiled; a safe place, was that possible? Megan headed for the windows and smiled again. Below where the bodies of the two men. The drop was around twelve feet, but like he had said, "They should break your fall."

She leapt out of the window and disappeared into the shadows.

TWENTY-NINE

The morning brought a slight frost that lay like a silver blanket on the garden outside her window. Judge Matthews sat in the study in her grand home, using the time to catch up on things before everyone rose from their slumber. Sitting at her desk, she sipped her first coffee of the day while news blared from a large wall-mounted flat-screen television. The office was large and modern, with plenty of windows for natural light. As she went through her e-mails, something in the news report grabbed her attention: it was about a shootout in an old disused tenement building.

Eyewitnesses explained how they saw armed men rush into the building and open fire on someone, and the reporter told how "person or persons unknown immobilised the men by shooting out their knees."

Matthews almost had a heart attack as her cell phone began to ring, but she just stared at it for a moment, as if gathering the strength to talk. She picked it up and pressed the answer button. "Yes – yes, I was just watching it. I don't know what happened. It wasn't me who sent them – yes, I *am* aware of what is at stake. Look, I never signed up for—"

The caller spoke, the voice was garbled but clear. Something the caller said made her tremble in fear, her gaze on the photograph of her family, and a lone tear trickled down her dark cheek. She put down the phone, and utter shock filled her face; her eyes looked at a large painting hanging above the fireplace, and she smiled.

Picking up her phone, she made an entry in its memory. Slowly, she stood and headed for the kitchen as sounds of her family moving about filled the hallways. Something was coming; she always knew the day would come, and she *had* to be ready.

* * *

McCall hadn't taken the subway to work for years. In fact, the last time was when her car was in the shop getting a tune-up. She had a nasty feeling it might be permanent; the insurance agent had said they wouldn't pay because her insurance coverage didn't include burning buildings. Plus, *she* was the one who had smashed the car into a burning dumpster. As she stepped off the elevator, she found Steel, Tony and Tooms with the young female tech, going through street-camera footage.

The tech was tall and slim with a ruby-red long-sleeved top and cocoa-brown skirt that followed her curves. Her short fiery red hair and vivid blue eyes added to the pretty picture. McCall wondered who had requested her as the usual tech – a geek called Adam wasn't taking the controls. Steel got up from his perch on the desk, which faced a large monitor on the opposite wall. He handed her a Thermos mug that resembled the one which had been incinerated in her car.

She smiled as she took the mug filled with fresh coffee. "Wow, thanks. Now all you have to do is replace my car, too." She grinned.

Steel smiled awkwardly and pointed to the screen. "Yes … well, Traffic sent over footage from the crash. We were hoping to get an idea of what had happened," he explained.

McCall sat in the spot Steel had just warmed and smiled enthusiastically, hoping for a break in the case.

"Man, I don't know why we couldn't do this in your office," Tooms said wickedly, knowing the cat was now out of the bag.

The tech turned to Steel. "You have an office?" she asked, intrigued.

He pointed at the monitor as if trying to change the subject. "Well, it's more a broom cupboard really."

McCall grinned again and shook her head at the childish antics. As the tech turned back, Steel threw a paper ball at Tooms' head, which bounced off and fell into the trash basket, causing Tooms to give him the bird with a haughty smile.

"So, did we get anything?" McCall asked, her eyes meeting the ones of everyone else. They all registered the same thing: confusion.

"Um … just watch," Tooms said, nodding to the young woman, who began the footage from the start of the scene.

They watched as the delivery truck pulled up, then suddenly the cameras moved away from the crash site; moments later, the cameras moved back in time to show the three men running from the scene.

"What the hell was that?" McCall asked, now displaying the same confused look like the rest.

"How could the cameras be moved, remotely or would that have to have been done at the source?"

The others didn't like where Stel was going with this.

"Hey man, you're talkin' about people in Traffic – that's other cops you're talkin' about, man. No way would anyone do dat," Tooms vented.

The tech shook her head as she went through the footage. They had been given footage from all the cameras on that junction, and all of them moved at the same time.

"I don't know. If it was done at the routers, then there should be signs of tampering – but to get them all to move the same time?" The tech shook her head.

"I'm not saying it was Traffic, but I'm wondering where it could be done, Tooms. Someone *did* move them, and I just want to know from where and how," Steel said, seeing the anger in Tooms' face at the thought of a cop doing such a deceitful thing.

Tooms smiled slightly and nodded. "Yeah, man, I guess you're right, so I guess we gotta check the cameras." He shrugged.

Tony closed his notebook and stood up from his chair. "I'll go check out the cameras and the systems room, and see if it can only be done from there," he said, shooting a look around the room.

Tooms watched his partner disappear towards the elevator.

"Whoever did this is making us chase our tails again; they want us to waste time looking at cops." McCall's theory was more hope than fact. The thought that cops might be part of this whole thing made her stomach turn.

"Go back to when the truck arrives, please," Steel requested.

The tech smiled at him with wide eyes that sparkled.

He smiled back, and she blushed and got back to the task. "Okay, so watch this. Our delivery guy comes in and parks," he said, pointing at the monitor.

Everyone looked him strangely, as though he had two heads.

"What?" Tooms asked, wanting to hear the rest of the idea.

"The driver parked – so, it's what they do. Don't you get it!"

McCall felt like going for her gun just to end his lunatic rant.

Steel stood there, hoping for some sort of stir in their thinking. "Don't you get it? He *parked* the truck." He was beginning to feel he was alone in the idea.

McCall and Tooms rolled their eyes, hoping he would stop talking riddles.

"Yes, you said that already … lots of times. So he parked his friggin' truck? So what," McCall barked with frustration.

Steel shook his head in disbelief. "Delivery guys don't park, they abandon, but this guy he parks, and I mean *parks*. If you watch, he manoeuvres until he is in the perfect spot, then he doesn't get out until the cameras move," he explained as he looked at the still of the box body again. "Where are all the other cars? The street is empty apart from that truck. Why?"

Tooms shrugged, sporting an uninterested look. "Who knows, man? Maybe they cleared the street for a movie shoot; they do it all the time," he shrugged.

Steel wasn't convinced. The whole thing seemed too staged.

"So, let's get this straight. You are saying the delivery man staged this whole thing, including getting his van smashed up – really?" Tooms bit back. Steel's crazy theory had worn him down.

"OK, why don't we ask him what he was doing there, and did he see anything?" Steel suggested.

Tooms looked at the report, then scanned the page with a distressed look on his face. "The driver – he never came forward. He's in the wind." His face darkened with anger and Steel smiled victoriously.

"Alright then, so the escapees had someone on the outside putting this whole thing together, someone with enough influence to make it all happen," McCall said, standing and looking at the board as she started to theorise.

"Yes, but who?" Tooms asked as he sat on the edge of the desk.

* * *

Captain Alan Brant slammed the handset on its cradle. He leant back in his chair with a look of exhaustion on his face. An urgent knock on his door made him look over to see McCall and Steel standing in the doorway.

"Is everything alright, sir?" asked McCall, worried about her mentor.

"It's this new chief of detectives – the man is phoning me every hour for updates on this damn case. Like we haven't got other crimes to solve." Brant removed a hip flask from his top drawer and took a small hit.

"What's he like, this new chief?" Steel asked, hoping not to pop the already pulsing vein in Brant's forehead.

"He's some hotshot who made his way up getting easy, lucky cases and kissing ass. Hell, it wouldn't surprise me if he was groomed for the position." He laughed at the very thought of it. "So, detectives, what have we got, just in case that pain in the ass phones back?"

McCall smiled sunnily before telling the Captain everything they had found so far: the video footage, the cameras, and the driver of the van.

Brant made notes as she spoke, so he had it on paper – the voice of the new chief was irritating enough to make you forget your own name, let alone what you were about to say.

"We are checking out known associates, family members, things like that. Financials are clean … no movement since the guys were put away. However, we know that something happened ten years ago that ties this all together. We just have to find out what it was."

Brant nodded; he was happy he had something new to throw to the chief to calm him. "OK, so what's your first move?" Intently, he regarded the two detectives, who were now looking at each other, wearing the same expressions.

"We need to go over the escapees' cases again. There is something we are *not* seeing," Steel affirmed.

McCall had to agree, but she needed coffee and fresh air.

THIRTY

Judge Matthews had gone about her normal day-to-day routine – going to the courthouse and meeting with other judges and high-powered people for coffee during the breaks she could fit in.

She was grooming herself for Chief Justice. She had her eye on greater things, and so did other people. Years ago, she had sold her soul to the devil to get a foot up, and it had worked, but like all things, there was a price. Her career had been fast, and influential people wanted her in place to make sure things were done or forgotten. Not far behind, Megan Armstrong followed in the shadows. Always on the hunt for her quarry. The judge had gone to her favourite restaurant to meet with her politician friends, which suited Megan as she could sit in the deli across the road. In a window seat, she kept a watchful eye on the judge as she laughed and put on that career smile.

Megan stirred her coffee slowly, the images of her angel in black, shutting the door on her before the firefight burnt into her mind. Who was he, and why was he protecting her? She took the business card from her pocket.

On it was the address of a local priest. Then she realised what he meant by "she would be safe" – it was a sanctuary.

Looking up, she saw the judge was now alone; her conversation with the men had ended, so why was she still there? She watched intently as the judge became impatient and nervous, and checked the time on her watch again, something she had done at least twelve times in the last half hour. Megan glanced at her own watch and noticed that it was nearly half twelve. For the past couple of days, she had always met the mysterious man at half twelve, but not today. Something was wrong.

Judge Matthews got up and left, her face full of concern, but for what? As Megan got up to follow, she noticed a Town Car pull up and the judge quickly got in. Admittedly, it was a fair walk to the courthouse, but that had never bothered the judge before; something had changed, so much so she was fearful of going out in public. Had the judge been tipped off to Megan tailing her? She didn't have time to think about it – she had something to do. She had a date with the judge, and it was time for payback.

* * *

THE COURTHOUSE STEPS were filled with law students, all gathering to enter and see how a case was being carried out. Megan smiled at her good fortune. She was the right age and was dressed as badly as the other students, so she would fit in nicely. All she had to do was get past security and head for the judge's chambers to wait for her.

The professor stood on the top row of steps and hailed all the students to follow her, and the gaggle of noisy teenagers gathered in a line, like sheep to a dipping.

The inside of the grand old courthouse held high

ceilings and carved pillars. Lawyers stood in groups, discussing golf-swing averages while others made their way to courtrooms to begin or continue cases. It was a hive of activity, a virtual mass of bodies rushing from place to place or gathering in waiting groups. Megan smiled as she got through the masses and headed off to the judge's chambers. She knew there would be some time before they were called to sit down, so she had time to leave her message for the judge.

The courtroom began to fill up just as Megan made it back to the group. She still needed them to leave the courthouse as she couldn't risk being caught on camera. As she took a seat in the upper gallery, Megan couldn't help but wonder which courtroom Matthews would be in, and she never had time to check. Megan thought she would have trouble finding the judge's chambers in the huge building, possibly stopped by a guard for wanding about. To her surprise, though, Megan had found it. She had also gotten in and out of the judge's chambers without being seen, then re-join the group with ease. The line of students had been so long it made it almost too easy to slip away and slip back in unnoticed. Megan looked around at the other kids who seemed to pay her no mind, as though she had always been with them. The group entered one of the courtrooms and took their seats in the Gallary above.

A large muscular bailiff with short hair walked up to the bench and took a deep breath before announcing the judge. "All rise for The Right Honourable Judge Matthews."

Megan smiled broadly as the judge walked through, carrying a glass of water. Her eyes locked onto the glass as she retook her seat. Now she had a better view of the judge, but she wondered about the message she had left and when she was going to get it.

Inside the courtroom, the temperature was boiling as the midday sun beamed through the windows; the room itself was like an oven. People adjusted their dress. Men took off jackets while women fanned themselves with whatever they could find in their purses.

The case she was working on was a man accused of stabbing his wife to death after an argument – a case Megan found fitting. As the proceedings went on, mouths became dry and clothing soaked with perspiration. Matthews wiped her brow for what seemed like the seventh time, but it would be the last.

"Bailiff, could you get an officer to go to Maintenance and find out what is wrong with the heating?"

The large man nodded and headed towards the door – glad to get some fresh air, if only for that moment.

"Go on, councillor," she beckoned the defence lawyer.

He was a tall thin man with black side-parted hair and a blue Armani suit. The man thanked the judge and continued his argument. As he spun his sales pitch to the jury, the bailiff returned and took his place by the door to the judge's chambers. The lawyer spoke clearly, using small understandable words and a calming tone. His manner hypnotised the jury like a cobra to a group of mice.

Matthews looked at the glass of water; the cool liquid looked refreshing, and her hand went to reach for it. Her dry lips could feel the cooling liquid upon them.

"But I say to you, ladies and gentlemen of the jury," he yelled, making Matthews and the others jump out of their skins.

She glared at the man's back as he faced the jury. Her hand was close to the glass but not enough to knock it over. She licked her lips and, as she reached for the water, something caught her eye.

One of the jurors, a large man with thinning hair

began to gasp for air and clawed at his open collar. Out of breath, he fell to the ground, his face pale and sweaty. Everyone rushed to his aid but ended up crowding him.

"Can everyone get back and give him some room? Please, go back to your seats," ordered the bailiff over the din as people moved back to their places.

The man was still conscious, but his breathing was laboured.

"Are you OK, sir?" asked the bailiff.

The man nodded slowly as he reached into his pocket for a bottle of tablets.

"It's too warm in here. I have high blood pressure amongst other shi … stuff."

The bailiff smiled and nodded. "Can you continue?" he asked.

He nodded, still looking like death warmed up.

Matthews rushed forwards with her glass of water and handed it to the bailiff, her expression one of concern. "Here, give him this." Her words were calm but firm.

The man sat up slowly and took a large mouthful of water; his eyes began to bulge as he grasped his throat as though something was wrong.

The bailiff slapped the man on the back and a cascade of water shot from his mouth, clearing the water from his windpipe. "Sip it, sir, or else that's gonna happen again."

The man nodded and took small sips. Matthews nodded and smiled as if to say "good job" to the bailiff.

"Are you sure you are OK to continue?"

He nodded again, the colour starting to come back to his cheeks as he retook his seat. "Yes, Your Honour … sorry, Your Honour."

She nodded and smiled. "Very well. Sorry, councillor, please carry on." Matthews turned as the bailiff brought her a fresh glass and a large water jug that he had found in the judge's chambers, and placed them on her bench.

As Matthews listened to the councillor go through his argument, she poured a fresh glass of the inviting liquid while maintaining a watchful eye on the proceedings. The heat was making everyone uncomfortable, including Matthews herself. She would wait until he had finished his argument, then call a quick recess while the problem was resolved. It would be pointless carrying on if nobody was paying attention.

Her eyes darted towards the double doors at the back, hoping to see the officer the bailiff had assigned to get the engineer, but it was wishful thinking, almost as much as the councillor cutting his speech short.

Matthews felt another drop of sweat hit her hand. She was in a suit and her robes, which was the same as being in a sauna. She picked up the glass of water and took a massive mouthful as the councillor droned on. As he approached the jury, his words heightened, and his voice rose as if to bring drama to the whole event.

The jury watched him intently as he went through how his client had been set up, how he wasn't even there when she was killed. Eyes fixed on him as though he were reading an exciting novel – all eyes except one set. There was a scream from the gallery, and everyone turned to see a woman standing, her arm outstretched as she pointed towards the judge.

Matthews sat, her eyes bulging; blood gushed from her mouth. Suddenly, she vomited a stream of red plasma that reached the desk of the accused; the poor guy behind the desk shot backwards, falling off his chair in the process.

The flesh around the judge's mouth bubbled, and pieces of bloodied flesh fell away as though she were melting wax. Matthews froze, her hands gripping the sides of her bench, her eyes still wide open. Then she slumped forward, her head smashing onto the bench and making a hard sickening cracking sound as bone met wood. The impact knocked over the glass jug, spilling the rest of the liquid.

Everyone ran out screaming – all apart from Megan, who just froze in place, her eyes fixed on the judge as she lay slumped on her bench.

* * *

THE SUN WAS HIGH, and the breeze had died away, leaving warmth in the air. Steel had finished his hotdog and was now watching McCall devour hers in a most unladylike manner.

He shook his head and laughed as she shoved the rest inside her mouth and tossed the crumpled paper into the trash basket like a champion basketball player.

"What?" she asked with a lost look on her face.

Steel said nothing, just stood leaning against a station wall. "Nothing. Come on, we have work to do," he said with a smile.

McCall licked the remaining ketchup from her fingers and headed for the entrance. They had just entered the stationhouse lobby when the desk sergeant stopped them and waved the two detectives over to him.

"Hey, McCall. Your captain said you and James Bond over there have got to go to the courthouse. Someone whacked a judge during a murder case," the desk sergeant shouted over the escalating noise.

McCall's face flushed red as she marched over to the desk to see if there was anything else. "What the … are we the only detectives here or what?" she growled.

The sergeant shrugged and smiled unsympathetically,

and the two detectives walked into the welcoming sunshine. It was a great day to take a walk, but the courthouse was on Chambers Street in the civic centre, which was miles away.

McCall headed for the subway whilst determining which route to take; she stopped and turned to see Steel reading a text message on his cell phone. "You comin' or what?" she shouted, losing her mental directions.

He just smiled and headed for the parking lot down the road.

"You remember I don't have a car anymore, right?" she shouted after him as he walked with the speed of a child in a toy store. She growled with disapproval and chased after him. Suddenly, it dawned on her: he might have actually brought *his* car for a change. She imagined an Aston Martin or a pumped-up Range Rover but, knowing Steel; it was more likely a Bentley or Rolls.

As she caught up with him, she found him looking at an old Ford F-150, and her excitement died at the sight of the dusty pick-up.

"You have got to be kidding me! *This* is your car?" she asked. Her voice sounded as though all the air had left her body. Steel turned to her with a puzzled look.

"What? This? No, detective, that is." He pointed to a far corner of the lot to a brand-new black Ford Mustang Shelby GT Coupe.

Her jaw dropped, and she could feel herself drool at the sight of the beast. "Wow, Steel ... I am ... actually ... not surprised, really." She turned a compliment into an insult – mostly out of jealousy. "Well, you said you had a car and, well, I am impressed you brought it," she grumbled.

Steel smiled smugly as he watched her walk around the shiny new car.

She paused for a moment – hold on, new car! "Steel, did you just buy this to piss me off?" She knew he could be insensitive sometimes, but this had taken the biscuit. She shot a look that could have melted the sun.

"What, don't you like it?" Steel slid his hand along the roof.

McCall was lost for words. Was he actually asking if she liked *his* new car while hers was in an ashtray somewhere? "Seriously, you're asking if I like your new car while I trashed mine saving your ass?" She fought the urge to either shoot him or damage the car, but the car was too nice.

Steel threw her the keys and headed for the passenger side. "Who said she was mine?"

* * *

THE STREETS WERE FILLED with the throaty roar of a V8 engine as McCall took her new baby for a spin. She had to admit she was taken aback with the whole thing. He had come through for her and had bought her a new car – and *what a car*. But she had to wonder: was this new car fitted with hidden police warning lights in the grill and other extras? How long had he had this planned? But the more she thought about it, the more it didn't really matter. She was happy, but she wasn't about to tell him that.

Steel smiled as he watched McCall out of the corner of his eye. Her knuckles whitened as she gripped the steering wheel every time the car's V8 engine gave a mighty roar.

* * *

As McCALL PARKED, she could see the media circus had started to arrive and was set up in what were the best places for good shots. As McCall and Steel approached the outer police barrier at the foot of the courthouse steps, she smiled. They had already cordoned off the building with a nobody-in-or-out policy to prevent the killer from leaving. At the door, two uniformed officers stood watch – a tall female officer with dark hair, blue eyes, and a secret smile for Steel and the other a tall man with a quarterback body and watchful eye.

"Morning detectives," the male officer greeted them as they walked up to show their IDs.

"Morning Officer … Hodges." McCall shot the greeting after quickly getting his name from his name tag.

"Morning, detective," the female officer greeted Steel, the smile never leaving her lips.

"Morning Elizabeth … sorry, Officer Lane." He walked in, leaving her with a widening smile and a good feeling.

McCall rolled her eyes and followed inside.

Inside the old stone walls, groups sat or stood in the wide corridors while uniforms took statements. Crying and loud mumbling was constant. Something terrible had happened – sure, they had been told a judge had been murdered, but there was more to it. McCall figured the large group of people had come from the crime scene, which now had two officers on either side of the courtroom doors to prevent anyone with a sick urge to grab a photograph. Steel looked at the groups, most of whom were teenagers, possibly students. Then he froze as he saw a familiar face waiting to be interviewed. He walked over to the young uniformed female officer who was waiting to carry out the next interview and moved in close to whisper in her ear. She smiled and nodded before he gratefully tapped her on the shoulder as a thank you.

He hurried towards the guarded doorway to catch up to McCall, who waited patiently.

"Sorry, was this murder interfering with your social life, Detective Steel?" she asked flatly, thinking he had just picked up another date.

Steel smiled at the thought she was mad at the idea other women gave him the eye, but he kept it to himself; it was more enjoyable to watch her squirm.

"Who the hell attacks a judge in a courtroom?" she asked as she pulled on surgical gloves.

Steel held open the door with a gloved hand, letting McCall in first. "OK, then!" His voice rang with surprise.

They both stopped at the sight of the judge slumped onto the wood of the bench and Tina standing some feet away. Blood had run down the sides of the front, and splatter marks lead to the defendant's desk.

"What the hell happened here?" he asked, as surprised as McCall at the sight of the remains of the judge, half expecting it to have been a shooting or something similar.

"Well, time of death is obvious, and we have plenty of witnesses. What we don't have is a suspect," Tina pointed out. McCall looked at Tina, confused by what she had just said.

Steel got closer, then quickly reared back from the potent overwhelming smell emanating from the corpse.

Tina nodded at Steel's assessment. "That's acid. As for the type, well, I will have to get her back to the lab first to find that out … uh, well, what's left of her anyway." Tina gestured the bench, then carefully walked around to get a better look in hopes of finding a clue as to how it had been delivered.

McCall pointed to the overturned water jug, thinking that may be a good place to start.

"Whatever it was, it chewed her up pretty good.

Luckily, we knew who she was ... Judge Carmen Matthews," Tina stated.

McCall nodded whilst wearing a look of disgust. "Okay, you get her back, and we will check out her chambers. She may have left something that might explain all this."

Tina waved over a couple of men in safety suits and buckets to collect the remains, even the fluid ones.

* * *

McCall and Steel made their way to the bailiff, who was still guarding the door of the judge's chambers. She could see the shocked expression on his face even though he was facing away from the scene.

"I am Detective McCall, and this is Detective Steel," McCall said, introducing themselves.

He looked at them and then the shields that they held up for him to see.

Steel opened the door to the chambers and stepped aside. "I think it's best if we talk in here. I think you could do with a change in scenery."

The officer nodded shakily and proceeded inside.

Steel beckoned the man to sit in one of the padded chairs in front of a large wooden desk. The man sat and smiled at McCall as she sat in the other.

"Can you tell me what happened?"

Steel left the room briefly but soon returned with a bottle of water from a vending machine he had noticed another time he had been here. He handed the bottle over and made a conservative search of the office.

The bailiff cracked open the bottle and drank with short sips. McCall smiled at him as if to tell him it was OK to take a moment.

"I have no idea what happened. We started proceedings as normal." He stopped as he remembered the juror getting sick. "Well, everything was OK apart from it being damn hot for some reason. She asked me to get someone to see the caretaker about it. Later, after I got back, one of the jurors well, he must have had a hard time with the heat because he dropped to the floor with breathing problems."

McCall had already turned on her digital recorder and was taking in everything.

"Did he leave?" Steel looked over at the bailiff, curious at the timing.

The man shook his head and took another hit from the bottle. "No, the judge gave him some water, and we carried on once he had retaken his seat. He insisted he was fine."

McCall glanced at Steel, who wore the same expression.

"Which juror was that exactly?" He shot the question as he sat in the judge's chair and opened the drawers of her desk to see if there was anything untoward.

"Number six … juror number six. Hell, you can't miss the guy – he must weigh two hundred pounds!"

McCall made a mental note to look for the man after they had finished with the room.

"So, what happened next?"

The man's face was suddenly filled with terror as the image came back. "Oh, God, it was horrible. I brought her a fresh glass from her chambers, and she refilled it; like I said, it was like a friggin' oven in there. Anyways, she took a drink …"

Steel watched closely as the man quickly put his bottle of water down.

"She began to spit blood; I mean it was comin' out like a fireman's hose. Then she just collapsed. I told everyone to get the hell out of there and radioed it in so nobody could leave." The bailiff looked at one of her pictures on the wall – an old picture from when she graduated from law school with another woman who was around the same age. "She didn't deserve that; she was a good judge and a good person."

Steel noticed a family photograph on the desk of the judge, her husband, and their kids. The thick oak frame sat neatly on a corner under a brass desk lamp.

"We will come back later. In the meantime, can you secure this room? CSU will probably want to come in just in case."

The bailiff was still shaking with shock and McCall made a mental note that the paramedics should take a look at him.

Steel had come up empty, but if there was something, he figured it would not be in plain sight. Outside the office, they could hear a commotion from frightened people. He got out of the chair and helped the bailiff out of the room, through the doorway and into the hallway, instead of making him look at the courtroom once more.

But something played on Steel's mind: how did the judge fit into this whole mess and what the hell was the girl doing there?

THIRTY-ONE

Tooms and Agent Lloyd sat in the briefing room, looking through files on the prisoners; they also had the paperwork on the guards and the bus driver - just in case they red-flagged.

Tony had sent a request to the Financial Department for anything on the guards. They had already found that one guard had taken a payday, maybe there were more. However, that would take time – or so they said.

Tooms looked over at Lloyd as she sat in the chair opposite. She wore a grey suit with a black blouse that had the first two buttons unfastened, probably not for his purpose, after all, he was married, but she got a lot of attention from the other detectives who seemed to have the same coffee breaks as she did. Her hair glistened from the false lighting above them. Though he had to admit she was a stunningly beautiful woman, she was damaged goods.

She caught him staring and smiled as if she had misjudged his attention. "Anything wrong, detective?" Her voice was soft and sensual.

Tooms leant back in his chair and squinted at her. "I am just trying to work out why you're here."

Lloyd looked puzzled, not really knowing where this was going. "I thought it easier than rushing back and forth between here and the office."

Tooms shook his head. "No, I mean this case: why are you here? If it's a federal case, we wouldn't be anywhere near it, apart from being your lapdogs, but we seem to be doing all the lifting on this. Plus, where's the rest of your team? Don't you normally travel in packs?"

Cassandra Lloyd nodded with an impressed smile on her face. "We all have our orders, detective, whether we like them or not."

Tooms sensed disappointment in her voice, as though she were on this case like a kid sent to the corner of the classroom for being bad. He knew there was no use pressing the matter; she wouldn't unburden herself, not to *Detective* Tooms, but she might to *Joshua* Tooms.

He smiled and shrugged as if defeated, then he picked up the file on the driver, hoping to defuse the situation. Lloyd watched him look quickly through the file, as if it were a buffer, and smiled at his attempt to change the subject. Then he stopped, and she saw his expression change. She knew that he had found something. He stood and swiftly scanned the files he had just brushed through.

"What did you find, detective?"

Tooms raised a hand to silence her before he lost his concentration. Lloyd leant forwards with interest as she watched him peruse. For a second, she thought Tooms looked excited by something when he grabbed two files and looked through them with interest, his fingers flying up and down paragraphs as he compared them with the driver's file. The files had obviously revealed something to Tooms that everyone else had missed.

He gazed at Lloyd with a surprised look on his face. "The guard who we found in the Hudson and the guard who was sat with the driver had both been transferred to the prison two days before. Someone wanted them on that bus, but the questions are who and why?" He stared at Cassandra Lloyd as she raised an eyebrow.

"We need to speak to the survivors in the hospital – they are the only ones who can tell us what happened on that bus." Lloyd threw down her file and sat back, so the chair rested on the rear two legs.

"Good luck with that, detective. We are waiting for the hospital to phone back to tell us when they are awake." Tooms stood and grabbed his jacket from the back of his chair. "Look, I am going to the hospital anyway, so you can come with me, or you can stay here. The choice is yours." He started towards the door, but stopped suddenly and turned back towards her. "Oh, by the way, it's either Tooms or Joshua. I think we have outgrown the formalities, don't you … Agent Lloyd?"

She nodded with a friendly smile, rose, and shook his outstretched hand. "OK … Joshua … let's go."

* * *

Nobody saw DC Williams cautiously enter the main entrance of the safe house. He nodded to the two armed men who sat around acting like bums, squatting, their .50-calibre Desert Eagles and H&K MP5K machine pistols hidden safely under their long coats.

He made his way up to the top floor to where his bother and fellow escapees had called home for the past couple of days. The corridors and staircases were dimly lit as not to bring attention to the outside world. The musky smell of an ageing building filled Williams's nostrils as he walked towards the last apartment. He tapped the door three times with his boot as his arms were full of groceries for the men. The lack of noise made Williams suddenly become uneasy. They couldn't have gone out during the day; the cops were looking for them. He tapped again, this time a little harder.

The silence continued. He was just about to throw down the bags and go for his keys when he heard the deadbolts and chains being taken off. The door opened slightly, and the familiar face of Tyrell peered round the door.

"What's up, man?" Williams scowled disapprovingly as he raced past his yawning brother, then relocked the door.

"What took you so long, man? Thought you mothas had bolted." Tyrell looked strangely at his maddened brother.

"Yeah, we were gonna take off to the mall or catch a friggin' movie."

Tyrell laughed at the silliness of his brother's statement.

Williams headed for the kitchen where he found Darius making chilli from items he had found in the refrigerator and cupboards. Darius looked excited at the sight of new food items. Tyrell eyed the man, puzzled, as he watched him check all the packets as if he had plans for the items, like making up menus.

"So, what ... you're a chef now?" Tyrell joked.

Darius shrugged and smiled dryly. "Before the cops grabbed me and locked me up, I was due to open a new restaurant. I guess someone didn't want some black dude stealin' their business, so they got me out the way."

It made sense to Tyrell what Darius was saying – hell, they had both bad histories, but they were starting on a righteous path before they got stung. Tyrell had to laugh. For years the cops had tried to get them, but the moment they were going legit they got them on something they never did.

As they cleared the stuff away, Williams looked around suspiciously. "So, where's the professor?"

Tyrell nodded towards the back room with half a glazed doughnut in his mouth.

"The man's been a bit of a loner since we got out; something is bugging him," Darius muttered. He had wondered about the teacher; he kept to himself, and he would slip out at night, sometimes for hours.

Tyrell looked at his brother and rubbed the top of his head to break a smile, but Williams' face looked troubled, more than usual.

"Hey man, what's wrong with you?" Tyrell asked as he placed the milk in the refrigerator door.

Williams glanced at the closed door.

"You remember that bitch lawyer who put you away?" Tyrell's face soured as he stopped on the way to the cupboards next to the stove.

"Yeah, hard to forget. She made a career out of screwing me, God-damn Councillor Carmen Matthews."

Darius looked at the two men, and his mouth fell open at the mention of her name. "She was your prosecutor. You got to be kiddin' me, man. Shit, she screwed me over as well, damn bitch," Darius growled as he impaled a red pepper on the chopping board with a large knife.

"Yeah well, she was a high-court judge." Tyrell gave his brother a sudden look of panic.

"What do you mean *was*?" Williams leant against the wall and shrugged as he stared straight into his brother's eyes.

"Somebody took her out this afternoon … in her own courtroom, too." Tyrell crossed his arms in defiance to the implication.

He saw the questioning look in his eyes. "You think I would be dumb enough to kill a friggin' judge ... in her *own* damn courtroom?"

"You do – you think *I* wasted the bitch!" Tyrell yelled in anger and surprise.

Williams simply shook his head.

"When you didn't answer, I thought you had gone to settle up, but I figure how you gonna get past my boys and the guards at the courthouse – especially with that huge ugly head of yours. I mean, man, cops would spot you a friggin' mile away."

Tyrell threw a damp dishcloth at his laughing brother.

There was a click, and the front door opened, and the hooded figure of the teacher walked in, his expression stony. He nodded in greeting, then disappeared into his room and shut the door. The three men stood open-mouthed. Williams shook off the confused look, and it changed to anger. He ambled to the door with his colleagues behind and opened the door.

"Hey, Teacher, where you been man?" Darius asked casually, as though it were a daily routine.

Armstrong, standing beside the door, shrugged; a wry smile broke from the corner of his mouth. "I have been to see ... an old friend." And with that, he shut the door in their faces.

The three men shrugged it off and returned to packing away the groceries until Williams stopped and looked at the front door, his eyes burning with rage. "Wait a minute. How the hell did that motha-fucka get out?"

* * *

STEEL AND MCCALL returned to the courtroom to be greeted by the CSU team sporting bodysuits and buckets.

The acid had reacted quickly and was turning the judge into soup. McCall headed for Tina, who stood to one side with the jug and glass in evidence buckets.

"What you got?" McCall asked curiously on sighting the two items.

"Not sure, but these things are made from plastic, not glass."

McCall shrugged, lost at the point her friend was trying to make.

"The acid would have melted the glass, but it wouldn't the plastic."

Tina gave Steel the thumbs up. "Gold star for you. My question is who brought the plastic to the party?"

McCall looked back at the judge's chamber. "Could it have been the bailiff? After all, he brought her the glass."

Steel pondered the question; anything was possible, and it would make sense.

"Let's go ask him, shall we?" McCall suggested and, as they began to walk, Steel received a text.

He stopped as he read the message, and his gaze moved to the courtroom doors. Distracted, he put the cell phone back into his pocket.

"Hey, Steel. you OK?"

He turned to face McCall and smiled. "Yes, sorry, it was nothing." He beckoned her forward with a flat palm towards the chamber.

McCall turned the handle and opened the door to an empty room.

"OK then, that's a problem." Steel joked, causing McCall to give him a look.

THIRTY-TWO

Tooms and Lloyd arrived at Manhattan Hospital. Its long sterile corridors shone with cleanliness, and overhead lighting made everything brighter, but the smell of disinfectant hung in the air like invisible smog. Tooms did not care for hospitals; he had lost too many friends in them, but then a lot had also pulled through. It only seemed like yesterday that he and Tony had rushed in with the medical team with McCall on a gurney. He'd been surprised that so much blood could flow from one wound.

That was their first case with Steel: a serial killer and a weapons-smuggling organization. McCall had taken a bullet in the shoulder after a firefight. A year had passed since that day, and he had never forgotten that day in the hospital – in fact, it was this same hospital.

The injured men from the crash were in separate rooms so they could not plan or confer. The last thing they needed was the same lie from all of them. Tooms knew that some would lie but, at some point, someone would tell the truth; it was inevitable.

Tooms and Lloyd met with one of the doctors. He was a short man in his mid-thirties. Black-rimmed glasses made him look like the sort of doctor who had all the answers. Tooms figured that they were clear glass instead of prescription lenses, a trick to make himself look more distinguished. His sandy brown hair, brushed neatly to the left side, was neatly cut.

"I am Doctor Clarke."

They all shook hands and exchanged pleasantries.

"I am Detective Tooms, and this is Agent Lloyd. Can any of the survivors talk yet? We need to get a statement."

The doctor pointed towards the last room on the right. "Miguel Sanchez is pretty banged up, but he is the only one who can talk."

Lloyd looked puzzled. Was it convenient or coincidental that only one of them could talk – but then it was her nature to be suspicious.

As they entered the room, they saw Sanchez in a full-body cast. Both his legs and right arm had been broken in several places, and his left shoulder was dislocated. Heart-rate monitors and morphine drip-fed into the cast like science-fiction movie devices.

"Miguel Sanchez, I am Detective Tooms, and this is—"

"You heard about the crash, didn't you? Well, sorry man, but I don't know shit apart from been thrown about like a piñata," Sanchez butted in as if to save Tooms the trouble of asking questions.

Lloyd walked to one side of the bed and Tooms the other. Tooms reached into his pocket and pulled out the digital recorder McCall made them carry, which he didn't mind so much because his shorthand sucked.

"What's that for, man?" the injured man asked, almost in a panic.

Tooms raised the device and shook it to show there was

nothing abnormal about it. "Don't worry man. You know us cops are too dumb to write, so we got to use these to get your statement."

Sanchez smiled at the quip and then coughed as he tried to get a lung full of air.

"All we want to know is what happened on that bus – a, anything you can remember, no matter how small or unimportant you think it is. Someone tried to take you guys out, and we want to know who."

Sanchez only moved his eyes and ared into Tooms' large brown ones. He could see that he was an honourable man. "OK, so where do you want me to start?"

Tooms switched on the recorder and placed it onto the small bedside cabinet to the injured man's right. "The prison, let's start from there." He watched Sanchez lick his lips, so he picked up the drinking vessel and placed the straw next to his mouth.

Sanchez sipped enough to wet the inside of his mouth and then he began his tale. "We were loaded on as usual, but this time it was different."

Lloyd regarded Sanchez intently, who was staring at Tooms. "Different, how?"

Sanchez' eyes shot over to her, which made him flinch with pain at the sudden movement. "It was the parole hearing bus. Most of us didn't need to be on it, but we were thankful for the time out, you know? The guard said they had to fill the bus or something."

Tooms coughed, making Sanchez look at him again; he felt the man's pain even when moving his eyes. "Miguel, just keep looking at me, man, even if she asks you a question, OK?" He noted a relieved look. "So, you get put on the bus, then what?" He gave the man another sip, then waited patiently for him to gather himself.

"We got locked down, but then the usual guard says he

has to split because he got a text – his mama is in hospital. Well, they loaded on some other guy who then sits upfront with the driver." Sanchez stopped to take a breath.

The meds he was on obviously didn't minimize everything, Tooms thought. "OK, you're on the bus, and it's raining," he prompted to jog his memory.

"Yeah, man … never seen so much friggin' rain. Was hard to see out of the windows, it was so damned thick, but I remember thinking that we were going the wrong way."

Tooms looked perplexed. "How did you know that?"

Sanchez smiled like a kid with a big secret. "Man, I have done that trip hundreds of times and each time, just as amusement, I would plot a getaway route. You know, if something happened and I got out. How did I know? Because I didn't recognize a damned thing. The street was different, and the stores, hell, even the coffee shop at the corner of one of the streets were gone. No, we were taking a different route."

Lloyd glanced at Tooms, who shot her a look of surprise.

"So, you're going along. Did anything seem strange or out of the ordinary to you?"

Sanchez seemed surprised at the question as if Tooms should have known the answer. "Yeah, first off, we were all put on the left, and the guys who got away were stuck on the right, near the back. Then there was the driver and the guard next to him screamin' at each other."

Tooms drew closer with interest.

"Why was the guard telling the driver he was going the wrong way?"

Sanchez tried to shake his head. "No man, the guard was tellin' the driver where to go, and if he fucked up, his family was dead."

Tooms' stunned gaze lifted towards Lloyd, who now held the same panicked look as he did.

"Then what? You're going along, it's raining, and the driver and the guard are arguing. Then what? Did the driver lose control of the bus because of the argument?"

Sanchez' face went white with fear as the memory came back to him. "No, the guard was looking at his cell phone and shouted 'now' to the driver and stuck a gun next to his head. The driver swerved and …"

Tooms placed the drinking straw next to Sanchez' mouth, and he sipped slowly to calm himself. With a soft sigh, he continued. "There was a loud explosion or something to the right-hand side, and the whole bus shook, and next thing I know we're on the side, hanging upside-down and being smashed. The noise, man. I will never forget the fuckin' noise. People screamin', the sound of the metal sliding along the ground like nails down a friggin' chalkboard, but constant, you know? Next thing I know, I am in here."

Tooms nodded with appreciation and reached for the recorder; as he went to switch it off, something Sanchez had said at the start began to bother him. "At the beginning, you said the trip was strange because not all of you should have been there. Who *shouldn't* have been there?"

Sanchez swallowed hard as he fought back the memory of the crash.

"What? Oh yeah, the four guys on the back row on the right. I know for sure they were not due for another year as they had theirs not long ago."

Tooms suddenly looked horrified. "Four guys … no, you mean *three* guys?"

Sanchez seemed puzzled. "No, man, *four* guys. Teacher, Darius, Tyrell, and Monster," he said.

Tooms looked at Lloyd with a terrified expression. "Shit! We have four missing prisoners, not three." His voice conveyed panic.

THIRTY-THREE

McCall put in a call for uniforms to check the judge's house for anything that might explain her murder. She had also a warrant request on her computer ready to go in case her husband refused. They were looking for anything, even hate mail. Normally, she would get another detective to do it; however, there was a shortage of personnel, which included the newest detective Jenny Thompson, who was on "personal time". The woman had had a rough year – they all had. Others had taken holiday time to cut down hours. So, McCall had to resort to the "boys in blue" to carry out the task.

Steel had found the bailiff; he had been in the bathroom, emptying his breakfast into one of the cubicles in the men's room. After being asked about the glass and the jug, he had to confess he never really noticed; he just thought the judge had brought them in.

After Steel had packed off the bailiff to the medics for a check-over, he joined McCall in the judge's chambers. "Find anything yet?" he asked hopefully, but knowing the judge was a smart woman who wouldn't leave something lying around.

McCall shook her head as she finished looking through the judge's jacket and purse. "Naw, nothing, just her wallet, cell phone … the usual stuff."

Steel walked around the large desk and sat on the thick leather office chair, his gaze fixed on the heavy wooden desk as if he knew it was hiding something within.

McCall watched as he started to search drawers, pulling them as if to find one that was locked. Suddenly, he stopped and looked at McCall as he tugged on a slim drawer and smiled as if he had won a prize.

"OK Steel, it's locked, so we wait to see if the key—" She stopped talking and her mouth fell open at the sight of the lock-pick set Steel removed from his inside pocket.

"Sam, could you check those books over there? There might be something useful."

She understood his meaning even if she didn't like it. If she didn't see him pick the lock, it never happened. McCall brushed a finger over the leather-bound books – law, law history, psychology, and numerous other volumes that would make her head hurt if she tried reading them. She turned quickly as Steel let out a victorious "yes!" but didn't know whether to be impressed or scared at the quickness with he had completed the task.

"First time lucky?" she joked.

Steel shrugged and smiled as he tucked the set back into his jacket.

She walked around to see what he had discovered. Inside the drawer was a mass of papers, some of the letters, but one note stuck out.

Ten years ago, you destroyed my life like acid you bitch, so now you will burn in Hell. Steel lifted it by the corners so not to disturb evidence. It was typed with a computer, the letters large 72pt Times Roman font.

"Well, that's chilling and somewhat poetic," he said.

McCall shot him a surprised look.

"In a bad murderous way, that is," Steel said shrugging.

She opened a clear evidence bag for him to place the document inside. As she sealed it, he continued to check the desk but found nothing of importance, only a couple of receipts for a local restaurant and other places she had probably put on her expense account. He closed the drawer with a disappointed look on his face; he had hoped for more than the note.

"We need to find out what she was working on ten years ago," McCall and Steel said in unison.

Steel leaned back in the chair and tapped the padded arms. "Does it strike you as odd that *ten years* keeps on cropping up? It wouldn't surprise me if she worked on one of the escapee cases in the past."

The look on McCall's face told him she'd had the same thought. Out of the blue, she asked,

"OK, so who's the girl?"

"Sorry, what?" Steel shook his head, as if to reboot his system to the here and now.

"The girl in the hallway… who is she?" McCall asked again.

Steel stood and walked over to McCall; his face had its usual stony expression.

"Ask me again after the case is done, will you?" His tone was serious but friendly. She nodded as if understanding, but he knew she wouldn't be done with it; she would be on his back until she got an answer. Trouble was – he didn't know either. He only knew he had been tasked to keep her safe.

* * *

"Captain Brant, are you any closer to finding the escaped men?" The Chief of Detectives' voice was dry and calm – emotionless some would call it.

"Not yet, but the FBI have put out their nets and pictures have gone across the board to every toll booth, gas station, train station, you name it. We have the word out."

There was a slight pause, as though the chief were gathering thoughts. "And the killer? Any leads yet?"

Brant was becoming tired of the same questions, but he knew he had to give him something. Since McCall's return from the courthouse, she had briefed him on the off-chance that he'd receive such a call.

"Two of my best are working on it now, and they are following a lead as we speak. They think it is some sort of revenge killing."

The pause came again, but this time Brant could swear he heard scratching in the background: fingernails rasping against something hard, like a desktop.

"Very good captain, but please keep me apprised of anything new. We need to keep people happy, don't we?" the voice on the other end of the phone said.

Before Brant could answer, the phone offered a dead tone; he was disconnected. He looked over at McCall and Steel, who sat on a long couch that rested against the back wall opposite his desk. He placed down the receiver and sat back in his chair.

"Chief's asking for updates again. I swear the man might as well get an office here; it would save the city a fortune on phone bills," Brant said.

McCall and Steel smiled, but they could see there was something eating at the captain.

"That's an idea … he could have yours," McCall said jokingly, turning to Steel.

"You have an office? I thought you were joking about that?" Brant said surprised at the news. McCall shot the captain a shocked look.

"What, haven't you seen it yet?" she joked, earning a dig in the ribs by Steel's elbow. Hoping to change the conversation, Steel interrupted.

"Anyway … this whole thing has something to do with an occurrence that happened ten years ago. It must have been big to have so many players in it. But we need to find it; whatever it was could be *the* key."

"That's a hell of a job; a lot happened ten years ago." Brant nodded as he weighed the task at hand. Steel knew it was a mammoth task, but he hoped all the victims intersected at some point, that something tied them all together. McCall glanced at the elevator as Tooms and Lloyd stepped off it.

"Do you think that the missing escapees are involved?" Brant said.

She nodded, and Steel sat motionless, as if not willing to offer an opinion just yet.

"It makes sense, they break out and kill the people who put them away. They would have plenty of friends and resources to pull it off on the outside." Brant thought for a moment as he struggled with the idea, then turned to Steel. "What do you think?" He eyed Steel who stood and absently brushed the creases out of his suit.

"I think we need to stop the killer because I don't think they are done yet."

* * *

McCall and Steel left the captain's office and headed after Tooms and Lloyd, who had entered the briefing room to check files. They walked in to find Tooms searching through a fresh stack.

"Hey guys, the financials for the guards haven't come back yet, have they?" he asked eagerly.

McCall shook her head, puzzled by the greeting. "No, apparently they have a bit of a backlog of cases. Why? Did you find something out at the hospital?"

Lloyd's eyes lit up as Steel entered the room, but his attention was on Tooms.

"The driver may have been coerced by the guard next to him, who, get this, had been put on the bus at the last minute," Tooms said with a curious grin. McCall's mouth fell open at the news.

"Not only that, but there were four escapees and not three, so we may be looking in the wrong places."

Steel felt Lloyd's stare and looked over to where she sat. He could see she was trying to smile, but his icy expression only brought a tear, which she quickly brushed away. "So, what did you guys get, apart from a dead body?" he asked Tooms, who obviously had not heard about the state of the corpse.

Tooms merely stared.

"Uh, not body… but soup." Steel amended.

Tooms looked confused.

"Somebody used a powerful acid to kill the judge. By the time we got to her, the ME was using buckets," McCall explained.

Tooms and Lloyd cringed.

"But we did find a note, which proves it was the same person. We are thinking it may have something to do with an event ten years ago," McCall said.

Tooms looked over to Lloyd, who seemed excited with

the concept. "All our escapees went down around ten to twelve years ago; maybe that is part of your connection. All we have to do is find the fourth runner, whoever it is, and find out when he was put away."

McCall smiled at Lloyd's theory and gave Steel a friendly slap on his left shoulder. "See, told you they might be connected with the escapees. Lucky us girls think alike, or you boys would be lost." She headed for the break room for a much-needed coffee.

Lloyd followed, sensing an awkward moment if she stayed near Steel. As she left, he did not move but followed her via a reflection in the large display monitor on the wall. He could see her twirl to look at him as if to see if he would turn, but he would not give her the satisfaction. All the while, one thought kept coming back: why the hell was she here?

Steel left Tooms as he strolled over to Financials while he headed for the solitude of his office. There he could think between the quiet of those walls. Besides, he had another little matter to see to.

He stepped inside and slowly closed the door. Every time he entered, he would stop, close his eyes, and breathe in the comforting smell of ageing wood and leather, scents that made him think of his home back in Britain. John Steel used to love his father's study as a child; there was something pleasing about it. So, when he had a chance for an office, he knew what he wanted it to look like.

He had searched on the internet and various dealers for the same type of furnishings. But then, why get reproductions when you already had what you needed? So, most of the furnishings were brought over from his father's old study. As he walked slowly towards the vintage cigar office chair, he let his hand brush the hard leather of the armchair and the wood of the antique desk. Gently, he sat and put his feet on the desk and took off his sunglasses, allowing natural light on his weary eyes. He closed them and drew in a long breath, held it for a couple of seconds, then slowly exhaled. Twice more, he did this before sitting properly at the desk and switching on his laptop. The screen blinked, and seconds later, the password protection box came up. He typed the password, then waited for the computer to finish the loading process.

He clicked onto the icon for the internet and opened his email account. Steel searched for updates to his private mission but found only junk mail. Closing the screen, he went for an internet search on the judge. She had been a prominent figure, so her career would be all over the web. His search for her cases was made simple by the timeline; all he had to do was find out as much as he could about her, starting twelve years ago.

As he combed through pages, he discovered she was a prosecutor and a hell of a good one at that. Steel could see how she'd been shooting through the ranks.

He made notes of dates of cases that were relevant to the escaped men. The information didn't show much, so he would have to find the original files. Sure, he could have telephoned for them, but he wanted to speak to people who might have known the judge to get a feel for her. Had she been fair or brutal?

He sat back in his chair and looked at the large monitor on the wall. Even though it was turned off, he used it to focus on as he let thoughts collect and sort. This was a strange case. To that, there was no mistake, but in the end, it would come down to something simple. It always did. However, one thing was clear, and the killer had left notes, which suggested they wanted people to know why they were killing all of those people. That would fit the escapees if it was about revenge, but if that was the case, why try and hold up the investigation? It was clear that someone was either trying to stop or hinder the case, made obvious by the attempts on McCall and himself. The more he thought about it; however, even that did not make sense. Whoever created the breakout had means and resources, but the killings were simple.

Also, if they had that many resources at their disposal, why not just skip the country and enjoy reading about it in the papers after a hitman did the work? No, there was something wrong; there was an element missing. He closed down the computer and stood, putting his glasses back.

The judge had seen over fifteen cases in the two years. Granted, not all were big ones, but nevertheless, she had won. For him, the judge was the key, and if he could find out more about the cases, he might be able to shed light on why they were doing this – and find the killer.

THIRTY-FOUR

As Steel left his office, he noticed Tony had returned from his field trip and was seated in the break room with Tooms, McCall, and Lloyd. Nobody noticed him silently approach as they discussed the case and built theories.

"So, the monitor room that controls the cameras has a staff log in place and a supervisor. When I spoke to the supervisor, she insisted no one had touched or moved the cameras," Tony explained before sipping coffee from a carry-out mug. "However, when I checked out the crime scene with Tech, they found control units attached to the cameras, which proves they were moved in that area, using some sort of remote."

Tooms exhaled a lung full of air as the complexity of such an operation went past the realms of his imagination.

"They probably set up a relay in a building, and the driver had the remote."

They all spun to see Steel in the doorway with the afternoon sun shining behind him, giving him a mythical appearance, like some sort of archangel.

"Could be. You have cover from sight and plenty of power from the building. Maybe the driver was simply the driver, and someone inside the building was using the remote; either way, I'll check it out," Tony advised, thinking it was the most logical idea.

"Thought you had gone out somewhere?"

Steel shook his head to McCall's question. "No, not yet. I was going over the judge's case list for the time period we were looking at. I'll see if it coincides with any of our escapees."

McCall looked at the time. It was now a quarter to four, and she felt disappointed that they had achieved so very little. She took out her cell phone and checked the display screen, just in case Tina had tried to reach her, but there was nothing new.

"Something wrong?" Steel asked as she tucked the cell phone back into her jacket pocket.

She gazed into nowhere and shook her head before looking over. "No, it's nothing. I thought Tina may have had something new by now."

Tooms gave a look of surprise. "I thought you said she was killed by acid? Tina may be good, but that stuff is gonna get rid of a lot. Hell, you already said they brought buckets!"

McCall cracked a smile. The more she thought of it, the more she had gotten her hopes up. Seeing the body like that, and running flat out, had taken its toll for the day. Her thoughts drifted towards a deeply relaxing bath and a bottle of Merlot she had bought the other day. "You're right, dumb call. I was hoping there may have been some evidence where she had been the hours before her death." She was hoping for a meeting with someone or a fight in a public place, anything to make the murder make sense.

Steel saw the lost look in McCall's eyes and wished

there was something he could do. His expression grew flinty as a thought crossed his mind. "McCall, come with me."

She looked confused. "Where are we going?" She was almost scared by a potential reply upon seeing his pissed-off expression.

"I think I may know of a way we can find out where the judge went." Steel looked around, suspicious of being overheard while McCall turned to the others.

"You guys keep on the guards. I want to know where they transferred from, what their finances are like … everything you can find. Also, one of the escapees had a brother – DJ or something … Tyrell Williams' brother. Find him and lean on him, see if he knows something." She looked back to see Steel at the elevator, waiting for the doors to open.

"It's okay, we got it. Now get the hell out of here before he goes without you." Tooms laughed and watched McCall walk speedily after him.

The elevator doors opened, and Steel used his back to hold them open while she scurried in.

"So where are we going?" she asked, expecting some shadowy alleyway meeting or the underbelly of a bridge.

"Church," he said simply.

McCall turned to him, perplexed. "Church?" Since when did he need to repent?

As the doors closed, Detective Bennett rounded a corner and watched the numbers on the display count down. Taking out his cell phone, he backed around a corner while he pressed the autodial. He waited for several seconds before someone picked up.

"Yeah, it's me. Look, we have a problem. Those two detectives are getting too close. You have to send more guys next time. They need to get it right."

He stared at the phone as it went dead in his hand. Whoever was on the other end, had hung up. Quickly Bennett closed down the phone and, after inhaling deeply, walked around the corner with a huge smile as if nothing were wrong.

* * *

Steel and McCall stepped into a cold breeze brought by the west wind, but the warmth of the sun made it bearable. The clear blue heavens were only spoilt by vapour trails from aircraft. As Steel put on his leather gloves, a homeless man dropped to the ground in front of them. He knelt to help the man up. His long raggedy woollen coat used to be green but now leaned toward grey while his jeans were nearly brown. The man – who McCall guessed was in his mid-fifties – had a long grey beard that still had streaks of copper and brown from his original colouring. "Are you okay, sir? Do you need any help?"

The man coughed violently and waved as if to say he was OK. McCall cringed as the man sounded off a harsh bark as if he might cough up a lung.

"No, son, thank you. I am fine, just lost my footing is all."

Steel helped the man to his feet, then reached into his trouser pocket and pulled out some money, gave the man a fifty, and wished him well.

As the man shuffled off, McCall smiled smugly and chirped, "You know that guy probably picked your pockets just then?"

Steel smiled as he brushed himself off. "Of course he did. I wouldn't expect anything less from Crazy Gus."

She looked down the street to see the man running off as though he were a marathon runner, then turned back to

Steel. "You know ... that guy?" She wasn't sure what to say or think.

"Yes, of course, I do. That time when we first met, when I went undercover ... never mind. The fact is he's a friend."

McCall laughed quietly to herself as if to say I'm working with a madman.

Steel reached into his pocket and pulled out a piece of paper, read the note, smiled as if he had gotten something right, then stuck it back away.

"Do you want to share?" she asked with a scowl.

Steel thought for a moment, then shook his head. "Ask me again later, but now we have a witness to talk to."

McCall didn't know whether to shoot him or let his maddening behaviour go; after the thought of paperwork and too many witnesses, she went for the latter. "OK, so where is this witness – the church?" She raced after Steel, who was swiftly heading for the parking lot. "And another thing, why do we always use *my* car?"

Steel smiled. He found her quite cute when she was angry, but he dared not tell her.

* * *

THE CHURCH WASN'T FAR from the 11th Precinct, but McCall wanted to drive there nevertheless. Besides, the vehicle was warmer, and it shielded them from the biting wind that was starting to pick up the more the sun was disappearing. She parked across the road from the old church. Its brickwork glistened from a recent restoration project Steel had funded. Inside it was quiet – even the noise from outside was muffled by the thick walls.

McCall entered first as Steel opened the door for her

and, as he entered after, he smiled at the sight of a priest knelt by the front row.

"Wait here for me, will you?" he whispered.

"Where are you going?" she asked quietly.

"Off to see an old friend, why?" he asked.

McCall would have screamed at him if they had been elsewhere. "I thought we were going to see a witness," she growled softly.

Steel stiffened and adjusted his jacket as though he were making himself presentable. "First things first, my dear McCall. Sometimes a little faith goes a long way."

McCall bared her teeth in frustration. "Steel, we don't have time for this."

He didn't hear her; he was already making his way down the aisle. She waited for a few seconds before looking round to see she was alone, then started following him - but leaving some distance between them.

The tall priest was in his mid-forties but wore it well; broad shoulders filled out the clergy apparel nicely.

"I hope you're not praying for my soul, father?" Steel joked as he approached.

The priest turned his head. "A bit late for that, don't you think, you murderous bastard? Besides, one has got to have a soul in the first place." He stood up, and the two men embraced like long lost brothers.

Not quite understanding what had just happened, McCall's jaw dropped. Then sShe coughed politely as to draw attention.

Thetwo men spun round to face a puzzled Samantha McCall.

"Oh, forgive me. F,s—

"Samantha McCall?" The priest stepped forward and kissed the back of McCall's hand; she looked into his deep brown eyes but didn't see the priest, just the man. "Johnny has often spoken of you."

Steel grabbed McCall's hand and pulled her away jokingly. "Yeah, yeah. OK, Mr Smooth Talker, behave yourself. You're meant to be a priest."

Gabriel put his hands together as if to pray and smiled. "You look surprised that he mentioned you," he said, noticing the strange look she was giving Steel.

She shook her head and smiled. "No, just surprised he had friends."

They both laughed, leaving Steel crossing his arms in defiance.

"Yeah, nice. Great to see you too old friend. So, where's the girl, locked in? A dungeon, I hope?" McCall shot Steel a shocked look when she figured out that he had the girl from the courthouse.

"Don't worry; she's safe. Actually, she is in the canteen … with, uh, the babysitter you sent." Gabriel's words faltered when he saw Steel's face creased with venomous anger.

He reached to the small of his back to draw the Barretta Storm Bulldog.

"But of course… you didn't send one. Did you?" Gabriel muttered at his stupidity.

Steel shook his head and got McCall to call for back-up.

The trio rushed for the canteen. It had been built for those to use after church, and it doubled as a soup kitchen for the homeless in the evenings. McCall put away her cell and removed her custom Glock, and pulled back the top slide, chambering one of the 9mm hollow points.

As they burst through the double swing doors, they found a short and stocky bald-headed man trying to drag the girl to a back door. He turned, holding the girl as a human shield; unfortunately, they were around the same height, making it impossible for Steel or McCall to find a target.

With their weapons trained, McCall raised her shield to identify themselves, just in case they were about to take out a cop – but then, a cop wouldn't need a human shield. "NYPD, put your gun down and let the girl go!"

The man had his Sig Sauer 320 to Megan's head, with no intention of giving either of them up. "Tell you what, detective, why don't you two put yours down and you let me get out of here? If not, you'll be picking bits of the girl off the walls." The man laughed cockily as if he held all the cards.

"That ain't gonna happen, so why don't you just do the right thing, so nobody gets hurt."

The man stuck the weapon firmly against Megan's head as if to show he meant business. All the while, Steel was looking for something to shoot; he was hoping just to injure the guy so he could be questioned but his main priority, of course, was the girl.

"The interesting thing about human shields is the person who is holding them is counting on the others, who need the shield alive or uninjured," Steel shouted, startling everyone. "Also, one other flaw in the plan is what happens to you if you do shoot. You are then open to getting your own head blown off. You see, there is no win-win for you really. You're not getting out with the girl, and you're sure as hell ain't fuckin leavin if she dies." His tone had turned grim.

"Stop, for the love of God. This is a place of peace, so please put your guns away." Gabriel rushed forwards to reason with the man. As he approached, the stocky man extended his arm to shoot at the priest.

His first mistake.

A loud explosion filled the room, followed by the gunman's scream as a 9mm round from Steel's Glock disintegrated the man's wrist bone. The effect: it propelled the hand away from his target and caused it to open as muscles were smashed. The Sig fell to the ground in front of Gabriel, who quickly kicked it to one side as he watched the man holding what was left of his wrist. Blood flowed freely through his fingers to the clean floor.

Steel and McCall rushed forwards to the girl to make sure she was okay. "Are you hurt?" he asked softly as he checked for blood.

She shook her head; her eyes fixed on the man on the floor.

"This is Detective Samantha McCall. She will look after you."

Megan's large watery eyes gazed at McCall, looked her up and down suspiciously, then turned to Steel. "You said I would be safe here. How did they find me?" she spat angrily.

Steel looked down to see a shield on the man's belt as he lay writhing. "I was wondering that myself actually." He turned back to McCall and the others as he suddenly realised something. "You all have to go now. He probably either has back-up en route or waiting outside. In the meantime, we are going to have a little chat."

Megan rushed forwards and hugged Steel. "I will be safer here with you," she said, suspicious of the others.

Steel smiled and pried her off him. He crouched down, so they were on the same level.

She wished at that moment she could see behind those sunglasses – to see into those eyes.

"You will be safe with them. There is nobody I trust more and, besides, McCall is a bit of a badass," Steel said with a smile and a shrug. Megan laughed and wiped her eyes, nodded, and walked over to the waiting arms of McCall.

"Sure, you don't need any help?" She already knew the answer, but thought she would put it out there. Steel shook his head as he picked up one of the plastic canteen chairs and brought it closer to the man. "Just get yourselves to safety. I will be fine."

The three burst out the back door, leaving Steel with the scared, injured detective.

"OK, now that we are all alone, what shall we talk about? Go on; I'll let you pick the topic."

The man watched Steel sit down and take off his sunglasses. At first, his eyes were closed, but then, as the smile faded from Steel's face, he opened them to reveal cold, dead emerald eyes. As the back door to the kitchen closed, the injured man's scream was closed off from the unsuspecting world. McCall turned to Gabriel, hoping he had an idea for a safe place.

"We can go to my friend's parish; it's out of the city, and nobody will find us there," Gabriel said. McCall looked concerned and peered behind her, then shrugged. "Don't worry. He has a way of finding people. Besides, he is a little busy," she assured Megan.

THIRTY-FIVE

Tony and Tooms arrived at the morgue. Tina had called them as she couldn't reach McCall on her cell phone. As they entered the double doors, she looked up from her latest customer: a twenty-two-year-old man with a hole where his brain used to be.

"Hi, doc, what you got?"

Tina pointed the scalpel to a filing tray behind the worktop that Tony leant against. He turned and picked up the evidence bag containing the judge's cell phone.

"That was in the judge's purse, the damn thing keeps going off every half hour, an alarm or something."

Tony lifted the bag and looked at the black, empty screen.

"Thanks, we will get Tech to look at it. Did you find anything on the body that may give a clue to where she may have been?" Tooms asked hopefully, only to have Tina look at him with a you-have-to-be-joking look.

"The acid compromised the body. The bad thing is the family haven't got a body to bury because the poor woman was almost dissolved. The killer used hydrofluoric acid, which will eat through pretty much anything, but you can't just pick it up from any hardware store, so your killer knew someone in the chemistry game."

Tooms nodded with a sickened look on his face.

Tony put on gloves, took the cell from the bag and pressed the power button; the screen illuminated with the usual apps. "It's unlocked." He raised the cell to show Tooms.

"As if she wanted us to find it?" Tooms' question got a shrug from his partner.

"Well, if there is something, I am sure Tech will—" Tony froze, and the alarm went off again, revealing a photograph of a picture over a fireplace and numbers on the bottom of the screen. "So, something tells me this is majorly important." He showed the photograph.

"Oh, great. Like we have nothing else to do, and it's nearly five, man."

Tony shook his head and headed out, laughing at Tooms' moaning. "Thanks, Tina, you may have broken the case." He waved as he stepped into the hallway with Tooms still yapping.

* * *

AGENT LLOYD SAT, reviewing the files Steel had requested. As he had left to go and see his witness, he had passed the list to the desk sergeant to give to her. He knew her federal "fast pass" would move things quicker than a detective's shield and smile.

The fifteen case files had been delivered within two hours, but she had a feeling the male desk clerk had been charmed by her seductive voice and had rushed them over personally. The man, in his early twenties, had left with a smile on his blushing face and ruby-red lipstick, courtesy of a kiss, on a napkin as a memento.

As she sifted through the case files, something drew her attention – two cases stood out as career makers, one was a hit-and-run case, which had nothing to do with the one they were working on, but the second was gold. She texted Steel with the information and got a short reply a minute later: *Check the main witness and who wrote the lead story ... THX.*

After a deeper search, she found the name of the main witness: it was the journalist.

"Steel you always were a clever bastard," she complimented him from afar as she read a few clippings. She stood and rushed to the captain's office, knocked and entered.

Brant, as usual, was on the phone with the chief and the conversation didn't seem as pleasant as before. "Yes chief, we are doing the best we can ... well, if you can find someone else to make this run quicker, be my guest." He looked over to Lloyd, who had a wide smile as she held up the file, suggesting she had something. "Look chief, Agent Lloyd may have something, so I am putting you on speaker." Pressing a button, he then placed the receiver on the desk.

"Under the request of a ... Detective Steel ... we got all the judge's case records for the years O-Three through O-Five. What we found was a case that made her career and put her in the running for judge. A top judge, who was going places, was knifed to death in an alley by her husband. Witnesses at the restaurant heard them arguing, and a fight broke out. She left, and he followed soon after."

Brant's expression showed that he recalled the details. "Yeah, I remember that case. Was there anything to tie that to the escapees?"

Lloyd nodded slowly as if what she had discovered was the case cracker. "The husband was no other than Brian Armstrong, one of our escapees – not only that, but the prosecution lawyer was Judge Matthews."

Brant could feel the tension on the other side of the phone – the chief might have to say "well done" or something similar – and he was loving it. "Great job, Agent Lloyd!"

She flicked a finger. "There's more. Steel asked me to check on witnesses and press articles. At first, I didn't know why. Then I learned that the main witness was a gym teacher who saw Armstrong enter the alley, then come back out later, looking anxious. He got into a taxi and drove off. Also, during the trial, one newspaper covered the story in-depth; in fact, some might say that the articles may have swayed the jury. It looks like McCall was right – one of them had broken out, seeking revenge for destroying his life."

There was a silent moment before the chief softly cleared his throat.

"Well done on some fine detective work, captain. Brant, find Armstrong and do what you have to, but bring him in."

The phone went dead, and Brant looked at Lloyd with a satisfied smile. "Well, I guess he won't be phoning again soon ... probably getting his press conference speech ready."

Lloyd laughed at the thought of him rehearsing in front of a bathroom mirror. "Do you think that Armstrong is done?" she asked, concerned with the already high body count.

Brant shrugged – he only hoped so.

THIRTY-SIX

Darius sat watching television in one of the back rooms. He was waiting for his favourite shows to come on after some boring chef program. He sat casually, with his back half on the back of the armchair and the other half on the arm; his right leg hung over the other arm. Beside him were a large bowl of potato chips and a cool beer can clutched in his hand. He was comfortable and ready for a lazy evening. Grabbing a handful of chips, Darius was about to shove them into his mouth when a news flash stopped him midway. A large picture of Brian Armstrong came onto the screen. The chips fell back into the bowl, and he sat up straight to pay attention to the story.

"Yo, fellas, get your asses in here!"

His yelling brought the others rushing in.

"The police are looking for this man in connection with three murders. He is considered to be highly dangerous, so do not approach him."

Tyrell turned quickly to find Armstrong behind them,

his face emotionless. He grabbed the man and pinned him against the wall, and Armstrong did not resist.

"What the fuck you do, man? You brought this shit on all of us. You know that?"

Armstrong peered directly into his flashing eyes. "You know I didn't do this – whoever set me up back then is doing this now."

Tyrell let him go and stepped back. "Yeah, thing is, Teacher, where you been goin' nights? We seen you sneakin' out. At first, I thought what de fuck, man's in the free world and probably got an itch. But now ... where you been goin', Teacher?"

Armstrong appeared to think for a moment, then shook his head; for him, it was personal.

"You killed a friggin' judge man, a friggin' *judge*," yelled Darius as he paced up and down.

"Everyone just stop and the shut fuck up. Look, the police are grasping at straws, and my name fits, but I don't know why. If we all stick together," he advised, urging them to see reason.

Tyrell shook his head with a disappointed look on his face; he was torn. He thought he knew this man, but what if he *had* done this? Then they would all go down for it.

"No, man, you ain't bringin' us or my brother into this shit. You're on your own, man. I would rather go down as an escapee than a judge killer." Tyrell shook his head.

Armstrong saw the looks in their faces, but none of them would meet his gaze. He nodded, understanding that Tyrell was just looking after his brother and the rest of them. Hell, he probably would have done the same. "I wish you all well guys, but just remember: I *didn't* do this. If they are willing to pin this on me, they will be after you as well. Leave the country, guys ... get the hell out!"

DC opened the door, and they watched the man

disappear into the darkened hallway. Quickly, he shut the door and bolted it before he tried to get back in. "What if he was right, man? What have we just done?" DC asked, scared and confused.

Armstrong stepped out into the dusk, the sky full of purples and oranges as the sun faded into the horizon. He pulled up the hood of his top over his head, looked around to make sure he wasn't being followed, then stuck to the shadows and disappeared down the street.

"Yeah, Armstrong just left the building. What do you want us to do? The others are in there," asked a detective in an unmarked car.

Bennett's voice blared from the cell phone speaker. "Stay on him, the others will follow later. Wait until they are somewhere public, then we can move in."

The detective ended the call and started the motor. Slowly, at a crawl, he stayed behind Armstrong.

THIRTY-SEVEN

Tony returned to the precinct while Tooms attempted to locate the picture. Tooms had gone to the judge's chambers first as that was the closest and, for all purposes, more secure: if you're going to hide something important, you want it to be safe.

He stepped off the elevator to find the room alive with activity – something was wrong. The detective looked around and finally spotted Lloyd at his desk, using the phone. He waded through the crowds of uniforms and detectives as he headed over. He drew in close to speak over the noise but was stopped by Lloyd placing a finger to his lips to silence him.

"Yes, it's important. Look, I am an agent from the FB—what do you mean, you don't care? He's busy ... hello, hello?" Lloyd looked at the receiver, shocked. "Bastard hung up on me. What an asshole," she barked, taking her finger away from the confused detective's lips.

"What the hell is going on?" he asked.

Lloyd opened the file and pointed to the arrest report

regarding Brian Armstrong. "Armstrong's arresting officers were Detectives Alan Carter and Jack Doyle."

Tooms shrugged, as if not getting the point. "Yeah, so we find them and warn them."

Lloyd shook her head but sported a large smile. "Better said than done. One of them retired and lives, God knows where, and the other …" She pointed to a footnote signature from the new Chief of Detectives.

"You got to be kiddin' me." Tony's mouth fell open.

Lloyd filled him in on what she had found courtesy of Steel's instructions. She repeated what she had briefed the captain and the chief on, bringing Tony up to speed. He had to agree it made sense, but who did Brian Armstrong know with that much influence?

That answer Lloyd had found in a different background check. She'd discovered that Armstrong was once Michael Adams, a "company" man until something made him get out, but he still had friends in dangerous places.

Looking at it, Lloyd could see how the pieces now fit together. The chief could most certainly be the next target, but getting to him would be almost impossible unless you had been trained to be a ghost, that was. The smile faded from Lloyd's lips; the more she thought about it, and Tony noticed.

"What's wrong? What did we miss?" he asked, the fear in her eyes chilling him.

Quickly, Lloyd went over the notes again and then threw down the file from Tyrell Williams. "Damn it!" She rubbed her forehead with one hand.

Tony picked up the file and read through it, then gazed at her.

"Tyrell Williams, his brother, has enough pull to get this

done. Armstrong probably used the escape to settle old debts. We need to find Jacob, Tyrell's brother."

He nodded in agreement. "True, but nobody has seen the guy since the breakout. Hell, he hasn't even been to his club lately."

Lloyd stood and put on her jacket. "*Someone* knows where he is."

* * *

A STRANGE UNEARTHLY mist hung over the cemetery at waist height, and the full moon gave everything an eerie glow – the sort of scene you would expect from a horror film just before undead hands started breaking through the surface of the ground. A lone figure made its way through the maze of headstones, moving slowly and with care.

Brian Armstrong stopped and looked up at the clear sky, liking how the blanket of countless stars presented such a beautiful scene. He took a deep breath and continued further in; he knew where he was going, and he had his goodbyes to say. Something in his soul said he might not get the chance to say them again. He walked up to a lonely marble gravestone, the lettering filled with black to help it stand out, but he knew every word by heart.

In memory of Julie Armstrong, Loving Mother and Daughter, Taken from us Too Early.

Armstrong shed a tear as he stared at the words "loving wife" and wiped it away with the back of his hand. He knew the truth, and one day he hoped everyone else would too, including his daughter. He bent down at the foot of the headstone and placed a yellow rose that he had taken from the bushes near the entrance.

"So, this is where you been comin', why didn't you say, man?"

Armstrong did not turn around; he had sensed he'd been followed. He just hoped it was either Tyrell or Darius.

"I never got to say goodbye that night. Our last words were ... well, not friendly ones, shall we say?"

Tyrell nodded as though he understood Armstrong's pain and placed a comforting hand on his shoulder.

"If you were right about what you said back there, we need to go. Your face is all over the place, man," Tyrell said.

Armstrong stood up and kissed his fingers, then pressed them onto the stone as if transferring a goodbye kiss to her. Tyrell put an arm around his shoulders like a brother and led him gently back to the parking lot at the front of the church where a blacked-out G Wagon was waiting for them.

As THE CAR SPED OFF, a shocked McCall sat open-mouthed in the church parking lot.

"You have got to be kidding me. That was Brian and the others," McCall mumbled to herself, disappointed she had missed them. She had seen the G Wagon pull up but waited in the shadows with the others in her car just in case they were noticed.

"What ... who now?" Megan gaze wandered aimlessly, confused by what McCall had just said.

"Look ... never mind, we have to get after them." She couldn't lose them, but then she couldn't be seen either.

"What about Steel? If we leave, he won't know where to find us," Megan said, concerned.

"If you haven't noticed, he always has a knack of turning up when he *is* needed," Gabrial said.

"Yeah, he does at that," McCall affirmed, then put the car into drive and sped off into the night.

* * *

Steel walked out into the parking lot and pulled on his leather gloves, his breath turning to mist as it met the cold of the night. The dirty cop had given him some information, but it was very little. Steel figured that was how they played it. You only knew what you needed to. But he came away with a name, one that didn't really surprise him: Detective Bennett.

He looked around and smiled. McCall's car was gone, so that was something. He wasn't about to stop and answer questions, especially as to why he had shot a fellow detective. Those were questions for later. No, for now, he had to find McCall and the girl, after which they had to locate and stop a killer. His long coat, a military-style wool trench with leather arms, collar, and shoulders, flapped in the wind like some demonic beast. He pulled it closed and buttoned up the cross-over closing.

The street was empty less for one unmarked vehicle with two men inside parked next to a children's playground; he couldn't make them out given the distance, but he knew they were the back-up for the hero Steel had left cowering in the church canteen, and not him.

"Some back-up," he thought. In fact, he was surprised they were still there.

Inside the car, the thin driver looked over to his large partner, who was eating a sandwich like it would be his last, pieces of chicken and mayo clinging to his large fatty chin as he shovelled in another mouthful. He eyed him with disgust.

"You eat like a friggin' animal, you know that?" said the driver. The large man smiled and belched loudly to add to the driver's annoyance.

The driver shook his head and looked through the side

window just in time to see a fire extinguisher heading for him. "Duck!" yelled the driver, trying to lean out of the way, but his hefty colleague failed to budge.

The two men covered their faces as shards of glass flew past. The thin cop felt himself being swiftly yanked towards the door; his head impacted the doorframe and then the steering wheel, while the man in the passenger side fought to turn to help the driver, but his size and the seatbelt held him in place. Half-conscious, the driver didn't feel Steel relieve him of his sidearm. Steel tossed the handheld fire extinguisher onto the ground and pointed the cop's gun at them both.

"Good evening, gentlemen. Now, if you would be so good as to take out your weapon and throw it onto the back seat ... using your other hand and holding it by the grip with two fingers. Thank you."

The fat fellow struggled to get his weapon but managed to do as he was told. Steel backed away from the car but kept them within gunpoint range.

"OK, gentlemen, what do you want with the girl?" Steel didn't really expect an answer, given one was half-dazed and the other was ready to soil himself.

"I don't know what you're talkin' about, man. Look you, idiot, we're cops so put down the gun," the thin cop muttered as he nursed his head.

"Funny, your partner was a cop as well – told me you were waiting on him – so, again, what do you want with the girl?" Steel's words were full of venom. He hated dirty cops, but ones who hurt kids he hated all the more.

"Fuck you. What now, you gonna kill us?" the thin cop asked defiantly, as though he were ready to meet his end rather than give up anything.

Steel smiled and shook his head. "No. We're just gonna have a little chat. Take out your cuffs, both of you. Now cuff yourselves through the steering wheel," he ordered as he pointed the gun at the thin cop's crotch.

"You have no idea who you're messing with," the thin cop growled.

"Oh, I have a fair idea. You see, your friend was most forthcoming on a couple of facts. It's amazing how compliant someone is once you have found that one thing that makes them crumble," Steel said with a hint of pleasure in his voice.

The two men looked at each other, hands still raised.

"For instance, you tell a guy you're going to shoot him dead, chances are he will be a hero and think 'go for it, it's quick, and it's over.'"

The two looked at each other, fear in their eyes and on their faces as they realised the man might be a nut job.

"But you threaten a guy with pain … and I am not talking breaking fingers, because that pain comes and goes…the kind of pain that stays. Take your friend … I threatened to pour red-hot cooking oil over him. Now *that* is pain that stays."

The fat cop lost control of his bladder, forcing his partner to edge away.

"So … so … what are y-you going to do-do with us?" The fat one stumbled over his words.

Steel walked forwards and smiled. "Just a little experiment to see if my theory is right."

The two looked at each another, fear turning to terror.

He walked swiftly back to the church, but soon returned with two large fuel cans and placed them close to the vehicle that held the two men, now shaking with fright. The thin one gaped at the cans and the stranger who now sat on them.

"So, is this your plan? Scare the crap out of us, then let the cops find us, yeah, right?" he asked.

Steel stood and shook his head. "No, not quite. You see, I don't intend on killing you at all." He picked up the cans and shook each to convey their fullness.

Again, the large man lost control of his bladder.

"OK, this is how it works, I ask a question and you answer. Simple. However, if I think you are lying, or you piss me off, you get a soaking. Got it?"

The men nodded just in case that was one of the questions.

"Great, so you said I don't know who I am messing with. My question is: who *am* I messing with?"

The two men shook their heads, the fear on their faces deepening, and the large one quickly replied, "We don't know, man; we just know it's someone *big*. We just get told what to do … I swear."

"Who tells you? Bennett?"

The man nodded, prompting the thin one to try and kick him. Then he smirked with confidence when he recognised Steel from Bennett's description. "Be on the lookout for a man dressed in black wearing sunglasses – you can't miss him. He's a British prick."

His smirk intensified. "What the hell you doin'? He's not gonna kill us. He's a cop, just like us."

Steel smiled, flipped the lid, and covered the men and car with the liquid. The powerful smell of gas fumes filled their nostrils, making them cough and their eyes burn.

"Are you fuckin' happy now? The guy is nuts, and you want to provoke him," yelled the large one.

"Like I said, I won't kill you," Steel said coldly. The thin one smirked yet again, as though he knew this cop was too righteous for such a deed. "But I won't stop you from doing it yourselves either," Steel continued.

The men's jaws dropped when Steel took out a flare he had gotten from the trunk of their car.

"The judge, she had files," barked the large one.

Steel moved forward, the flare firmly grasped in one hand. "What sort of files?" he demanded.

The large man shook his head as he fought to catch his breath. "I don't know … I just know she had some evidence or something, and that's why she was getting up the ladder so fast."

Things were beginning to slot into place slowly, but he needed those files. He realized these cops didn't know much if anything; if they did, they would have found them by now. Steel thought for a moment. He knew that the boys were searching for something to do with a painting. Maybe it was a safe.

"What did you want with the reporter's research? It was you two who took it, right? I remember the description. Nice touch with the fake moustache by the way," Steel joked darkly.

The men grew silent, but it didn't really matter; he had what he needed. Taking the other can, he soaked the ground around the vehicle, then lit the flare and stuck it into the big man's mouth. "You hold the flare, and only he gets hurt. You spit or drop it … and, well, happy Fourth of July."

Steel walked away, leaving the two men screaming for help. His face was like stone; emotions had left him as he had left them. He pulled out his cell phone and pressed the caller menu for Tooms, then waited for him to pick up.

"Tooms, it's Steel. Did you get anything in the office?"

There was a muffled response.

"Meet me at the judge's house. I think I know what we are looking for." As he switched off the phone, Steel hailed a cab going by.

The driver stopped and watched him as he

approached. The cabbie waited until Steel had gotten to the window.

"Where you goin' to, man?" asked the driver when Steel stepped up to the window, hoping for a big fare on a slow night.

Steel gave the judge's address, hopped in and sat back, and the cab sped off. As they turned a corner, the night sky was illuminated by an orange glow.

Steel smiled. "Two less dirty cops to deal with." He rested his head against the cushioned headrest and sucked in a long breath. For all he knew, that was just the beginning.

THIRTY-EIGHT

McCall followed the G Wagon for what seemed like hours. At first, she thought they were lost, but then she figured it was to make sure they weren't being tailed. The German 4x4 took the side and main streets that made no sense.

"Where are they going?" Megan asked, both confused and excited.

"It's a normal trick to see if you're being followed, the trick for us is not to be seen to be following," McCall said. Megan looked at McCall with a childlike grin, as if she were getting on a ride at Disneyland she wasn't supposed to be venturing on. Then she peered forward and quickly thrust forth an arm in case nobody had noticed.

"Look, they're parking!" Megan said.

The vehicle had pulled up opposite a nightclub. Bright lights from a huge monitor lit up the street as it advertised the club and future events. Normally, there would be a queue of people that was only surpassed by a book signing from the author of that popular wizard kid. Above the monitor the words ORION usually blazed in blue and red neon, but tonight the large screen displayed other business.

"That must be DC's club," McCall said as she pulled back the top slide enough to see a glint of a brass casing, then re-holstered her weapon.

As they watched, four men got out and headed down an alley. She figured that was the back entrance to the club. "OK, you guys stay here and wait for the cavalry," she ordered as she sent a text to Tony Marinelli and another to Joshua Tooms: *Suspects are at the Orion Club.*

"What if the cavalry gets here too late?" asked Gabriel as he regarded the girl sitting on the back seat.

"Take my car and get to the precinct and ask for Detective Bennett. He will take care of her," McCall instructed him.

Gabriel repeated the detective's name as if burning it to memory, while McCall opened the car door and went to get out. "Good luck, detective. I am sure the cavalry won't be too far behind."

McCall looked back and winked at the priest, then shut the door and ran across the street into the shadows. She leant into a doorway, trying to conceal herself but still have good visuals on the club. It wouldn't be easy getting in. The place was locked up, and she needed entry – and when she got in, what then? She was alone. Damn, where was Steel when you needed him? She felt a vibration in her jacket and pulled out her phone, and saw the text from Tony: *I am en route with Agent Lloyd. Steel is with Tooms at the judge's house.*

She sighed and put away the phone and got ready for a long wait.

* * *

BROKEN STEEL

THE CAB CARRYING John Steel pulled up outside the home of the late Judge Matthews. He paid and got out, telling the cabbie to keep the change. As the yellow cab sped off, he turned to see a bright pair of headlights. As they grew closer, he saw it was a black Dodge Charger. Its paint job glistened as the streetlights reflected off its sleek shape.

Tooms parked and got out, his stride towards Steel heavy and strong. "McCall tailed the escapees to a club downtown. It's owned by Tyrell, William's brother DC."

Steel nodded as he took in the news, knowing that she would not go in alone, not without some sort of back-up. He rested a reassuring hand on Tooms' shoulder. "You know we don't have a warrant for this, so what makes you think he will go for it?"

"Have a little faith. He will go for it. Besides, we don't need a warrant if we have his consent."

They walked up the winding path, and Steel rang the bell. It took a while for someone to answer; it was one of the daughters. Her eyes were puffy from too much crying.

"Hi, I am Detective Steel, and this is Detective Tooms. Is your dad there?" His words were soft and gentle, and he offered a small smile of understanding.

The girl opened the door wider to let them in. Steel and Tooms thanked her and followed her to the judge's study, where they found Mr Matthews sitting in his wife's chair. He knocked twice on the white glass door to attract attention with his gloved knuckles.

Matthews looked up, not registering their presence at first.

"Mr Matthews, we are here from the NYPD. We're very sorry for your loss."

Matthews sat there, holding a photograph of his wife; fresh tears rolled down his face. "Have you found my wife's killer yet? You found that bastard Armstrong?"

Steel stepped forward and stood in front of the desk.

"We are doing all we can to catch the people responsible for your wife's death; however, we need something from you." Steel's tone was gentle but firm.

Matthews looked up at the stony features of the black-clad cop. This strange man wore sunglasses during the night. He sensed the coldness of this man before him and realised he, too, had lost someone.

"Who did *you* lose, detective?"

Steel clenched a gloved hand as memories flooded back. He could almost smell the gunpowder in the air, hear the faint cry from his mother before she was taken. His eyes blurred as he saw his wife, her beautiful pale skin glistening under the sun on a cloudless summer day.

He wanted to touch her once more, but the image grew hazy as her eyes clouded. Steel stumbled backwards as he crashed back to reality, his hand outstretched as if to grasp something. He gathered himself, and as he dropped his arm to his side, he noticed Tooms staring curiously at him in the window's reflection.

"My world was taken from me many years ago," Steel finally replied.

Matthews could see that his pain was nothing compared to the strange detective's and, for a moment, he felt better at someone feeling worse.

"What do you need, detective?" Matthews replied. Steel looked towards the picture over the fireplace that he had noticed upon entering the room.

"We need to see the contents of your wife's safe."

THIRTY-NINE

The nightclub was in partial darkness because DC had only a few lights on. He had closed the place for the night, even though Tyrell had said not to. DC, however, figured a firefight and people dying would be bad for business. No, it was easier to put a sign on the door that advised closing was due to a private party, which he did from time to time. The clubbers didn't mind as he would have a happy hour the next day to make up for it.

A long, mirrored corridor brought the guests from the paying booth to the main dance floor. The nightclub was large, with a huge bar that stretched along the left wall. It had blue neon lights on the front and mirrors lining the back wall. An assortment of bottled spirits and liquors sat on glass shelving, which filled the back wall and covered most of the mirrored wall space. The dance area held a glass floor that resembled something from the seventies with colour-changing panels. Seating surrounded the dance floor like a coliseum, and the DJ's booth was at the far rear, right-hand wall. This was elevated like a preacher's pulpit. High above it all, heavy metal trusses held the lighting and speakers firmly in place. Darius looked at his watch. It had been at least an hour since they had entered the club and he was getting anxious.

"OK Tyrell, what now?" he grunted, still not convinced that bringing the teacher back with them was a brilliant idea.

"We lay low for a while. We have another safe house – you'll like this one. It's out of town, a nice quiet place. We bide our time, wait for things to cool down. We got money, passports, and a plane out of here. All we need now is lady luck," Tyrell explained as he stood behind the bar and racked up shot glasses.

"Sorry, boys. Looks like you're fresh out of that one," came a voice from behind them.

Everyone spun around to see McCall, Lloyd, and Tony walking in with bulletproof vests and weapons drawn. McCall ordered Tyrell to step away from behind the bar and waved her custom Glock towards the others. "OK, hands up where we can see them." McCall ordered.

The four men raised them high and Darius shot a look of disapproval at Armstrong.

"This is all your God-damn fault, man," Darius growled.

Armstrong said nothing.

McCall walked over to him while the others covered him. Tony had his 12-gauge combat 870 shotgun aimed while Lloyd gripped her 9-mm Sig.

"Brian Armstrong, you are under arrest for murder and escaping police custody." She would read him his rights later when there was less of a crowd. She could not believe the charges herself, but all the evidence pointed to him.

"You know I've been set up, detective – what am I saying? Of course, you do. You're with them," Brian Armstrong said, angry at his choice to stick around.

McCall said nothing, simply cuffed the others with Tony's and Lloyd's handcuffs that she had gotten from them earlier. Once they were in cuffs, she started to breathe again; she'd been holding her breath in anticipation of trouble.

"Detective, you called for back-up?" came a voice from the corner of the room near the entrance.

McCall looked over as the other two walked towards her. Out of the shadows strolled Bennett and six of his men: the cavalry had indeed arrived, prompting her to raise an eyebrow with amused surprise.

"A little over the top, Bennett. You expecting trouble?" she joked, wondering what they were all there for. "How did you get your team together so fast?" Casually, she slipped her hand towards the drop-leg holster where her pistol sat.

Bennett and the others were armed with shotguns.

"Uh-uh, detective. Step out where we can all see what you're up to." Bennett smiled as he quickly aimed the 12-gauge weapon.

His team responded similarly. McCall and the others wouldn't stand a chance against so much firepower. They would be turned into mist before they could do a thing.

"So, it was you all along. Why? What has this to do with you?" Her question was laced with venom; she had been betrayed by the very man she was going to send the girl to. Her heart froze. Had he gotten to them as well? She couldn't say anything, in case she let the cat out the bag. If he didn't mention it, she knew they were safe – for now.

"What's the plan, Bennett? We die in a shootout, but you were too late to save us?"

Bennett smiled and rocked his head back and forth. "Mmm, something like that yes, but don't worry. You and your team will get full honours." He laughed, and his team members went around and disarmed McCall and the others before taking up various posts in the venue.

"Why, Bennett? You used to be a good cop. What happened?"

Bennett thought about McCall's questions as he absently scratched his head with the barrel of his service weapon. "Things get done, and careers get made. For years, I have been bustin' my balls and for what? Two failed marriages and nothin' to show for it."

She could see the fire in his eyes, yet he was a shadow of the man she'd known.

"Why do you ask? Simple. I have money in my pocket, and I am going places. What about you, McCall?"

She couldn't answer. The question had never entered her mind. But now that she considered it, she didn't mind; she was where she wanted to be and if someday she moved up, great.

"At least I'm not dirty, whereas you'll go to jail for this, and you know what they do to cops in there." McCall said with a bitter tone.

Bennett laughed. "Who's gonna stop me? You?"

Bennett and his team spun as the front doors swung open and a six-man Strategic Response Unit or SRU rushed in and surrounded Bennett and his men.

"Nicely done, detective, nicely done," clapped a figure in the shadows.

McCall saw the man's silhouette break from the dimness. It was the Chief of Detectives himself. Sure, she was used to the Feds taking over, but never 1PP.

He was tall, well dressed in a thousand-dollar suit, with nicely styled hair. He was garbed for a press conference, not a bust. Was that why he was here – so when they walked out with the bad guys, the press would be making him front page and not them?

"Well, you and your team have done an excellent job, really. But rest assured, we have got it from here." The chief spoke with a broad smile and pearly-white teeth.

The only thing missing was the forked tongue, McCall thought. "Respectfully, sir, I have some questions for Detective Bennett."

The chief rubbed his hands as if to calm himself. "And be assured, detective, we shall get those answers for you."

McCall became uncomfortable with the situation; something was wrong. Suddenly, the lights went out, and they were plunged into darkness. The room was silent as nobody dared to move – just in case people with guns nervously opened up at any sound.

The darkness was quickly broken by a floodlight that shone in the centre of the room, engulfing them all except support members in the wings. Everyone shielded their eyes from the blinding light.

"The thing that I could not figure out during this whole case was why everyone was separated on the bus. Now, we all thought it was planned that way for an escape, but it wasn't, was it?"

Bennett and his associates gazed around to pinpoint where the voice was coming from – all except McCall and her team who had their gazes firmly fixed on the others. McCall's looked on in surprise as the chief marched over to Bennett.

"You said it was done. You said he had been taken care of – you idiot!" The chief's face reddened with a mix of anger and fear.

"Chief ... it was *you*? You did all this?" McCall shouted, feeling physically ill.

The chief ignored her as he was too busy looking around for the intruder. "Who is that? Identify yourself," screamed the man.

McCall smiled, and he noticed. He rushed towards her and grabbed her by the shoulders. "You know who that is, don't you? Tell me who it is!"

McCall could see the panic in his eyes. "A nightmare, a wraith … a pain in the ass."

The chief shoved her aside as the voice boomed over the loudspeakers once more.

"It wasn't an escape; it was an assassination. What better way of getting rid of all three men? If they were shanked in the courtyard, it would be too obvious, and questions would be asked, but an accident? How perfect."

The booming voice made it impossible for them to get a fix on the man in the shadows. It echoed around the room as it streamed through speakers; the stranger had a microphone. The chief offered a slight nod towards the DJ booth, hoping that one of the SRU team had seen it and understood.

"But something went wrong, didn't it? The bus missed its mark because it was too wet outside. But it didn't matter, did it?"

The chief laughed to himself at the silly theatrics of the situation. "Why didn't it matter … Detective Steel?" He stood still, but the smile fell from his face; he knew his men would be close.

There was a muffled grunt, then another. The chief listened carefully, hoping to see lights come on and Steel lying on the ground with a blade in his chest, but there was nothing, just silence. Then from the other side of the room came another muffled grunt, then the clatter of metal hitting the ground. More silence.

"Detective Steel, I hope you have made plans to get out of here … because how is it going to look if you and your team walk out and I'm lying dead on the ground? They will mark *you* a criminal." The chief was starting to sweat, and his collar felt like a noose. "Answer me, damn it! I am your superior."

The silence was broken by a subdued sound to the rear of McCall, whose eyes were firmly fixed on the chief and his men.

"It didn't matter, because their escape forwarded you another opportunity to tie off loose ends."

The chief smiled cockily as if Steel's ramblings were mere speculation and theory. "An ex-teacher, a journalist and a judge. Really, how would killing them benefit me?" He motioned for the rest of the men to surround him.

"When we got the financials from everyone ... oh, brilliant job of clogging up the works with pointless stuff, by the way," Steel said.

The chief's fake grin turned into a snarl.

"Anyway, when I got them, I found that our first vic had no income, so how was he paying for the apartment, his food, everything?" Steel's voice continued to echo through the multiple speakers, making location impossible. "He was being paid off. His career as a teacher was coming to an end due to injury, so you found him and recruited him. The task was simple: be a false witness."

The chief and the others said nothing, but everyone gazed furtively around in case of a surprise attack.

"The journalist, I liked that one. You fed him false information, and he put it to press. The trouble was, he found out. What could he do? He couldn't say a dirty cop had given him false info, or he would be laughed out of court. Then you found out he was going to do a story on Brian Armstrong. This you could not allow."

The chief began to clap, the smile and expression on his face showing that he was impressed by Steel's work. "A brilliant story, detective, most brilliant. However, why the judge?" He felt confident Steel would have nothing; all his ramblings were pure conjecture.

"The judge, well, for her, we have to look back. You see, as a cop, you had to make yourself shine, so having several criminals who you could not put away just wasn't doing it. So you set them up, quite well in fact."

The chief nodded as if he had been complimented.

"The first one was difficult. Hell, you had never done this before – frame a crook and then what? You needed a prosecutor, a damned good one, one who was going places so her record would shine especially if she had a slam-dunk case against Tyrell Williams. You found Julie Armstrong."

Armstrong felt the cuffs tighten around his wrists; all he wanted to do was leap across the room and rip out the chief's throat.

"Then you had Darius Smith. You had done it before. You knew the lawyer would jump at the case. Hell, she had been told she was being looked at for Chief Justice. Another slam dunk. She makes the press once more."

The sudden silence was followed by a muted sound.

"They had a witness each time who could place them at the scene. The trouble was that she recognised Andy Carlson as the witness from the Tyrell Williams case. The tabloids had been blowing up the hype quite nicely, and it was only one reporter who had the facts."

The chief took a silk handkerchief from his breast pocket and wiped his nervous brow as beads of sweat trickled down.

"Julie worked it out, didn't she? She'd threatened to come clean, but that would destroy everything she had worked for. Cases would be questioned, and the cost on retrials would be in the millions ... and you reminded her of this, didn't you, chief?" Steel spat the words as if the sentences containing them were poison. "How long had you had her followed before that perfect opportunity arose – an argument between husband and wife in a packed restaurant with plenty of witnesses to confirm that argument? But you had to be sure, so one last job for the witness who would see Brian Armstrong enter the alleyway."

Another pause filled with silence. The men surrounding the chief trained their weapons into the darkness, held ready to engage the next target.

"Sorry about that. Just had to get a drink from the bar; it's very warm in here," said Steel from the shadows. The bodyguards swung round to the bar and opened up; flashes of lights and sparks flew, and the sounds of mirrors and bottles being vaporized filled the room.

"Stop shooting, you idiots!" yelled the chief as the last shell casing hit the floor.

They heard a new sound, that of laughter.

"Sorry gents, I could *not* resist seeing how dumb you really were," Steel chuckled.

DC flipped the bird towards the darkness as thanks for decimating his bar. "Anyway, back to the case ... where was I? Ah yes. The problem: you needed another prosecutor, a hungry one, and so along came Matthews, or as she was then called, Baker. She was everything you needed, but most of all, you had something *she* needed: a case that would send her into the eyes of the people who mattered."

McCall looked over at Armstrong, who was taking it all in. Everything became clear; he hated himself for believing she could cheat on him.

"She won the case and was quickly propelled into career mode. She became a puppet for you –you would decide who lived and who died, and she couldn't take that so she kept the files from the Armstrong case because it would show that you handed her thirty pieces of silver, not a life-changing case. In fact, she kept a lot of files, including the Tyrell and Darius cases."

The chief could feel the veins in his forehead throb, and his skin warm as his blood began to boil. "Will someone *please* shut this asshole up?"

McCall and the others dove for cover as the remaining gunmen opened fire into the darkness that surrounded them. Sparks flew when metal hit metal as shots impacted metal beams, railings, and just about anything in their path. The firing only stopped when all shotguns and pistols were empty.

"Did we get him?" asked one of the armed men as he fumbled for a magazine from the magazine pouch attached to his belt.

"Not quite," said Steel, making the men look upwards in time to see his black-clad form drop onto one of them.

He contacted the hard glass floor, the sound of his left leg shattering as he broke Steel's fall muffled by his screams of pain.

Steel still crouched, spun and slammed the legs of another man, who then crashed onto his back. The glass comprising the floor splintered as his head struck it. Now a four-on-one fight, none of them were going to wait for a turn.

The foot of a tall, stocky cop swung up as he hoped to catch Steel under the chin, but he merely fell and rolled backwards, out of the way. Steel grabbed a bar stool, and it met with the stocky man's leg, breaking it at the knee.

The man screamed and fell back against the railings of the seating area, his hand striking something metallic; he grasped it and found it was one of the SRU M4 rifles. He screamed and opened up.

The cop was propelled backwards from close-range impact; pieces of bone and bits of flesh soared through the air as the metal-jacket rounds punched holes through parts the Kevlar vest could not cover. What was left of the man smashed to the floor and a fountains of blood shot upwards. The thick body plasma oozed from the many exit wounds and turned the dance floor a deep red.

The chief turned towards the injured cop, drew his service Glock, and put a hollow-point round through the man's head. "Stop shooting my men, you idiot," he spat as he put the weapon back into his shoulder holster.

McCall gazed over as a huge man stepped from the shadows and grabbed Steel. The giant, who stood nearly seven-foot-tall, was a mix of flab and muscle. His face was covered in shadow, but that mammoth form couldn't be missed. He lifted Steel off his feet, then threw him like a rag doll against what was left of the bar. Sparks and flashes from frayed wires and cables, as well as small flames, courtesy of broken spirit bottles, illuminated the bar.

"My bar! You set fire to my God-damn bar, you motha-fu—" DC screamed.

DC never got to finish the sentence as Steel flew past him, towards the shadows. There was a crash and a groan of discomfort from Steel.

"Your boy's not doin' too well, is he?" DC asked McCall before she spotted her mark: Bennett.

She ran full pelt at him as he searched his pockets for more cartridges. Bennett looked up in time to see her boot swing round in a roundhouse. His head snapped to the side from the impact, knocking him to his knees. He spat plasma mixed with saliva, then looked up at her with evil in his eyes as he wiped away the blood and spit hanging from his mouth in one long strand.

"Is that any way to treat a friend, Sammy?" Bennett laughed.

McCall threw a punch, but he grabbed her fist, failing to see her extend her leg and kick upwards, making him a soprano. Bennett fell forwards, the air thrust from his body, but he had enough to give her a backhand across the face, which sent her sideways. She used the force of the hit to carry out another roundhouse, which took Bennett both by surprise – and in the jaw. There was a spray of blood and teeth before he collapsed on the floor unconscious.

"You ain't no friend, and you ain't no friggin cop." She stood over him and spat a mouthful of blood at him.

The giant was now swinging punches as Steel, who was backing out of the way, something he knew he could only do while he had the ground. As they came into the light, Steel's heart sank when he recognised the giant from a previous encounter, which had started with Steel hanging upside down in a warehouse and ended with Steel dropping several full barrels onto him.

"I remember you. You're that guy from the steelworks – you're the only man to beat me, you fucker."

Steel smiled cheerfully, then shrugged. "Well, small world isn't it? I guess you must be Monster?" He hit the rail to the seating area. He had a couple of choices: jump over it or roll out of the way and start this dance again.

"Why don't you just kill him already, you big dumb fuck? We didn't break you out just to dance with people, you idiot," yelled the last remaining guard of the chief's, who was backing off to nowhere while he slapped his last clip into his 9mm Glock.

The monster turned towards the guard and headed for him.

"Um, I wouldn't shoot him," Steel yelled, but the warning came too late as a shot went off, followed by a scream. He shook his head as he imagined the giant tearing the man's arms off and then clubbing him to death with them.

Suddenly, the doors burst open, and a team of SRU filed in with Tooms at the rear.

"Nobody move! Hands in the air," shouted Tooms, taking no chances until the lights were on, and they could see who was who.

The lights floor light came on, and Tooms found his colleagues and his quarry.

"Oh detective, just in the nick of time. Arrest Detective Steel and the others. We have found out that they have been working with the killers all along."

Tooms looked at the chief's extended hand of thanks. He smiled and slapped the cuffs on him – to the chief's utter surprise.

"What are you doing, you idiot? It's them you want," the chief yelled, irritated.

Steel walked over to the giant as he stood there, ready to take on the whole police force.

"It's okay, this one was with us," Steel lied to the SRU sergeant.

The monster looked down at Steel, lost for words.

"You know, *Tiny*, you have potential. Don't waste it. Now, get out of here." Steel handed the man a business card and watched him leave.

McCall walked up to Steel, who was watching as the real cops took the chief's men into custody.

"Why did you let him go?" she asked, but Steel didn't move or blink. He was busy watching the bad guys being corralled.

"Guys like him aren't bad. They are just made to think they are because they're so big. You give them a purpose, and they could amaze you."

They both watched Tooms lead out the criminals, with the chief in the lead.

"You want in on this party?" McCall asked Steel, but she knew the answer would be no. The press wasn't his thing.

Steel watched them disappear through the door and smiled with relief that it was finally over.

As they stepped out, under the night sky, the chief was screaming his innocence to the masses that now lined the street. Camera crews from news stations stood ready for anything to transpire.

"Ladies and gentlemen, I can assure you that this is a misunderstanding and I will be back in the office tomorrow. The events inside this building tonight will come out for all—"

Suddenly, DC's voice, yelling at Steel about his bar, came over the large monitor above the front door for the crowds to see.

"To answer your question, sir, yes, we saw everything."

The chief looked around to find captain Brant standing by a large police prisoner transport with a large grin on his face.

Steel strolled over to meet with Tony, McCall and Lloyd, their clothes torn and bloodied, but all were alive. He stopped and inhaled clean air at length.

"So, case closed. The three will go back to jail until their hearing, but I don't think they will be there long." McCall smiled. At least *something* good had come out of this. She followed him as he made his way to the three escapees.

"So what happens now, detectives?" Armstrong asked with a glad-to-be-alive look.

"Well, I am not sure, but you can bet there will be

another investigation. Until then, you three will go back to jail, but this one will be more like the Ritz."

The men laughed while they looked at the others being loaded on to the transport.

"In the meantime, I know someone who wants to say hello." Steel turned towards McCall's car and waved.

Armstrong gazed round to see a young woman approach slowly, and a tear ran down his cheek as he realised who she was.

The girl's pace quickened into a run. "Daddy!"

Armstrong ran towards her. McCall went to stop him, but Steel put an arm across her path; she looked at him, confused.

"They have been apart too long. Give them this. He deserves it."

McCall nodded and smiled.

Lloyd walked up to Steel, who was obviously feeling pretty good about himself. "So, mission completed … just like old times, huh Steel?"

He nodded but didn't look at Agent Lloyd now standing next to him.

"Yeah, just like old times. You using me, not telling me what the hell was going on. So, who the hell is Agent Dalton?"

Lloyd smiled self-consciously she wondered how long he had known. "He works for me at the company; he was quite new and green, so he was the perfect choice." She offered a smug grin.

Ever since she appeared on the case, he had thought something was wrong. The company didn't get involved in such things; they left that to the feds. "So, are you Echo or is he?" Steel nodded towards Brian Armstrong.

Lloyd stood for a moment before answering. She could lie, but then he probably already knew the answer and was just playing with her. "He is, or rather we are. I have known him for a long time. He has done a lot for me in the past. Friends help each other out, remember?"

Steel nodded as he watched father and daughter reunite.

"He was in the company for a long time, and they say he was the best."

Steel watched them with mixed feelings of happiness and jealousy. Brian Armstrong had something he would never have: a happy reunion with his family.

"He probably still is, less for you, of course, Mr Steel." She smiled, taking pleasure in saying his name again.

They turned to watch press members rush and take pictures of the police transport before it took off back to the precinct. Steel smiled, satisfied: case closed, less for the paperwork.

"What's next for you, John? Coming back to do some *real* work?"

Steel reached into his pocket and pulled out the piece of paper that Crazy Gus had given him. He unfolded it and read the note and smiled.

"No, Cat, I have a promise to keep."

Cassandra Lloyd looked at Steel as he put away the note and pulled his coat tight around him as the night breeze began to pick up.

"It's funny how you said friends help each other out," Steel said.

She gave him a curious look, not knowing what the point was. "What do you mean? He and I were … are friends."

Steel smiled as he saw she missed the point. "I thought you were family. After all, you were his wife's kid sister," he said softly, then walked away, leaving her shocked and open-mouthed, not knowing how he had found out.

FORTY

The dark of the night brought with it a biting wind from the west. The city was silent, or as quiet as it could be at midnight. Cabs drove slowly here and there, hoping for lost tourists or anyone who had missed the last train. The Bronx at night was not the place to be, especially alone, but he paid it no mind. The figure dressed in black made its way through dimly lit streets towards the address on the piece of paper. Steel stopped and took note of the street names. Earlier, he had looked up the route on the computer and memorised details such as street names, at least as much as he could. He was heading for a house that belonged to some player named Bulldog. He had checked on this Bulldog to see what he could expect. The man was twenty-six and spent most of his time running around with gangs or doing time. His rap sheet read like a shopping list: drugs, prostitution, attempted murder. All in all, he was a low life.

Steel wore a quarter-length leather military-style black coat over a black polo shirt and black trousers and boots. Leather military-style gloves with carbon knuckle protectors covered his hands from the elements. He soon found the place. Men and women hung around the front, playing loud music and drinking. He stayed in the shadows as he assessed the situation and thought through a plan. They would be armed; he would be surprised if they weren't. Two large men guarded the front, each around six-three and built like they had spent too much time in a prison yard. The alleyways probably held more men farther in to discourage people from entering.

***

Normally, Steel sought a way in that would be as less bloody as possible – normally. His only concern was the girl inside, not any of the scum who surrounded her. Steel walked straight up to the front door. He watched as the men closed together to create a barricade, but he was ready. The guard on the left reached out to grab him. Mistake.

Steel grabbed the man's fingers and bent them back before he had time to react, then produced a sidekick to the man's knee, which brought him down. The second man swung for Steel with a massive fist, but he had grabbed the injured man and pulled him up by his belt. The big man's hand contacted his colleague's face with a nasty cracking sound. The battered guard spat blood and swung at the other man for hitting him. Steel watched the two men fight each other in the street, forgetting about the man who had caused it all.

Steel moved inside, hoping that the larger of the men were outside. As he made his way down a long corridor with four doorways, a man stepped through one of them and received a palm to the throat. He stumbled back inside before Steel closed it after him.

Red, low-intensity bulbs gave the whole place an evil lair feel, as if a demon lived there and not a low-life nobody. Another door opened, and a man stepped out doing up his belt. He saw Steel and went to cry out, but Steel kicked high into the man's jewels. The man folded inwards, and Steel brought up his knee into the man's chin. The man stumbled back into the room and Steel carried on down the corridor.

Three doors were at the end: one to the left, one to the right, and one straight on. Steel knew he didn't have time to search all of them; plus, one mistake could cost the girl her life. Behind him, a door reopened, and the bloodied man came out, spitting red plasma. Steel turned and slammed the man against the wall.

"Where's Bulldog and the girl?" he growled.

The man, only in his late teens, shook his head, a look of utter fear on his pale face.

Steel grabbed the man's jacket and, using the wall, lifted him off the floor. "Don't make me ask again."

The terrified man scanned Steel's stony expression and the sunglasses, which merely reflected his own face. "He's in the middle room, I swear."

Steel put the man down and pushed him forwards. "Show me."

The young man looked at Steel with fear. Steel figured there were two reasons for such an expression: number one, he was lying and Steel would kill him for it or, number two, he was telling the truth, and his boss would kill him for telling Steel about the location.

"No, please, you can't make me."

Steel looked at the kid who was playing the big man and wondered how many people had pleaded with him before he did something brutal to them. "Sure, I can. Now open the door, or I'll feed you to the nice people in Harlem."

The young man looked down at his tattoos and knew he wouldn't last two seconds there – if he was lucky. Slowly, he walked towards the door, his hands shaking. Sweat streamed from every pour in his body. His steps were deliberate and measured, and he hoped that this was all a dream. His hand grasped the doorknob, and he opened the door.

Inside a brightly lit room, the man called Bulldog sat on a leather couch surrounded by four women, all dressed in bikinis. Bulldog was a bulky man with black hair and a football shirt that hung from his baggy jeans. A sleeveless denim jacket covered his back, and a red patterned bandana was stretched over his egg-round head. He was ugly and full of tattoos and scars, but Steel thought the extras probably improved his looks. The square office had two doors, the one where Steel and the tattooed man stood and one way back at the right wall. The room wasn't grand. There were no carpets or rugs, or a spectacular wooden floor. It resembled a broom cupboard with a desk. The couch sat along the left wall by a wall unit that was lined with cheap booze.

"What the fuck do you want?" Bulldog yelled angrily as he looked at the young man, not registering the blood streaming from his mouth and nose, just that he stood there in *his* room. It wasn't until the girls screamed that he noticed the blood and hastened for the back door but found it locked.

As the door opened, a guard was greeted by a smash to the face with the tattooed man's head. The stunned guard fell to the ground with the tattooed man on top of him. Steel leapt across the room and vaulted the desk, hitting Bulldog in the chest, knocking him and a chair over.

He grabbed Bulldog by his sleeveless jacket and slammed several punches into him to render the man half-conscious. The guard, now on his feet, was ready to run but was distracted by a strident cough from Steel.

"If you run and tell the others, I won't chase you, but I *will* find you. Now, shut the door and sit the hell down."

The man obeyed without question.

"Which one of you is Naomi Sanchez?" Steel asked the girls as he held a bleeding Bulldog.

A sweet-looking nineteen-year-old girl with dark hair and eyes that sparkled with innocence raised her hand shyly.

Steel walked over to her; she seemed tiny compared to his large build. He smiled as he said, "I am here to take you home."

"You're dead, you hear me – dead," yelled Bulldog as he struggled on the ground.

Steel walked over to him, knelt, and removed his sunglasses. Bulldog froze in fear as he stared into cold, soulless emerald-coloured eyes. "Been there, didn't like it. If you make a move on this girl or her family, I promise you this: you *will* want me to kill you." Steel put his glasses back on and led the girl out, using the back door and leaving a shaking Bulldog lying in his own mess.

* * *

Garry Sanchez sat with his wife on a sofa in the motel that Steel had put them up in. Only the sound of the television broke the silence. His wife held a photograph of their daughter, a pretty girl in a purple prom dress. Her tears had run dry hours ago. The food that Sanchez had ordered sat undisturbed on trays on a small window-side table.

He stood up and looked out the window into the dark night. There were no stars above, no moon to brighten the city. He released a deep sigh of disappointment. He had been promised by the stranger that he would find his little girl and, so far, they had heard nothing. Sanchez turned around to his wife, who was sitting there, looking lost and alone. He wanted to comfort her and tell her it would be OK, but how could he make such a promise to her?

There was a knock-knock-knock on the door. Sanchez looked over, expecting hotel staff to come in for the plates, but nobody said anything. Again, three knocks on the door, but no words were spoken.

"Who is it?" he shouted, suddenly in fear of his wife's life. "Hello, who's there?" He began to move towards the door, but his wife grabbed him by the arm to hold him back.

"It's fine, it's probably a waiter who can't speak English or something."

Sanchez motioned his wife to retake her seat while he sorted it out. He headed for the door.

"OK then, what's the problem?" He pulled open the door.

Lara Sanchez watched as her husband stood in the doorway. She rose; fear ripped through her body as she walked towards him. Then, as he moved to the side, she saw a miracle: her little girl had come home.

FORTY-ONE

The next morning saw a blood-red sunrise. It hadn't taken long for the news of the chief's arrest to be all over the media and tabloids. He'd wanted his face all over the media, and now he'd gotten it.

The chief sat in an interrogation cell. In fact, he had sat there for quite some time. He knew this trick well and what it was meant to do; he had done it so many times before, but never in such an elaborate place. He sat back and waited.

The chief was bathed in shadows; he was little more than a silhouette, but the white of his eyes and teeth stood out like the Cheshire cat, waiting to appear. He glanced over at the sound of a loud click. The door was being unlocked. Metal hinges squealed as the heavy door swung open. Then ... Steel walked in. The room was dimly lit to give it a more intimidating feel. Steel liked this room, not because it was way down in the building's bowels and soundproofed, but because the lighting was just right to help play on the nerves of the individual. Steel pulled out a chair and sat without a word. He placed a large A4 notepad on the metal table, then simply watched.

The chief looked about the room, confused. If this was an interrogation, why wasn't he asking any questions? Then he sighed and shrugged.

"I know exactly what you're doing, Steel. Trying to make me talk. Well, I got news for you, you arrogant prick," The chief said.

Steel continued to sit there in his black pinstriped suit. An expensive high-collared shirt clung nicely round his neck.

The chief smiled and sat back. He knew he could do this all day. The dead-silence trick was meant to provoke a response, even a little one. Interrogators recognized that people had to talk; nobody could sit with someone and not talk, even if it was only to utter one word. Steel sat as still as a Greek statue – motionless and staring straight at the chief, or so the chief imagined because Steel had on those damn sunglasses. The chief started tapping the desk to break the silence. Steel smiled as could tell the man was close to breaking.

"I know you don't have the brains or the balls to think up this operation, which means you work for someone ... people who can change careers or cover things up."

The chief sat there, eager to hear Steel's theories. "If not me, who then?" The chief was happy it wasn't him who had spoken first.

"Do you work for? SANTINI?"

The chief laughed out loud at Steel's shot in the dark. "Who – sorry, never heard of him," he replied snidely.

"The organisation called SANTINI – you work for them. They helped you get up the ladder. You couldn't do it by yourself, so you got your powerful friends to help you." Steel's tone was solid and firm; he'd not raised it a decibel.

The chief remained silent, smiled and shook his head.

"I have heard that that organisation is the main runner, that all others answer to them," Steel said, leaning back in the chair as if to rub the chief's nose in it. "So, tell me how long you have been working for SANTINI."

"I do not work for anyone or anything called SANTINI. They are weak. They have no vision. We work to expand ourselves, whereas they simply wait and then die. We want to rule while they hide in the shadows and trade quietly. They are almost extinct while we expand."

Steel had come across this organisation once before, on the Neptune cruise ship several months ago. These were thugs and bullies. "OK, who do you work for?"

The chief leaned back and said nothing, but then he didn't need to because Steel already knew.

Steel peered through the chief's old arrest records. "You were a good cop once. What happened? They offered you power and control?"

The chief just smiled. He was older now. Yes, there'd been lots of surgery, mainly for the cameras; nobody liked an old-looking chief. His whole life from twelve years ago had been planned. They had seen the potential and offered the apple of knowledge like the serpents they were. All Steel saw now was a marionette that had had its strings cut; he'd served as the sacrificial lamb.

The chief sat with a smug expression, which made Steel think he had excepted this end – or that he was hoping for a phone call that would get him out.

"Answer me this. Why the girl? What was special about the girl?" Steel asked.

The chief leant forward and beckoned Steel closer.

Cautiously, Steel bent forwards.

"The powers that be didn't want to kill her. They wanted to recruit her. Her mother had promised her to us long ago, but sadly her husband talked her out of it. Oh, she had a change of heart all right, just not what you thought, detective. That girl is destined for great deeds; it's in her makeup."

Steel eyed the chief critically, and a look of shock turned to anger. "You did something to her in the womb?"

The chief shook his head, and a cruel smile tugged at his lips. "No, she was engineered before that ... everything a true warrior needed. Later, she was reintroduced into her mother to complete the cycle. Two strong family members, agent and lawyer. Brains and brawn."

Steel felt ill at the thought that they could do such a thing. "How did you know it would work?"

The chief shrugged, but the cruel smile remained. "Because they said they had done it before."

Steel stood, pushing the chair away with the back of his knees. His hands rested on the table to steady himself. The chief just looked at him with that same smile and Steel banged on the door to signal he wanted out.

The door opened, and he walked out, passing the female officer at the door. He stopped for a second and regarded her. She was stunning, with cocoa-brown hair that was tied up at the back and deep chestnut-brown eyes. Steel took one last glance at her, his mind elsewhere. He'd taken notice because she somehow seemed familiar.

"Make sure he doesn't leave," he ordered, then headed towards the exit.

The officer said nothing. Even if she had, he wouldn't have heard it.

He needed air. Steel made his way up and pushed through the crowds of cops like he was drunk or drugged.

BROKEN STEEL

As he walked outside, the cool morning air felt good on his skin. Now he had questions, too many of them in fact.

He needed to find the girl and warn Armstrong, but as the breeze swept over his face, his mind began to clear. He smiled and shook his head. She would be safe because he knew exactly where she was; the company had her. That's why Lloyd was there to take her to them. Steel laughed to himself, shaking his head at the whole mess of it all. But then the smile faded as the image of the female officer sprung into his head. Yes, he *had* seen her somewhere before. But *where?* Then, as the cool air began to clear his head, he started to remember a woman he once knew – a young temptress he had met on a boat trip from hell.

Steel spun around to face the precinct doors, and sudden shock lined his face as he realised that that same woman was now guarding the chief downstairs. She had changed the colour of her hair, but it was *her*.

Steel raced inside and made for the stairs, and hoped he wouldn't be too late. As he entered the long corridor, he noticed there was no guard outside the room. Steel slowed and walked towards the room – the door was wide open and the all the lights on, as if for effect.

Inside, the chief sat with his head back, pieces of brain and bone fragments, creating an abstract pattern on the back wall. Steel noticed that on the table was a tube of lipstick. It stood on its base with a glossy black lipstick bullet showing.

They had gotten to him, and he had let them. Behind him, the sound of footsteps echoed in the concrete passage.

"Oh, shit, man, who did this?" Tooms said. Steel could feel everyone looking at him, but he simply stood there.

"There was a female officer watching the door. I went to get some fresh air." He turned and saw suspicious looks from Tooms, McCall and Brant.

"So, a cop did this?" Brant said.

Steel shook his head. "No, she wasn't a cop…she was something else. She works for that organisation I told you about. The chief knew way too much." He noticed the headline on Tooms newspaper that was clutched under one arm. He only saw a few words, but he could guess the rest.

"So, I guess Chief Doyle made the front page after all."

"Did he tell you what happened, why he did it?" Brant asked, hoping to have some sort of explanation for the new chief.

Steel thought for a moment, then shook his head. "He didn't say anything we didn't already know. He did confirm it was another organisation that was responsible though," Steel lied. He couldn't tell them about the girl or anything else the chief had surprised him with. It wouldn't be long before CSU, and the ME would be down to do their job. Soon after that, he would be in front of Internal Affairs, explaining how this had happened.

"Why did you leave the room? Was it something he told you?" McCall asked, confused.

Normally, he would be in there until the perp had told his life story and more. That was one thing Steel was good at, getting people to talk. But he had left to get some fresh air? Things didn't add up for her.

"I couldn't look at him anymore. He had done so much to so many people just to get power, which he later abused," Steel snarled.

The others could feel his anger. The man who had sworn to uphold the law abused it in the worst possible way and nearly gotten away with it. If the bus crash had worked as it was meant to, none of this would have come out.

The group stood to the sides as the Medical Examiner,

and the CSU team exited the elevator and began their investigation. Steel moved to a quiet part of the corridor and spoke to an investigator from IA to get his side before he got CSU's version.

"Detective Steel, this is Detective King," Brant introduced the two detectives. He had requested an outside investigator so the investigation could be shown to be impartial and fair.

Steel shook the man's hand; he had no dislike for, or bad feeling towards, him or his job. "Hi, John Steel." He gave the man the once-over. The man was in his late thirties with a military presence about him: straight, strong back and head held high. He reckoned he used to be in the marines.

"Detective Arthur King," he said with a deep gravelly voice.

Steel raised an eyebrow and bit his lip. He so wanted to say something but thought it best not to. He would save that for later.

Tony walked into the small observation room next to the interrogation room, just to get some space. He couldn't believe what was going on, how things had fallen apart. He walked around the room with knotted fingers wrapped around the back of his head. He exhaled at length and looked through the two-way glass at the CSU team as they took samples and photographs. Suddenly, a flashing red LED light caught the corner of his eye. He turned to the monitors that were normally on to show that the interrogation room was in use; the monitors were off, but the cameras were not. He smiled as he realised the whole thing had been taped. This could prove Steel's story or doom it. He traced the hard drive to a server upstairs and took the number of the camera.

Upstairs, Tony found the feed to the cameras in the

interrogation room. As he watched, he saw Steel leave, but moments later, a woman came in. The chief struggled as she put a suppressor on her weapon. The hairs on the back of his neck tingled as she moved to the camera and blew a kiss before putting one between the chief's eyes. Tony Marinelli looked blankly at the screen as if it didn't compute what he had just seen. Steel would be cleared with this evidence; however, Tony had also listened to the audio. He looked at the captain and the rest, making their way into Brant's office. He made two copies of the tape and locked them into his top drawer. Tony sat for a moment, observing the group through the window. His gaze fixed on Steel.

"Who are you, Mr Steel? Who are you *really*?" Tony said, as an uncomfortable feeling shivered down his spine.

Dear reader,

We hope you enjoyed reading *Broken Steel*. Please take a moment to leave a review, even if it's a short one. Your opinion is important to us.

Discover more books by Stuart Field at https://www.nextchapter.pub/authors/stuart-field

Want to know when one of our books is free or discounted for Kindle?

Join the newsletter at
   http://eepurl.com/bqqB3H

Best regards,

Stuart Field and the Next Chapter Team

The story continues in:

Blood and Steel by Stuart Field
To read the first chapter for free, head to:
https://www.nextchapter.pub/books/blood-and-steel

Lightning Source UK Ltd.
Milton Keynes UK
UKHW041326201020
371876UK00004B/729